Mr. America's Last Season Blues

MR. AMERICA's
Last Season Blues

A Novel by John McCluskey, Jr.

Louisiana State University / Press Baton Rouge and London

1983

For three flying in the sunship
Malik Douglas, Jerome Patrice, and John Touré

Designer: Albert Crochet
Typeface: Linotron Trump Mediaeval

A portion of this novel, Verse Superstar, Line 3, appeared
as a short story in *Obsidian*, IV, Number 1, under
the title "Forty in the Shade."

LIBRARY OF CONGRESS CATALOGING IN PUBLICATION DATA

McCluskey, John.
Mr. America's last season blues.

I. Title. II. Title: Mister America's last season blues.
PS 3563.C343M7   1983   813'.54   83–7968
ISBN 0–8071–1120–1

Mr. America's Last Season Blues

VERSE

SUPERSTAR

LINE 1

ROSCOE AMERICUS, JR., slipped easily into the morning's rhythm. He loped down the steep bank of a hill and, his path hugging closely the hillside, started his three-mile run around the park. The morning dew made a soft sponge of the grass, and by the time he would lean into the first curve, his boots would be soaked. He had thought to wear two pairs of socks this time, however. He had started jogging in boots because that's what the boxers did. The extra weight was good for the legs. For twenty yards he lifted his knees high in a prancing trot, then resettled into his comfortable jog, a jog to weave thoughts through.

He ran the three miles three times a week, nine miles of punishment he by now regarded to be as silly as it was necessary. There was the whiskey to be burned out of his system; there was the relentless fat gathering along his sides, across the butt. Roscoe was trying to ease up on the scotch, on the heavy eating he had always done. No man worth anything wants to destroy himself in that slow soft way. Certainly no former athlete wants to balloon into some bubble of useless flesh. No, stop that mess now and get sharp again. Get together to go fifteen rounds with, say, Larry Holmes, to go head up with the meanest on the Pittsburgh Steeler defensive frontline. He clapped his hands several times, the claps like rifle shots through the morning quiet. It was going to be hot today, the heat's promise already there in the metal smell. Good, good. The flab would drop away as easily as a good stripper's front.

A honk from the highway above, a flash of teeth, and the wave of a hand. Roosevelt Sweatt sped past. Worktime. Tote that barge, Rosie, lift that bale. Rosie at the post office, slow Rosie on the basketball court. Rosie would be at the bar at four-thirty, sipping Jack Daniels and bitching about his boss. Get a little drunk and you land in jail. Roscoe snorted, letting his arms dangle at his sides as he headed down the longest stretch in the park.

The girls would be up by now. During the night, Grace might have joined Charlotte in bed, sleepwalking in to nuzzle her mother's back. When he had slept there, Grace would force her way between him and Charlotte, her feet pushing him to the edge of the bed, digging at the small of his back. In her own bed, Mayisha, the older daughter, would be drawn up into a ball, her top sheet drooping to the floor. And Charlotte, an early riser, would be sleeping a little later this morning. It was two weeks before she'd have to start teaching gifted sixth-graders in a special summer session. This week, aside from the girls, there was little pressure for her to rise and fly with the sun's first assault on the bedroom blinds. No man now.

Roscoe had moved out a month before. He found unfurnished rooms just a few blocks from the North Star Café, the bar he owned, and moved his trophies, stereo, and favorite chair there. He still saw the girls once a week. The father in him lived on, though the husband in him had died months ago. On the morning he left, there had been no sweet release, no fresh breath of freedom. Immediately he was caught by the uneasiness of a man who had pushed through one stubborn door and, after hearing it slam behind him, realized there were so many others ahead.

His move started as a time-out to think, a space in which to trace back, through the years to the source of decay. But no source had been found or understood yet. For the past month he had asked himself what went wrong in the marriage and hoped that a little distance would help him discover answers. He had told Charlotte he needed time to think. But that had been a clumsy lie. It was over.

The park was usually empty so early on a weekday morning. Soon Scottie would be at the swimming pool, the park's heart, mopping the floors around the lockers. Or Tucker and his gang would idle around the picnic table nearest the pool, sporting cheap highs, and starting a tonk game. Roscoe was pleased that he would have the park to himself for a few brief minutes. Except for Nora and Teddy. He could see the old faithfuls were at it again in a clump of shrubs behind the pool. Day in, day out, whenever the spirit hit them they would start their wild, wild loving. No one in town had ever seen anything like it. The coldest cynics turned away and claimed that the bad wine made the couple do such things. The two of them would walk into the bar together, Teddy propped on Nora's arm. They would order, then sit at a booth in front of a window. No one ever knew what would set them off— an old Etta James ballad, a word overheard, a thoughtless bump of thighs? There would be the sudden lurch and they would be at it hot and heavy with hands fondling, with long, wet, and smothering kisses. Teddy breaking from the clinch to draw on a cigarette before resuming the passion grip. Idle children would cluster at the window to point and cover their snickers. Serious drinkers, weary of conjuring love's possibilities, would yell for Roscoe to kick them out. Which he never did. Usually he interrupted them, faking roughness, and asked them to reorder. No loitering on the premises, he would say.

Impossible lovers, too, they appeared, with Nora in those limp beady sweaters stretched across her huge breasts. Her soiled skirts, her rundown shoes. Her hair was stiffly straightened, and she dared anyone to stare at it too long. She could whip most of the men in the bar. Had fists like Sonny Liston's. Six inches shorter than Nora, Teddy, the loverman, was a miracle that kept returning after more cruel defeats any one life could bear. He wore pants too short, shirts too dull, and glasses too small. And here they were at eight-thirty, lying on a blanket, the thin soles of their shoes peeking out from the bushes, their legs intertwined, their hands busily stroking and kneading. Roscoe had long liked their sudden urges. He called them Romeo and Juliet. The lovers were good shameless company this morning.

Roscoe laughed and hollered. "Do it, y'all! Let it all hang out!"

He ran on, blowing heavily, letting his lips flutter and make that snorting noise that horses make. Breathing was the key. Keep the legs in shape all you want, but if there was no rhythm to the breathing you were working against yourself. There was a trick to everything, the Old Man liked to tell his sons. And Roscoe had learned a trick of distance running only after the end of his football career.

Now he zigzagged through the wet grass. The Wisconsin game,

it was, years ago, and two minutes left in the game, and he, Roscoe Americus, Jr., picking up a fumble at midfield and lumbering toward the goal line. Even at 6'7", and weighing 255, he was swift. Eighty thousand fans on their feet and screaming their lungs out in the freezing rain. He was cut down from behind by one of Wisconsin's quick halfbacks. Maybe he should have made a lightning cut at the last second and left the back to spit grass. Ohio State scored in three plays anyway, but the glory could have been sweeter for him had he scored. An offensive and defensive tackle, he went on to make all-Big Ten that season and second-team all-America his last year. The knee was still good then. Strong.

Then the Cleveland Browns drafted him, and during summer camp the knee went out as it had done during the last half of the final game with Michigan. The Browns kept him around that first year, but, when the knee showed no signs of healing completely, they released him. No other team picked him up, all-American or not, and he drifted to the Canadian League where he played for a year. Weather would be the excuse he would give for leaving Toronto, but it was the hurt of not playing in the big leagues that forced him out. He drifted to the lucrative carnival of professional wrestling, and, when that soured in two years, he returned to Union City.

When he settled home, no one let him forget that he had failed. High school buddies talked endlessly and awkwardly of his successes. For those first weeks back they talked about how he had knocked fullbacks unconscious, how he blocked like a crazed bull and sent men to the sidelines in twos. They scratched their throats and speculated on what he would have done against the Chicago Bear frontline had the knee not betrayed him. But he grew weary of such talk. "Man, that's the past. Let's talk about now. Where's all the fine foxes that used to be here in town? Y'all chase them away with tired conversations?" But old fans were not easily sidetracked. They were the same ones who had driven the hundred or so miles to Columbus on frosted Saturday mornings, getting to the stadium early enough to pat him on the back when the team charged out of the tunnel for the pregame calisthenics. They were the same "home boys" who called his room after the games, bar noise in the background, to congratulate him.

These men knew he would make it big with the Browns, the way Jim Parker did with the Colts. Then they could drive to Cleveland on Saturday mornings, brave the icy blasts off the lake as they rooted from the bleachers, and be back home in time for work Monday morning. His failure had wrecked their holidays, he figured.

Another car honked as it sped down the parkway. Roscoe waved, not turning this time. From the other side of the park he could see Nora and Teddy standing now. Teddy shook out the blanket and Nora straightened her skirt. Roscoe was halfway through the course now and feeling a little tired. He needed more work. He had so far to run to get back to where he wanted to be.

He jogged around the basketball court and passed Henrietta, Lenora Jones's oldest girl. She was walking to the bus stop. At the sound of Roscoe's fake loud kiss, she suddenly hunched her shoulders as if slapped on the back. Then, instant dimples. "Mr. Roscoe, you getting crazier everyday. My mama done told me to watch out for you."

Only seventeen, she would soon be a real heartbreaker, judging by the switch of her hips, the flutter of the eyelids, the pout nicely put. Just like her fine mama. Make a rabbit hug a hound, make a do-right man do wrong. They're starting earlier, it seems. Worldly-wise these young girls were becoming in this town where the winds of change swirl devilishly, winds that bring the smells from the mills where the men sweat and daydream plots for the young girls going to meet the buses on fresh summer mornings. The girls used to be less sassy at that age, but he liked today's version much better. He carried her smile with him as he headed toward the parking lot which fronted the swimming pool.

And where was the Old Man now? Maybe he was resting. After all, you can't expect a ghost to run with you. Besides, that last visit must have taken a lot out of him, getting excited that way. Roscoe had never grown truly comfortable with the Old Man's visits. The first time it happened, ten years before, he was lying

9

on the sofa, eyes open. He had awakened slowly as he was often awakened by the wash of soft night noises, not knowing whether the sounds were dreamed and, after listening on, pressure building in the chest, wondered whether he had caught a miscue of a clumsy burglar. Through the wall, however, stepped Roscoe, Sr., "the Old Man," as his two oldest sons had called him during the last years of his life. He came into the room, rubbing his hands together as if he had just won heavily in a poker game. He stood there in that four o'clock darkness. *"Tell me something, son. Tell me about your life. I won't ask you if you're happy. I'll just ask you if you still got the fighting spirit."*

For five minutes Roscoe had lain there. But the figure of his father did not go away and the question was repeated. He smelled no cigar smoke, though he could see his father take something from the corner of his mouth and flick off what seemed to be an ash. Propped on both elbows, Roscoe spoke to his father, the pauses filled by Charlotte's fitful turnings.

Just three days ago the Old Man had walked in again, for perhaps the thirtieth time. His visits had grown more frequent over the past two years. Everjean, Roscoe's woman, had just left his room, and Roscoe was standing in the window, smoking. His father slipped in behind him as softly as the insistent notes from a never-say-die blues.

"Do you love her, son?" he asked. Roscoe shook his head.

"Well, if you don't love her, don't let her come between you and your family." The Old Man slipped his thumbs beneath his suspenders and slowly ran his thumbs up and down.

"At least you got good taste. The way that woman put together, she make a catfish gnaw a bone. But, Jr., you got to settle your family affairs first, you hear? Your family is more important right now than all the stray pussy between here and Georgia."

"I'm grown, Daddy."

"I can see you grown. I can see you a man. I raised you to be a man. You can be a bigger man if you do right by your family. Don't let things just drift on, son, the way you do. Letting that

10

happen just weakens the nerve, makes you baby-soft. You lose a lot when you run from decisions, when you doubt your nerve."

"I'm not running away from anything. Charlotte and I are separated. Real soon we'll have to sit down and say what we know is true, that our marriage is over."

It went on like that, the Old Man, over twenty years past the grave, laying down his law. Roscoe, Jr., had never mentioned it to his brothers or to his sister. For all he knew his father made the rounds of the family, and the other children were too embarrassed to talk about it, afraid of being called crazy. The Old Man had told Roscoe, Jr., that even though he was the oldest child he was the one who kept making a regular fool of himself.

But Roscoe ran on, slowing to beat on the hood of a Buick parked in front of the pool. Inside, two other morning lovers sat close. They looked like Mabel, Joe Mixon's flirty wife, and Skip Glover.

"Break that mess up!" The woman squealed, grabbing at her throat. The man jumped, too, and Roscoe's laughter rumbled through the quiet. If Joe Mixon ever found out about his wife, she and Skip would make the next day's news.

A little more to go now, just a little. He liked to sprint the last one hundred yards or so. He believed that running or any exercise did no good unless it hurt. So on he drove, pushing hard, harder. He wondered how he must appear, twenty pounds overweight lumbering along with only a trace of the big cat speed he was known for. An ache grew beneath the ribs and a dull pain gathered between the eyes. Knees high, he crossed an imaginary goal line, this man who never got the glory of a running back, this man who instead was once exiled with his bum knee to wrestling in high school gymnasiums in industrial villages.

Then he walked, gasping, panting for breath. Could death start like this? Do you pick the way you will die in some sudden moment and hold that secret with you until the right time? Automobile crash, a war, in a peaceful sleep? After a three-mile run in an old sweat suit, dreaming of the past, desperate for breath, heart near bursting? What dignity and rage there? Who would find him out here—a junkie straying through the afternoon, a kid playing centerfield in the little league? He snorted at the corny self-pity. He caught and held a breath for five seconds, let it out, panted five times quickly, then gathered another breath for five seconds. By the third deep breath he would be OK again. He could see that Romeo and Juliet had finally left the park, that Scottie had shown up and was napping next to the deserted pool, two hours before it would open. The day was settling to fulfill its dreary promises.

Julius and Pete stumbled their drunken, loud-laughing way to one of the picnic tables along the hill. A quick time-out on their way to cut grass and trim shrubs at Doc Jefferson's place, Roscoe figured. A little nip of grape in the park to help get the day going. One of them waved.

"Hey, Big Roscoe, what you training for—the Olympics?" Their cackles ricocheted around the park.

"Y'all go to hell," he said. Their laughter died. Julius and Pete would have all that joy-juice sweated and burned out of them by noon.

He began to sing "Summertime" loudly. He was thinking of the scorcher of a day coming on, of a dark and cool place and Everjean's fingers first digging, then slow walking down his back.

For the past week, late mornings were going to Everjean. Roscoe would knock softly on her door, knowing that Mrs. Johnson, the deacon's wife, was watching all from her window across the street. Once, just after he had knocked, he had wheeled to smile at her before she could duck, open-mouthed, behind her curtains.

Everjean would open the door, and on the hotter days she'd greet him wearing only the short and thin, powder-blue robe. Four long thick plaits sprouted across the front of her head, her crazy morning crown. The first time Roscoe saw those plaits he told her that they were "cute." "My mama told me that the only cute things in this world are monkeys and babies," she had said, but kept them anyway.

"Hey now," he would say as he walked inside and she would smile faintly, then kiss him on the chin.

12

Her small house was cool and dark, and she'd hand him a can of beer wrapped in a napkin. She'd sip from a can herself while finishing housework. She was very slow at cleaning house, even though Roscoe might have called two hours before to tell her he would be over. But she didn't want to appear indifferent about such things, so she never stopped what she was doing. He sprawled on the couch, watching figures on the TV screen or humming snatches of a tune off the radio.

"You break any records this morning, Roscoe?" she asked from another room, her voice carrying even over the noisy vacuum cleaner. "I saw Claudette at the shopping center yesterday, and she say she saw you the other day just huffing and puffing around the park."

"Huffing and puffing, huh? I know I didn't look that bad."

"I'm just reporting what Claudette said, now. You know she see everything and half of what ain't supposed to be seen. Turn the fan up if it ain't cool enough for you."

"Jean, you go shopping with your hair like that?"

She cut off the cleaner, then leaned in the archway separating her dining room from the even smaller living room. Barefoot, she scratched the arch of one foot with the big toe of the other.

"You know I've got more sense than that. I wear my pretty turban when I don't feel like being bothered with my hair. I had to go pick out a couple of pieces for the trip."

"That's three weeks away. You packing already?"

"You know how slow I am," she said, giggling.

"We're only going to be there a couple days. See the falls and then check out Toronto for a couple days. Maybe we can even get 'way north of Toronto to one of those back bays on Lake Huron."

This time she ran the side of one foot across the instep of the other. "I just want to look good when I'm out in public with you, Roscoe."

She turned away, Roscoe studying the legs, the hips. She wore nothing beneath the robe. Then he quickly thumbed through a magazine.

The Housebreaker. They were calling her that when Roscoe gave

13

up wrestling and returned home single, chasing every available woman in town. Two years older than Roscoe, Everjean had a two-year-old son and no husband. For a whole year he saw her often, and he had no plan beyond that year, simply the good times they both needed, wanted. Then he left. Roscoe had discovered Charlotte. Everjean eventually married Lank, her son's father.

"Where's Stone and Wanda?" he asked.

"They supposed to be over to their cousins. Stone probably somewhere talking to that fast Smith girl. That boy at the age now where it's hard to do anything with him. He needs a man to keep him in line. I can argue with him all I want, but at seventeen he keep trying me with his mannish self."

"Yeah, they try to get up in your face about that age."

He always felt that Jean's complaints about Stone's wildness were meant to tug at his sense of responsibility as a longtime lover, a daddy substitute. Yet he had never raised it directly with her. Stone's father was Lank, who had moved out of town after he and Jean divorced. Stone was Lank's responsibility, Lank's and Jean's. Roscoe could be a father to only his own. Besides, Stone barely returned Roscoe's greetings whenever they met on the street, and that coldness made Roscoe a little uneasy. Even his friendly kidding never got through to the boy.

"Ooh, Lord, I'm finally through." She lit a cigarette and dropped down next to him. He stroked the back of her neck. He wondered how things would be different if he had made the pros, if he had made big money. Would he still be here now, with Jean? Would he be with a big city version of Jean, the same spirit with more stylish makeup, stylish job, and fashionably jaded motions? Would his lover then live in rooms that smelled richly of fresh-cut roses or, like here, of coconut from a single stick of incense burning slowly down? He shifted on the couch, still stroking her.

They made small talk about the upcoming trip to Niagara Falls, about the blistering heat outside. Then he stroked her shoulder, her arm.

"Jean, your skin soft as new butter," he said. "Have I ever told you that?"

"About three or four times a week is all." She slipped a finger beneath his shirt, fingered his navel.

"You got something good under that robe, Jean?"

"More butter," she said, helping untie the knot in the robe's belt. "Lots more."

Roscoe laughed and reached to close the blinds. The stern edge of this morning's light followed him even here.

Taped to one corner of the bar mirror, its edges curled, the blown-up photograph in the bar was a good one. Roscoe couldn't imagine one any better. The picture was in color, and he was in the middle of the ring, holding the stiff dummy of a Canadian high over head, by the neck and thigh, his mouth open, begging the crowd for their quick verdict. The choices were simple: let him down easy or break his back. Still an impressive pose because the Canadian was no featherweight. He had tipped the scales around 215. The crowd had chanted, "Kill 'em, kill 'em!" He had body-slammed the chump. Maybe the photographer should have caught that, too, because it was hard enough now to convince the bar customers, most of them fanatic followers of his football career, that he had even been a wrestler, not to speak of the fact that he had been a very good and popular one.

Roscoe turned from the photograph and slapped the bar. "Don't look so bad there, do I, Wilson?"

The slightly younger man in a security guard's uniform squinted, then looked from Roscoe to the picture. He had done this dozens of times.

"Yeah, I guess that's you all right. You got your head shaved there, but I can tell it's you by the knock-knees. Look, you been telling me all this time that you was the world's heavyweight wrestling champ when that picture was taken. I ain't never heard of no black man being anybody's wrestling champ. Basketball, football, boxing, or running—any of them. But wrestling? Naw, uh-uh."

"I know you ain't, Wilson. But you're talking to the original asskicker supreme. Here's some quick education for you. You never know where you can learn something, so listen close. I was the North American heavyweight champ of 1964. See that other picture over there? That's the championship belt I'm wearing."

Wilson leaned further over the bar, his tongue licking along the edges of his moustache. In the color picture, taped to another corner of the mirror, Roscoe was in red, white, and blue striped trunks and held high overhead a gleaming belt. Sweat glistened on his chest and face, and he was grinning like crazy. "I see that picture, but where is the real belt now? That's what I want to know."

"Somebody else got it now. You see, I wasn't smart enough to retire while I had it. Some short Italian about your size lucked up and beat me, so I had to give it up."

"Man, you was a fool! I would have pawned that big pretty sucker before I gave it up. Or at least hid it and claimed somebody stole it." Wilson laughed, reared back, and slapped his chest. "Tell me again what they used to call you, Ros."

"Mr. America. I just changed the ending of my last name and came up with it. The fans ate it up. I had it written all over my red satin robe. I was the superstar. In some places I'd bring along this short white cat and dress him up like those Uncle Sam pictures you see. Fake beard, blue coat, red and white striped pants. The whole thing. They wanted to see my butt kicked at the same time the dummies figured the patriotic thing for me to do would be to win, heh-heh."

Roscoe motioned for Inez, the waitress, to take care of a man who had just taken a seat at a corner booth. Then he brought Wilson a whiskey to help his beer along.

"But that's the past, Wilson. I don't like standing around talking about those times much, because it makes me seem lazy, like there ain't more good days left. The past ought to teach you how to keep those good times coming and coming."

"You going back to wrestling or what?"

Roscoe shrugged at the baldness of the question, the half-tease he knew to be lurking in its creases. "Wilson, a comeback ain't nothing but a word. I could take a month, get back in shape, and

16

whip all them sissies parading around calling themselves wrestlers."

"I could be your manager, man. Except I ain't gon' dress up in no damned red, white, and blue."

Roscoe went on, looking off. "It'd be just like George Foreman coming back now to put some dignity back in the ring. I'd come back and be just as good as ever."

"One thing, Roscoe. Was you a good guy or a bad guy? That's about all I know about wrestling, you see. I see cats pushing one another around the ring, throwing dropkicks, and getting bit and hit all upside the head. But there's always a good guy and a bad guy. Which one was you?"

"Simple, Wilson. I was the good guy most of the time I was champ. When it was time for someone else to be champ, I took a turn at being the bad guy. I'd go after them with chairs then, claw at their eyes and stuff."

"So it was all a fake? Man, I knew it was. I just wanted to hear you say it. Yes, sir, straight from the horse's mouth at last."

Wilson never quit prodding. Roscoe shook his head. "I didn't say that. It was the crowd that thought about good and bad. I was the same Roscoe right along."

"Aw, man. Go on."

Roscoe walked to the jukebox. Is this what retired magicians go through? Wilson always pushed to discover whether the sport was one great comic dance or real head knocking and eye gouging. Couldn't blame him, though, the way some of them come on so sloppily.

He dropped two quarters in the slot. The few Thursday night customers were always stingy. They'd order their beer, an occasional sandwich with fries, maybe, but that would be it. Sit in silence, they would, bitching about low pay or an evil woman. For many the North Star Café was a kind shelter from the harsh rain of their lives. So he kept the music going, playing one of the old songs reserved at one side of the selector panel. The Roscoe tunes, folks called them. They were his favorites from over the years, and, when the songs started up, the older customers howled or clapped in sudden recognition. The songs conjured pieces of dreams for them, other keep-on-keeping-on times, relief from creeping loneliness. The nonsense passing for music these days didn't stand a chance, they agreed. The younger patrons winked at one another, nudged ribs at these ancient codes of style. This time Erskine Hawkins' "After Hours" started up with the piano rolling.

"Hey, Wilson," Roscoe asked from the other side of the room, "you think this place needs a happy hour? Drop the prices on the slow nights, know what I mean? Maybe one night have it so the women get their first drink free?"

"Nothing wrong with the idea. Just kill off all the competition is all it will do. But, hey, let me go back here awhile and try my luck at the pool table."

Roscoe cleared off a table that Inez had not been able to get to. She was waiting on a couple who had just walked in. Newlyweds, he guessed, because they were holding hands. He was pleased. He liked the café to be big enough for the world, not just for the steelworkers and mailmen, a man's place smelling of iron and sweat, but a place where love might not be drowned out, where love could be found, too, dazzling the eye like a new coin on a grimy floor.

He hummed along with the song. Too many folks who didn't care were running the bars these days, folks who simply wanted to sell watered-down liquor and house a couple of video games in a dim corner. Offer a jukebox with tasteless music, they would, like Chippie's place a block away. Talk about a no-class joint! Chippie had the money to help if he wanted to. Young junkies dropped in there for a dash of sweet wine, and the customers were always bothered by some kid hustling hot jewelry or color television sets. Such owners were no better than the thieves; they took the money and ran. But the Old Man had taught him that a business should say something about the man. Like his home. That's why Roscoe had spared no money to equip the bar with comfortable booths in elegant dark wood rather than the simple pine tables that offered themselves to the monotony of carved initials. Style was the reason for the burnt orange drapes, the large pictures behind the bar. So much went back to the father Roscoe had struggled to love.

Roscoe returned to his high stool behind the bar and sipped scotch and milk from a large coffee mug. This would hold him through the rest of the long slow evening.

"You still got today's paper somewhere around, Roscoe?" Inez asked. "I forgot to check my horoscope this morning. This might be the day I come into some big money or run up on a good man." She shook her head, then pointed at his mug.

"By the way, too much of that stuff in your cup can make you dumb and ugly."

"Well, I guess I better watch it. 'Course, just the ugly part bothers me, Inez. If I don't get no smarter, just let me stay good-looking."

"Well, go on now." The small woman laughed loudly and moved back to a table popping her fingers, job-proud. He liked Inez. She had come home from Detroit with a divorce, two children, and a drinking habit. Wearing a bright red wig she had come in one night with friends and had played Bill Doggett's "Honky Tonk" six times, dancing alone near the jukebox. In a good mood that night, Roscoe had walked over and offered her a weekend job. Called her Red, though without the wig she could be the twin of great singer Betty Carter. The fact that she was stone drunk had nothing to do with anything. The job would straighten her up or he would. On the job, she didn't touch a drop of liquor and always reported on time. Quick with the lines, she'd go toe-to-toe with the best rappers and liars in the bar. Occasionally, on slow nights, she'd imitate Diana Ross doing "Come See About Me," or Aretha Franklin doing "Respect." When Roscoe quit the mill to go full time at the bar, he brought her on five nights a week. He was proud, too, in some strange way, that he had never tried any funny stuff with her. Woman as friend, the newness of it for him.

He caught the phone on its second ring. Letitia. "Roscoe, we still practicing tomorrow afternoon? I don't think I'll be able to make it. My auntie in the hospital in Columbus, and my mama want me to help drive up and back."

"Well, yeah, we were going to practice, Tish . . ."

"We sure need it after that last dance. We sounded so pitiful, Roscoe. Now my auntie got to go and get sick."

He tried to sound cheerful. "Don't worry about it. Go and see your aunt. We'll put it all together after you get back."

"OK, I'll get the girls and tell them that it's off for tomorrow. I'm sorry. We'll never do any good at this rate."

Letitia was in a hurry, stayed in a hurry. Seventeen now, she wanted to be a *Jet* magazine pinup by her next birthday. By twenty she wanted to be a world-renowned model and would sweep through her twenty-first year starring in a movie opposite Billy Dee Williams. Through it all she would establish herself as a singer of ballads in the Gladys Knight tradition. Roscoe had never known a girl so young who had mapped out her life so completely. Of course, all the young ones wanted out, wanted to escape the town's dull rhythms, the quicksand routine of work, gossip, and boredom. Few escaped, however. They returned ashamed, victims of a harshness they were not shrewd enough to handle. Roscoe wasn't sure all of them needed to leave, but he was pulling for Tish.

As manager of Toejam, a small band with a trio of girls doing the vocals, he wondered, too, how far down the road they would go. Letitia sang lead backed by the quiet, thin Sandra whom the girls had nicknamed Retha for the strength she kept in the high notes. Then there was Jonetta, the short plump girl with the husky tenor voice. They had performed at a few dances, but Roscoe, taking over as manager from trifling Emerson, promised them tours of the bigger towns and cities, whispered recording contracts at them. They were slowly putting complete faith in him.

The scent of his aftershave lotion ahead of him, a man came in and ordered a bourbon with beer chaser. Roscoe served him grudgingly, for he had long suspected the man, C. C. Passmore, whom they all called simply C. C., of scribbling all that nonsense on the walls of the restroom. He had not quite figured out how to catch the man in the act. Saying little to anyone else, occasionally talking to himself, C. C. would belch loudly after his drinks and head for the john. At the night's end, Roscoe would notice a new verse on the stalls or over the urinal. The last one was "I hate murderers and crooks. I not crazy." Once a month Ripple would have to wash the walls down.

Maybe Roscoe would pretend to use the phone when he heard that first belch. He'd give the man a minute before he would crash in to catch him in the middle of a misspelled word. He couldn't, after all, accuse C. C. without evidence. ("Say, you the dude writing all that tacky shit in the bathroom?") C. C. could get an attitude, sue him for libel. He seemed a nice enough fellow, keeping to himself mostly, though occasionally opening up to Inez or one of the other customers. But no matter how nice a customer, the cleanliness of the entire bar was much more important.

Wilson returned from shooting the quick game of pool in back. "Say, Roscoe, I caught that singing group of yours at the Legion last month. They gon' be around town anywhere Saturday night?"

"Nothing happening this week. They're scheduled to be out of town for the next two weeks."

Wilson leaned closer. "Folks whispering that you and that fine Letitia got something going on. Say when she sing about her fine man she talking about the big superstar himself."

"Folks ought to mind their own business. She's young enough to be my daughter. Roscoe don't rob the cradle."

"I'm just telling you what they saying. 'Course me myself, now I might be a little less understanding, you know, when it comes to something that fine."

Roscoe frowned, bent forward. "Well, Wilson, since you brought up the band, I might as well tell you I'm planning to cut them loose. I need to spend more time around here. Toejam will have to make it without me pretty soon . . ."

By the time Roscoe heard the first belch, the quiet C. C. was off his stool and moving to the men's room. Roscoe waited for a few minutes, then walked in to wash his hands. The man was in a stall humming, the door closed. Roscoe lingered, trying to make out the tune, washing and rewashing his hands. He heard no scratching on the stall walls and left, cursing.

Inez was leaving. The booths were clean except for the young couple's. On the slow nights he let her leave early to get back to her children. "See you tomorrow, Babycakes," he shouted to her. When the door opened, he could see someone peek in over Inez, then move on. He decided it was time to close up. You couldn't work miracles on Thursday nights.

Then C. C. emerged from the men's room, whistling. He ordered another beer. Roscoe didn't smile when he took his money. Not only does he dirty my walls, but he keeps me here late. Then Roscoe went in back and told Ripple, the scar-faced rackman, to clean up.

"Been closed, Ros," Ripple said. "These tables been quiet for the past fifteen minutes." They turned out the lights over the tables and came back to the front. Wilson and C. C. were still at the bar.

"Wilson, I've got another idea for you," Roscoe said. "Poetry. I been giving it a lot of thought. I think once a week I'll open the place for folks to bring in their poetry to read. A little poetry for the people. Huh, what do you think about it?"

Wilson shrugged. "Never know what people around here will take to. Who would have thought they'd get all hopped up on those plays that girl with the funny-sounding African name had them doing in the streets a couple summers ago?" He drained his bottle of beer. "Try it."

"Yeah." Roscoe turned to the silent man. "Say, C. C., what do you think about poetry?"

"I don't know. Maybe. I don't read that much, but I'll listen to anything once." Short brown teeth for a smile.

"And I'll try anything once," Roscoe said more to himself than to anyone else. He began to wipe off the bar, whistling now. Wilson soon left and C. C. belched his way through the door. Roscoe rang out the cash register and with the money in dirty cloth bags moved toward the front door. Ripple held the door open, and Roscoe paused in the dark and silent room. In two days one of his brothers would be visiting from Chicago. In a week he would be forty years old.

LINE 2

FOR MONTHS NOW an idea had been shared by three members of the Americus family. At least, the idea had struck Baby Sister, Irwin, and Roscoe, Jr., at about the same time. In his most recent call from Chicago, Irwin, the third oldest, had casually mentioned a family reunion to Roscoe. A few days before that, Roscoe and Baby Sister, the youngest, had touched on such a notion during a phone call. Like milkweed in late summer, the idea had been blown about among them, not yet taking root. But slowly it was fixing itself deeply, growing. Did the other far-flung Americuses feel the same spirit?

Since their mother Earline's, funeral, the five sons and the daughter had drifted apart. Although they had grown up a close and tight family—"Mess with one Americus, you got to mess with them all!"—they kept in touch rarely now. Perhaps among them all there now blossomed a vague need to share their loves and lives, a need that memory nourished, even threatened with too much richness. It had been sixteen years since they were last together; twenty-one, if Emmanuel were included.

As he waited for Irwin's plane, circling somewhere above the dark clouds, Roscoe thought back to the rainy afternoon of the funeral. The children, fatherless and motherless then, were crowded into the rusting, red Buick Dynaflow convertible as they returned from the cemetery. There had been the rain off and on all day, and Baby Sister, only ten years old then, commented that rain was proper on the day of Earline's funeral. The whole world should be sad that day, and certainly the sky should cry. Rain had started as the bronze coffin was lowered into the narrow hole, the drops sounding like heavy fingers drumming on wood. The same nervous drumming on the convertible roof as they weaved their way home.

Earline had been ill for months, though no one suspected the extent of the cancer. Roscoe was on a pro wrestling tour when he got the news of her death, and he canceled a week of matches to fly home. Since he was the oldest, there were many decisions he

23

had to make. Big Brother, the model, the one to be imitated but never duplicated. Driving home from the cemetery he wondered what the brothers and sister could learn from his life at that moment. Avoid failure. And if you do happen to fail, then what? Take a lifetime to think about what might have been? Laugh at it, dust yourself off, and try again?

His brothers had watched him play high school ball, and Chris and Emmanuel had tried to follow in his huge footsteps. They chose different positions as their size and temperament dictated, Chris going to flankerback and Emmanuel to linebacker. "Americus boys are bigboned and tall as Georgia pines," the short father would say. Half of Roscoe's honors eluded them, though their pictures, too, would hang in the high school's Hall of Fame.

Emmanuel was always the quietest one, the slowest to laugh. Except for Roscoe, he was heavier than the other brothers. Thickly muscled, he threw the shot in track and hit big fullbacks head on with the fury of a thunderclap. He'd had two girl friends before his senior year in high school, going with each a minimum of two years. Settled type, the second son, finally, a stranger to his own brothers. He was a disciple, a follower of the highest order. He would have never made a leader, but as a disciple, as a believer, he was fearless. He joined Tried Stone Baptist Church at the age of seven, and, though the ministers came and went, he was always there in the first rows, attentive, rapt. At his father's funeral he did not shed a tear, and he missed his mother's funeral, two years later, because he was still chasing his father's killer. No one knew · where to reach him. Or how.

Irwin tried the band. Music was his first love. First trumpet in the high school marching band, he was, and on his later birthdays Earline would bring out the picture of him grinning, dry-lipped, his band cap too small, his jacket too tight and showing two inches of wrist. First chair, also, in the high school orchestra. When the Old Man bought Irwin his first trumpet, Roscoe, Jr., taught him to box, taught him how to throw a sucker punch in the clinch to cool out a larger opponent, how to block wild looping hooks and tap-tap-tap some poor fool's chin. Irwin's friends did not understand the singlemindedness with which he practiced, and therefore took him for a chump. But he rarely had to put Roscoe's lessons into practice, since so many bullies could figure that fighting one of the younger brothers might trigger the wrath of Roscoe.

Cha-Cha. By the age of five Chris was called Cha-Cha for his fondness for the spicy relish served with greens. The relish was actually "chow-chow" but young Chris pronounced it "cha-cha." Later, friends would guess that the name came for his obsessed dancing, but they were wrong, though the new myth did no harm. He was the most outgoing of the brothers, the one with the easiest smile, and the quickest to get the slap on the back. The Old Man had high hopes for Chris, since the boy displayed such a brilliant quickness with words and kept his buddies in stitches and at bay. The father had always wanted a lawyer in the family though no one ever knew why. He was convinced that Cha-Cha would go to law school and then enter politics, going all the way to the U.S. Senate.

Chris never sat still in a classroom, however. No, his feet, hands, eyes moved with an energy that his wiry body could barely contain. He soon became the best dancer in town. Before he was twelve, the Old Man's doubts, already mounting over three years, were not to be denied. By then he'd walk past his son's room where rhythm 'n' blues tunes would be playing loudly. The father, a lover of good blues himself, would tell Chris to keep it down. He'd pull the stub of a cigar from his mouth and pause as if to say something else, then walk slowly away.

Nervous Chris, as Roscoe, Jr., remembered him, clipping out the Charles Atlas ads from the comic books and sending away for the secrets of an intimidating physique like his two older brothers. The Old Man told him that the secret lay in mashed potatoes and gravy, hot buttered biscuits, plenty of chocolate malts, and hard work. But the Charles Atlas ads in comic books sounded more exotic, called the true secret "dynamic tension." Cha-Cha gained two pounds one summer and lemon-sized biceps for his trouble. He caught passes with one hand and offered tacklers the resistance of a boiled spaghetti strand. During the off-season, he grew a thin moustache, reigned as king of the dance floor, and drifted to fancy clothes and a quick jackhammer rap.

After a semester at Tennessee State and two years of moving around the South, Cha-Cha wrote a long letter to Baby Sister explaining that he was a disc jockey working out of Shreveport, Louisiana. Then each year a tape would come (his best show of the year?) from places like Knoxville, Dothan, Birmingham, Valdosta. And each year Roscoe would listen to the tapes in his sister's living room, and he and Baby Sister would roar at Cha-Cha's wild jokes, puns. Together they wondered how long he wanted to stay on the microphone. As they grew older, DJ's either went up to higher, off-mike positions or out.

In the red Dynaflow, that rainy afternoon after Earline's funeral, Roscoe, Jr., stared out of the window. The rain had stopped for awhile. In the middle of the street was a Chevy convertible with its radio playing loudly and two boys in sleeveless shirts sipping bottles of beer, their heads bobbing to the music.

"Those jitterbugs act like they got less sense than we did when we were coming along. Tyrone, I hope you ain't acting that crazy."

Tyrone, the youngest brother, was fourteen then, nicknamed Dodo by Irwin. Earline said that he might be the smartest of all the boys: "Catches on real quick to things." Growing up he didn't seem to be the fighter the other boys were. But again, like Irwin, he didn't have to fight that much. When he did, he usually won, screaming, spit flying, tears streaming, his teeth flashing, as his opponents grew weak from fear, figuring they had awakened a mad man whose passion knew no limits. At first the problem had been getting him to fight back. He had balked at dares, at sticks placed on his shoulder and slapped off by some loudmouth. But if the Old Man heard about it before Tyrone returned home, he'd stand in the door and drive Tyrone away with a leather belt. Once he chased him back to a playground into the startled arms of the boy who, with a looping left to the head, had sent him running home. The father's simple logic was that a boy who ran from fights would flee them for the rest of his life. The better the son with books,

26

the more he'd have to learn that. But Tyrone was no coward. He simply feared the wild demon in himself, a demon far beyond his control once freed. His legend grew, and other boys made friends with him eventually, blunting their fear of his sharp mind by calling him *weird*. He didn't mind this because he knew he had to allow them something or he would be doomed to isolation.

It was Tyrone's studying that marked him early. Reading, always reading. The Old Man and Earline had long been accustomed to buying books, cartons of books, if the children said they wanted them. Tyrone read so much that Earline took him aside once to talk of the nature of men and women in the way she thought the Old Man would approve, the Old Man eleven months dead by then. But Tyrone at a tender fourteen didn't need such lessons, because what the few sex encyclopedias in the public library could not tell him, Portia, Mrs. Thomas' fast sixteen-year-old daughter, could show.

College presented no problems for him. He finished Morehouse in three years. He also discovered gin in Atlanta. From that point his life took two surprising directions. First he went to Chicago and tried to play the blues guitar. No one knew much about those two years in Chicago until Tyrone, a little high, told Irwin how an old bluesman told him, "Son, you got the right idea. You got a good head and good fingers. Now you just got to live those blues so you knows what you talking about when you sings them. Right now you just copying somebody else's feelings." Tyrone thought the old singer had had too much bad bourbon and bad luck. At any rate, after the Chicago saloons he wound up in the navy.

The Old Man had hoped for a lawyer in the family, and by that day in 1965 it was down to Tyrone and Baby Sister.

"A lawyer is a good thing for a person to be," the father would say, looking off. And no one had the nerve to ask why to that except Baby Sister who raised the issue casually one day, looking squarely at her father.

"It beats the steel mill," was all he said, postponing the conclusion of the matter. Not always an easy one to figure out, the Old Man.

Ruth Anne, known as Baby Sister ever since the day she was brought home from the hospital, rivaled Tyrone in intelligence. She was also good in music and was a fine sprinter on the summer playground track team. Although the Old Man had heard of the woman lawyer who worked on the big desegregation suit before the Supreme Court in 1954, he never recognized such a possibility for his own daughter. He was content to spoil her, a girl-child, strange to him. He surrounded her with pinks and easy pastels.

"I think that even Daddy would release us from some of his daydreams now," Roscoe had said in the car.

"You're probably right, Roscoe," said Cha-Cha. "Especially since it don't look like no lawyer coming out of this family."

"How you know?" asked Baby Sister. "You still have to wait on me and Tyrone before you can say that."

The older brothers smiled at her loyalty to a dream now remote. Over the radio's static came an old song, "Shake a Hand," a favorite of Earline's. They were silent as the song played. And the rain, starting up again, smeared the windshield. A woman rushing from the hairdresser's, a newspaper as an umbrella over her hair freshly done. Two boys hurrying home from the swimming pool, their already wet trunks swinging from their belt loops, their towels now dripping turbans. Like the song, like death, the rain had caught the world by surprise.

When the song ended, Roscoe cleared his throat, noticing Irwin in the backseat wiping his eyes. "We'll keep the house. I think it'll be best to rent it out.

"Let's talk about it later, huh, Roscoe? Business can wait a little taste."

But Roscoe was struggling with the Old Man's words: "To give up the house and land is about the same as giving up all claims to the history of the family in this town. Just remember where you was raised at and who raised you. Respect that any way you see fit, but respect it all the same. If both me and Earline go, y'all keep the house." The father had said that only days after adding a new room on the house, and the children had listened restlessly, not understanding, not needing to understand the need for legacy.

28

Rent it out, yes. Rent out the house, then Baby Sister and Tyrone would live with Earline's people, Uncle Tootie and his laughing wife, who lived on the other side of town. But the house would
still be in the family, and with the other rooming house the Old
Man bought some years before his death, the houses would soon
pay themselves off. Roscoe had decided this on his own. Convinc-
ing the others would be the problem.

"I think we should talk about it as soon as we can. It's no disrespect to talk about this business today. It's disrespect if we don't
make a good decision. The point is that we keep the house, see.
It doesn't matter right now who lives in it as long as we keep it.
Then maybe one of us will come back and live in it."

"That mean you going to make the first move, Roscoe?" Cha-
Cha asked.

"Well, this wrestling thing might go on for awhile. I'm not crazy
about running all around the country every month. Maybe I'll get
tired of it . . ."

"Then you're coming back?"

"What you trying to say, little Chris?" Roscoe asked.

"I'm not trying to say anything, Roscoe. Both of us know how
hard it is to come back to this place to live. Mama, Daddy, Tyrone,
and Baby Sister were the only reasons we came back when we
did. I just don't think we should talk about that sentimental
stuff . . ."

"We don't need any arguments," said the precocious Baby Sister. She shifted in the front seat, shaking her head. The peace-
maker she'd always be.

"No argument, Baby Sister," said Cha-Cha. "I'm just saying
what's in everybody deep down, that's all. We're living our own
lives now or just about to. Which is what Mama and Daddy would
have wanted. They never wanted us to hang around home if we
didn't want to. I know what Daddy said about not giving up the
house and all, but he did want us to stand on our feet."

Irwin coughed, turning away from the window. "I guess we should
think about it, especially if nobody's going to come back. I mean,
that seems pretty clear in everybody's mind now. Finish school

and go see the world. Who's going to be here to collect the rent, pay the taxes?"

"We'll find a way. We have to keep the house."

"That's not the question, Roscoe. We're talking about who." Cha-Cha again, squirming.

"You want me to jump back there on you, man?"

"Relax, Roscoe," Irwin said. "We do have time to think about all this. There's no sense getting worked up over something the way we've been feeling today. Are both of y'all forgetting that we buried our mother just a half hour ago?"

He recalled that they came to another stop and the music from the radio seemed to grow dimmer. Static from lightning coming closer. That was the way the big family picnics ended. When they were growing up, there was only one state park nearby that black people could safely invade. Once a year the Americus' and first cousins would go to Jefferson Lake with mighty slabs of spareribs and countless ears of corn, and on the banks of that man-made lake they'd fight mosquitoes, play poker, drink beer, and fish, while the children swam under the watchful eye of one adult. They'd argue, too, with the heat which only families can conjure. Then they'd make up and eat and eat and eat. Roscoe remembered Uncle Bennie with the freckles, Mama's youngest brother, on his fourth ear of corn, saying, "Corn is my birthmark." And as the afternoon slipped into quiet evening the men would turn from beer to bottles in brown bags and look differently at their wives. Arguments over the cards would flare up, then die down, and the children would steal through the adult gossip and scour the woods for frogs or stray, shameless lovers. Then after the inevitable buildup of clouds, thunder could be heard rumbling from faraway, and one of the children always mistook it for a herd of motorcyclists on the highway. But clouds grew darker, and they would douse the fire, call the children, and pack quickly. The rain would catch them minutes later on a two-lane country road and the ride home on that glistening ribbon of road would be shortened by Aunt Pokie's stories of haunts and hungry preachers. Amid the pulse of the windshield wipers, the voices crowded the car, Roscoe then remembered.

The rain stopped then and the sun flashed. Baby Sister was the first to point out the rainbow. But by the time the car turned into their neighborhood and after they had wished the silent wishes their young lives demanded, the rain returned through the sunshine with the vengeance of a betrayed dreamer.

That crowded car, the rain, and the steamed car windows that needed to be wiped clear at every stoplight—those were the anchors of the moment as he waited impatiently for the jet from Chicago to taxi off the runway, then up to the gate. Roscoe tried to imagine how much Irwin might have changed in the three years since he had seen him.

Irwin, a big-time dentist in Chicago, was coming home to buy ten acres of land across the river, land to sink roots into. Long-distance roots ripping through his perfectly green suburban lawn, beneath the concrete maze of interstates, pushing toward home. The country plot would be a place for his spirit, Roscoe imagined, though the body would be in Chicago performing a root canal or sipping twelve-year-old scotch next to a swimming pool that collected bugs on its still surface.

Roscoe watched the tunnel and saw his brother slowed in the crush of other passengers and their well-wishers. At thirty-six he still looked the most like Earline. He had the rounded face, the full cheeks that everyone teased him about when he was younger. Baby fat, they called it. He wore a tailored suit and shoes with heels not too high, tastefully trimmed sideburns—all this as it should be for Irwin, the most practical one.

They hugged on meeting, stepped back to check one another out, then shook hands warmly.

"Don't tell me I don't know a stone-country boy when I see one," Roscoe said. "Always knew you had a home jones. You're giving up Chicago, huh?"

"I haven't seen you in four years and the first thing out your

31

mouth is some trash. Look here, you know why I'm back. To see you and Baby Sister, close the deal on that land, and hop a quick jet back to Chicago."

Roscoe put up both hands. "Just jiving, Baby Brother, just jiving. How's the family? You brought them back once for the Fourth of July, and nobody's seen them since. What was that—three–four years ago? You think we going to eat them up or something? I bet them two girls about as tall as you are now." They started toward the baggage claim.

"Everybody's fine, Roscoe. They'll be coming down with me next time for sure. That's a promise."

Roscoe glanced at him. "Next time?"

"Yeah, they got a right to see the land I'm buying and my crazy brother, don't they?"

Roscoe laughed. "Well, they ain't missing nothing if they don't see that sorry-assed bottomland you're going to get sucked into buying."

"Is it that bad?"

Both knew the extent of Roscoe's lie. They had never found any bad land across the river. Roscoe had driven past two of the three lots last week. Thickly wooded, beautiful land. Nice tax write-offs. Spending money on the pretty land to keep money, as Roscoe put it.

"Give any more thought to a reunion, Roscoe?" Irwin asked as they pulled out of the airport parking lot. "You'll have to be the one to call it, you know."

"How come?"

"You're the only one to bring all six of us back together. Either you or Baby Sister, the oldest or the youngest."

Roscoe laughed. "Well, you right about Baby Sister, at least. She's the clearinghouse for the family, right now. All of Cha-Cha's tapes, Tyrone's postcards and Emmanuel's letters go to her. Not me."

"How's she doing, man?"

"Give her another year and she'll be through with law school. Everybody's been rooting for her. It took her five years, you know,

32

with a course here, two there. She worked, raised two kids, and kept her husband in line. Her ulcer's under control. Shit, we ought to give her a medal."

Irwin nodded. "What's Raymond up to?"

"Same as usual, still quiet, never saying too much. I think he's been a little afraid of me ever since the day of their wedding and I got drunk and told him he'd better treat my sister right." Irwin laughed, loosening his tie. "She want us up to Dayton for dinner tomorrow night."

"Good. Can I see Charlotte and the kids, too?" Roscoe shrugged, kept his eyes on the road.

"I can't stop you."

"Well, the girls are still my nieces, right? And Charlotte's still family, too. Y'all haven't started anything legal yet."

"Naw." Then for the rest of the ride back to town Roscoe kept the conversation on Chicago politics and the violent streets there, on Ohio State's Rose Bowl chances in the fall.

The next morning, after receiving directions from the smiling real estate agent, Roscoe and Irwin drove out to look at the three most promising wooded plots. The brothers told the agent that they would prefer to look alone first, not wanting to be bothered by any aimless chatter. They crossed the river, low at that time of the year, then followed its course for three miles down the twisting road.

Irwin held the map while Roscoe drove. "Turn here," he said. They were looking at the plot that Roscoe hadn't seen. Sudden hills loomed on either side of the narrow road, cutting off sounds. But as they drove farther, the hills gradually leveled off to thick woods.

"Hot damn, you going to get a forest, Babro! This reminds me of the land in Georgia, the way Daddy used to talk about it. Except the dirt ain't red."

The woods dropped suddenly from the road, back to a mile or so off the road. Then they slowed along a wire fence, down in a few places.

33

"According to the map here and that agent's description, this must be what we're looking for," Roscoe said. "You got the whole length of the fence and clear back to the other side of the trees."

In that country quiet they climbed into the field and looked around. Soft explosions from distant motors, they heard. Tractors? Pickups hauling tools? A chicken's clucking from somewhere. Roscoe yawned, stretched, and looked around again.

"Babro, you hoping oil or something up under this land? It's pretty land, but I doubt if any expressway going to come down through here anyway soon. And that's how you make a killing on it, unless you sell it to some slick country club builder or something. Then again you can always build on it, farm it."

"Farm? What would I know about farming? I have a hard time growing a cactus back in my office. Aside from Mama's garden, no one's farmed in this family since the first Americus left Georgia. Look at it this way, Roscoe, we'll always have land to hunt on."

"OK, 'we.' If you don't make the reunion next year, I probably won't see you for another three–four years and you know you don't like to hunt. Couldn't hit a barn from ten feet with a shotgun. Remember that time you hit Mr. Phillips' hound with buckshot? Clean missed the rabbit and got ol' Bilbo. I thought that dog never would stop howling."

Irwin spat. "Well, it's just good to keep in touch with the town and the area," he said, mostly to himself. "Aside from saving me money with the taxes, it'll do that. Maybe give me an excuse once in a while to come back and see your ugly self and talk with my pretty sister."

Stick in hand, Roscoe was stabbing at bushes. A fat rabbit darted, then another. "They're carrying babies this time of year," Roscoe said. "By Thanksgiving those babies will be almost full-grown."

They traced the contours of the land as best they could. The wooden markers were the victims of the weather. They neared a stream. Irwin stuck the toe of one muddy boot into the water, mumbling something about water being a blessing to the land, something Roscoe did not understand and did not challenge. Then

34

the silence, not a Chicago silence or a small-town silence, but the silence of the land before the coming of men. It was a Georgia silence before dawn, before the motions of the old folks across the land, before the peek of the sun and the first gentle burst of sweat.

"I wonder what the Old Man would think of this?" Irwin said. "When he was alive, if a 'blood' ever dreamed about buying land over here, somebody would wake him up and make him apologize. Rednecks had all this under lock and key."

Roscoe nodded and Irwin went on. "Funny, I wasn't always sure what the Old Man liked about what I did. I mean, I don't really know now. I can see him saying how proud he was that I'm a dentist, though secretly he'd prefer me to be a lawyer. Wanted everybody to be a lawyer."

He looked at Roscoe for a cue, for understanding. Roscoe was a little surprised at the statements. Irwin was always the cool, aloof one. He planned everything carefully, even, Roscoe was afraid to admit, his feelings.

"I'm saying that I never really knew Daddy."

"Helluva time to spit it out, Babro," Roscoe said, stopping.

"Well, yeah, I guess the land, this land here, reminded me of him in some way. All during the plane ride I thought of him and why I was buying land back here when I could just as easily have bought some in Illinois."

"I thought that, too. But what was your answer?"

"I'm not sure I've figured it out. But along the way I had to admit something I've told you before. That little slewfooted man scared hell out of me every day that he lived."

"What did he do to you, Irwin?" Roscoe asked, knowing the love mixed with fear and respect the father could create just standing before them, hands stuffed in his back pockets, chin tilted up and lips pressed. "You and Tyrone were the most spoiled, next to Baby Sister. All three of y'all were born with the silver spoon in your mouths."

Irwin nodded. "I don't know what he did do. I mean, specifi-

35

cally. Daddy was behind us in just about everything we did. But somehow we were never close, you know. I used to think about this years later, and I felt bad about it. I never knew how the rest of you felt or if you wanted to even talk about it. After we got away none of us kept in touch that much, at least as much as we should have. Anyway, whenever I tried to remember back, it was like fighting through a cloud, and there would stand Daddy, and I'd recognize the voice but it would be a stranger in his clothes waving at me."

"Bullshit, man. You still talking that off-the-wall jive you learned in some funky lecture hall. Daddy ain't never done nothing to you except break his neck trying to keep you fed so you could go off to school and make lots of money and marry some foxy high yellow and come back to buy this little piece of land . . ."

"I should have known you'd take his side, number one son and all. You must have been the closest, I don't know. You're just like him except you're three times as big."

Roscoe moved on, grinning. "You forgetting how I used to bop you upside your head when you got out of line as a kid?"

"I'm not a kid now."

Roscoe took a lazy swing at Irwin who slipped it, stepped in to give Roscoe a hard shove. The grins on their faces hardened a bit. There was the father between them, a sudden memory to be controlled. In the flesh, in the afternoons of their pasts, he would step in to break up a fight and force apologies. Now he was a shadow that forced them to struggle over their definition of the real.

"Babro," Roscoe said, "you done come home to lose your mind."

"I'm not losing anything. You're just like Daddy. Just because you could whip us and was older, you thought you owned us."

Roscoe was hurt, not simply by that part about the father—all the sons were capable of digging up special hurts the father inflicted—but that Irwin, even in teasing, connected him, the oldest son, to the father so closely. He swung again, out of this hurt, and caught Irwin with a light slap on the head. Irwin swung back and missed. Then kicked, missing again. They stepped back to measure themselves, to take stock of demons driving them on so

36

crazily. As their excited breathing died out, they heard the soft steps of someone else in the field. Together they wheeled.

A man, straight and white, walked toward them. He walked tentatively, as if tiptoeing up on them, though they had turned to look at him. Their fury died at their feet for he held a shotgun, loosely cradled. He was dressed in faded coveralls with a dull red sweatshirt with a long tear through one sleeve. He wore no hat and the breeze barely moved his thin hair. He spat brown.

"What you doing on this here land?" he asked.

Irwin looked from the man to Roscoe. Neither brother doubted that the gun was loaded. "We're out here looking over this land. The real estate agent back in town told us it was for sale."

"You buying this land?" he asked, his eyes catching both of them. Flat eyes. The question was casual, as if asking their ages. But the gun made any question a threat.

Roscoe nodded. The man's lips curled back. "Ain't nobody buying this here land and I done told them that. No white is going to buy it, no nigger neither."

Roscoe looked beyond the farmer to see how many troops he had brought. But there was nothing, unless barefoot boys with double-barrel shotguns hid behind those trees in the distance. No house in sight, no smoke, no baying of hounds. Where had the man come from? He must have risen from the earth.

"You boys get back to town now and tell them what I said."

Shaken, Irwin backed up. "Roscoe, come on," he said, reaching for his brother's arm. Roscoe stood his ground staring at the man, watching his hands on the gun. The man stepped back, as if making space to square off better. He spat again and showed short teeth.

"You tell them just what Caudill said." Then he backed up a few steps, turned, and walked toward the line of trees.

"Come on, Roscoe," Irwin shouted. "That sonofabitch looks half crazy."

Roscoe turned as if dazed and followed Irwin back to the car. "Damn it Babro, how did you let me forget my gun? I was crazy as hell to be out here without my heat. My reflexes must be slowing up." Both stopped to look back at the farmer. The man had stopped near the trees, half turned to watch them, shaded his eyes with one hand.

"We'll be back," Roscoe shouted. "I'll personally drag your ass off this place!"

Although they were out of shotgun range, Irwin was still nervous. "Come on, man. Let the law handle it. I'll have his ass in jail so fast he won't know what hit him."

In spite of himself, Roscoe laughed at his brother's words. He glanced at him and before they got to town had remembered that before the farmer showed up, they, two brothers, were on the verge of fighting.

"Virgil Caudill's a little touched in the head, if you know what I mean, but a good ol' boy who wouldn't harm a flea." The agent shook his head, let a wry smile play across his mouth.

"Touched hell," Irwin said. "He had a shotgun with him. I want him off the land, and I want him arrested for threatening us with a shotgun."

"I can understand how you feel . . ." the man began.

"Can you? Do you?"

The agent leaned back, glanced at Roscoe as if for help. Got none. Reached to get his cigar stub and relit it. "That man and his family have been squatting on land out around here for years. They run 'em off one place and they just pop up in another. Like weeds. Nobody knows where they come from, nor, for that matter, how they eat. Once in awhile folks will see ol' Caudill around town working here, working there. But for a long time nobody will see any of those people—they got about eight dirty-faced kids."

When he saw that the two brothers were not listening, he switched tracks. "So you liked tha land out there, huh?"

Irwin nodded. "I didn't fly from Chicago for a picnic. I'm ready to swing a deal, but I want that man off the land, Mr. Armbruster."

Roscoe, Irwin's heavy shadow through all this, glanced at his brother. He liked his tough talking, though he was a little surprised that Irwin had decided to buy that plot without looking at the others.

Armbruster cleared his throat. "Don't worry, Mr. Americus. Caudill and his crew will be off that land by the time this deal is closed. Don't you worry."

Before they left with his promise, Armbruster praised Irwin's taste in land, his wisdom in investing in land. "A shopping center, a highway, something was always going up or through the boom-town's outskirts. Besides, you couldn't beat the good bottomland soil. Good for farming, good gentlemanly farming—no farming? You have to excuse an old West Virginia boy like me. Then good for hunting, huh? No hunting either? Well, anyway, I've been trying to get big Roscoe here to buy some land out there for years. But he ain't budged yet." Dry grins as they left.

At the bar, they sat in a booth and drank in a silence interrupted periodically by the soft collision of billiard balls from the back room. No doubt, Fat Daddy, the flabby shark in a solitaire eight-ball game, hitting for invisible agitators, missing for invisible suckers, and laughing to himself all the while. The bar, clean as it wanted to be, awaited steelworkers getting off at four. Sipping whiskey, Roscoe and his brother talked of other afternoons that promised so much. Shadows lengthened and ghosts walked.

"Do you think that you and Charlotte will get back together?" Irwin asked, sipping his bourbon through a straw.

"What do you mean?"

"Roscoe, stop playing dumb. You and your wife have separated, remember? You have two girls, huh? As a matter of fact, I really came all the way back here to see those girls, not to see your ugly face. You've got to remember that you never was good at telling lies."

Roscoe eyed evilly two customers who came into the bar. They were cheapskates, who usually bought a beer or two, then tried to game up on some more. He served them their beers and re-joined Irwin.

"Telling lies? Is that what you were saying, Babro? No, I never was good at it. Still ain't and I'm not trying to lie now. Charlotte and I have closed the door on it, man."

It was the first time Roscoe had heard himself say it. In past weeks he had shut the thought out, hoping for luck to turn their situation around. But good luck was something he was usually short on.

"Daddy would be proud of both of us, Roscoe. I mean, we both have tried hard at this family thing, and it seems to be falling apart. The way Evelyn and I have been going . . ." Irwin shook his head and smiled. "It doesn't seem like families are what they used to be, huh?"

"Ain't this a mess? We're sitting here crying in our liquor because it seemed that the oldtimers had more lasting power, more loyalty. You don't remember all those good fights our folks had? The time Mama took us to her folks for a month and told Daddy he'd have to walk on water before she would move back? And I know you can't forget that after Daddy died six—dig that, not two or three—but six fine strapping women around town started claiming that he had given them plenty of good loving through the years?"

Irwin shrugged, sipped again. "You think he held out on us? Or you think them women want to put some mess in the wind?"

"Mama would have put a hurt on him if she ever found that out."

"Do you really think Mama would have put the Old Man out of the house?"

"She would have pitched a fit, Irwin. We'd probably have to call the law, since I know for a fact that six of us couldn't get her off him."

They remembered the photographs. Earlene was a big-boned woman from north Georgia. Athens. Her large frame and erect carriage made her appear a full head taller than Roscoe, Sr. They were actually the same height, but she looked taller even with the Old Man keeping some kind of battered hat tilted on his head. All those yellowed pictures with them shyly holding hands. Mama: on a different level, wife. Or them in other pictures stiffly hugging

40

as if the camera imposed an unbearable formality on them. Mama smiled brightly out of those days of too-long dresses and strange hairdos. Mama, who could only birth boys—though it was Tyrone who later explained that the male sperm determined the sex of the child—who birthed boys big and loud until Baby Sister, bigger and louder in her way, came along. She'd be the one Old Man would spoil "rotten." He would sleep out in a hollow log for his only girl and dare the wind to play around her too much. Mama, in her quiet way, checked such madness.

"It wouldn't change my feelings about the Old Man one bit, if I found out he'd been messing around for true."

Irwin looked long at his brother. Shrugged, this cool one with both feet on the ground, shrugged and traced an *I* through the sweat of his glass.

"I don't know. Maybe if I found out he had, it would give me something to blame my running around on. You know, something corny like 'Daddy did it so what do you expect from me, world?'"

"You creeping around much up there in Chicago?" Roscoe asked. He would never suspect Irwin as a playboy.

"It's nothing to worry yourself about, Roscoe. Just a woman while I call time-out from my marriage. I'm sure you know what I mean, huh?" He paused, shifted in his seat. "Maybe Baby Sister has some more things from Emmanuel, huh? After all is said and done, Daddy has controlled his life more that anybody else's in the family."

"Look, Roscoe, between us we see quite a few folks. You in this bar and me in the office drilling teeth, we see all types close-up. Strong ones, weak ones, for-real folks, bullshitters, fake messiahs. But tell me where have you ever found anybody to come up to our own Emmanuel? I tell you, I ain't."

Roscoe shook his head. "You got me there. I haven't either."

"And as quiet as it's been kept, where have you met anybody like the Old Man? Like yourself? Especially you, who should have been on television playing against the New York Giants, throwing blocks for Jim Brown back then. You should have been kicking ass and taking names out there on the field. But that knee

41

held you back. A fluke, wasn't it? But you came home, got married, opened a bar. We thought running this bar was beneath you with all your talent. We looked up to you because we didn't have half your athletic talent . . ."

"You and your damn lecturing, Irwin. One drink always did have you talking silly. Here, let me get you another drink so you can pull yourself together."

Before Roscoe came back with the drinks, he stopped to play the Temptations "Ain't Too Proud to Beg" and Jimmy Witherspoon's "Love Is a Five-Letter Word."

He settled back into the booth. "Let's freeze that 'beneath me' stuff. I like what I'm doing. I'm not starving. Folks can't get enough of this place. I'm not going to lay around crying over my knee for the rest of my life. Besides, I might surprise you and get on television one of these days. It takes time to heal. But say, check out the tunes, man. My own private collection on the jukebox."

"Are you the only one that plays them? You're going to lose money like that and run out of space, too. You might have to get another jukebox."

"No big thing. If I like something, I like it and to hell with the rest. Anyway, they just don't make music the way they used to. I can't stand that singing they're putting out these days. It's worse for you than bad wine."

David Ruffin's voice wailed from the jukebox, and Roscoe turned to study the late afternoon street. Stranded on the corner and in a floppy hat stood a bony solitary boy who glanced at every car passing as if hoping for a driver to sweep him up and into Chicago, New York, or Los Angeles. Out of boredom, the boy's eyes played across the behinds of the girls getting off the bus from work. Occasionally one would giggle over something he'd say. But they kept walking. Big-city pool halls may have been more on his mind, or other women with more finesse in their hip walks. A thick roll of twenty-dollar bills in his palms. It was all there, yes, in his stance, his look, the tilt of his head, and the way he held his wrists behind his back.

Roscoe looked at his brother. "I'm checking out a woman, too.

It started out as a time-out, like you put it, but she's got a couple kids and a lot of problems of her own. It's like being in the battle all over again, except I can walk away a little easier."

"That's the way it starts out, but you get wrapped up in those troubles like an octopus got you, and you wonder what you've gotten yourself into trying to get away from home."

Roscoe laughed and waved a hand. "Come on, Irwin, or you're going to start crying in your drink. We'd better get up to Baby Sister's quick or she'll call us a bunch of names. You know how she is about being on time."

Each time Roscoe saw Baby Sister she looked more and more like Earline, too. Big boned, yet she had grown up lanky. And the weight she gained after her first child did not hurt her. She was a very attractive woman of twenty-eight. The smiles of her brothers were testaments when they walked into her home.

"Hey, Foxy," Irwin said before lifting her off the floor in his bearhug.

Dinner was a happy affair with Raymond and Baby Sister filled with talk and her special shrimp gumbo. Even Raymond got the spirit, talking more than Roscoe had ever known him to talk. The couple gasped when the brothers told them about the encounter with the farmer. The possibility of the reunion spurred the greatest excitement, however.

"How are y'all planning to get everyone back?" Baby Sister asked, turning to Roscoe. "It's been years now since we've all been together. I think the last time was Mama's funeral."

"Y'all?" Roscoe asked. "You make three. All we have to do is get Tyrone off that damned submarine, get Chris off the radio in Alabama, and throw a net over Emmanuel out there in Utah somewhere."

"Lightweight stuff, huh?" she said, smiling. "Look how hard it was to get Irwin back for a few days and he's just in Chicago. If it wasn't for that little piece of scroungy land . . ."

"Watch your mouth, Sister,"

43

"... we wouldn't see him today, eating my muffins like they going out of style."

Irwin faked hurt surprise. "Actually, I've been back scouting the town. I might come back here and set up practice, you never know. I could probably make more money here than I can in Chicago anyway. And be safer, too."

"But seriously, you know Emmanuel will be the problem," she said. "After all this time do you think we can get him back here for a family reunion?"

"Somebody'll have to go out there and rope him."

Baby Sister frowned. "That old man he's after probably been dead for years. He probably died from fright when he looked around and saw that speck way behind him, but steady coming on. He probably knew that the speck would grow larger and larger and sooner or later destroy him. He probably chose the sooner and went off to the side of the road and died. Just curled up and died. Emmanuel probably just walked on by, not believing he could be cheated so easily."

Raymond shook his head. "Ruth Anne, your imagination can turn wild sometime."

Baby Sister's smile was faint. "Maybe so. One thing I know for sure is that Emmanuel is now chasing a ghost. A year or two after he left town, maybe not. But now, his goal is the search, not the man."

"Somebody's going to have to go get him," Roscoe said after a moment's pause. "And they'll have a fight on their hands, too. He wants to bring the Old Man back to life. To come back empty-handed—whew!"

"He's not the only one who ever tried to bring Daddy back. All of us did that in one way or another. Here, I have something for both of you to read."

She went quickly into the kitchen and brought down an envelope from the top of the refrigerator. She dropped it on the table between Irwin and Roscoe. "That was his last letter. It's about four months old."

Roscoe took it, Irwin leaning to read the large script over his shoulder:

Dear Baby Sister,

He turned back from California. My bus got caught in a blizzard in Donner Pass. We sat up there for four hours before we could creep on into Reno. I remember there were footprints leading off somewhere. His? He was on the bus ahead of mine. I had that on good faith from the ticket clerk in Sacramento. I figured they would be stopped, too. So while everything was stopped I walked up ahead to find him, but I didn't. They must have gotten through before the snow hit real bad. The snow came up above my knees.

There wasn't hardly any snow to speak of in Reno. I checked all around but there was no sign of him. I thought maybe he got off back in Tahoe in all that snow, but the driver said no. It took me two days to find the driver of the bus. He was in a casino dropping quarters in a slot machine. Lucky for me he had a few days off. Of course, he acted like he wasn't supposed to say too much about who he dropped off and where. But I think he knows the man I'm after. I trusted him and I could tell by the way he answered my questions that he could be trusted.

Anyway I'm close to him now and I should be home in a few weeks.

Yours truly,
Emmanuel

Irwin sat back and wiped his forehead. "Are there others?"

His sister nodded, then went back to the kitchen and this time returned with more envelopes, some of them yellowing. She opened them and handed them one at a time to her brothers.

April 29, 1975

Baby Sister,

Although this letter will miss by a couple weeks, I want to wish all of you a Happy Easter. It stays cold out here all the way to late May. Then the summer comes on burning the grass brown.

I'm back in Salt Lake City working at a motel on Wells Street. I'm one of the cooks. I don't mind it much, but it doesn't pay as well as construction. I don't know how long I will be here. I've been here in this town so many times already I've stopped counting.

On Easter Sunday, I had the day off, spent it in my room, mostly watching television. There's a woman I sometimes see when I'm

45

here. Her name is Jessie. She reminds me of Annette, Raymond Smith's oldest sister.

I don't know how long I'll be here. I hope not too long. Mays is here somewhere, if not in town no more than ten miles away. He's probably somewhere around the Great Salt Lake wishing that were the Pacific Ocean and he could swim to China and leave me here. I keep asking around to see if anyone has seen him, but folks just hunch their shoulders or screw up their faces as if they're tired of me asking. Sometimes I think I get a little tired myself. . . .

May 3, 1973

Baby Sister,

My thirty-second birthday was spent winning $500 in the slot machines in Reno. You'd like the town, so would Chris the way emcees talk up a storm before the shows in the flashy nightclubs. $500 is a nice present to myself, don't you think?

The people here are tourists from Minnesota, Kansas, and places out this way. They play these machines while they're drunk out of their minds. No wonder they can't win. They go to the clubs and don't even know who they're listening to. Last week I ran into a man out here from Ohio. He claimed he heard of Roscoe and that monster Ohio State team. He asked what Roscoe was doing and I told him my brother was running a plush bar back there, if he quit football. The man said he would stop in there when he got back there and shoot the breeze with Roscoe. Of course, he was probably just saying that to make conversation.

The big mountains a few miles from here look like one big curtain of rock. Old Mays is somewhere up there, I think. Somebody told me they saw him hitchhiking around Lake Tahoe yesterday. They said he looked bad, like he was on his last go-round. Well, we'll see. I'll leave here tomorrow. On into California. I'm glad it's not January because the snow up there is something else. Knock out traffic every other day. They say a Black man found the best pass through these mountains almost a hundred years ago and they named the pass after him. Beckwourth was his name. Wonder if he was after somebody, too?

June 2, 1968

Hey Baby Sister,

Yesterday in Sacramento I was standing in a crowd watching a parade. I saw a man who looked like Mays. I kept my eyes on him all during the parade trying to inch closer. When the parade ended I tried to follow the man as he walked away. You couldn't imagine how I felt. I was sweating as I ran through the crowd. I had nothing

46

but my bare hands! That's as it should be, I figure. Just me and him and bare hands. He walked that slow walk, with his head tilted to the left and down. We were coming up on an alley and I pushed him in. I threw him up against a wall, my thumb just below his adam's apple. The old man had been too frightened to holler or anything. He just stood there hands raised, eyes bulging, mouth wide-open, his wine-breath on my face, words caught deep in his throat. His dirty brown teeth. I felt sorry for him, I didn't know what to say. It wasn't Mays. I ran.

The brothers were silent. Outside a car door slammed, and footsteps were those hollow knocks on the pavement. Roscoe spoke first. "So what's Chris saying on those tapes he sends back?"

Baby Sister wiped at her eyes. "Well, the latest one I have is six months old. The next one should be coming any day now. He's turned down some good office jobs just to stay on the mike. He loves the attention; y'all know that. At his age you'd think he knew better, but you Americus men don't know when to quit. I have the tape all set up. I figured we'd get into all this tonight."

On that tape after the shouts through the first bars of an up-tempo tune, after the whistling and handclapping through a refrain, came Cha-Cha's voice soft and clear. A ballad slipped under it. He was on a telephone hookup with a giggling teenager. "Woman was made out of the rib of man. Not from his head so that she may top him, not from his feet to be trampled upon, but from his side to stand mightily with him, and, most of all, from his heart to be loved. Do you understand me this evening?" A metallic voice squealed, "Talk trash, Cha-Cha. Talk trash!"

They laughed, imagining their brother too excited to sit down during his shows, dancing around the control booth in designer jeans, bright T-shirt, and leather cap.

"That fool don't miss a trick," Irwin said. "And what about Tyrone?"

"Tyrone is still on a submarine somewhere in the Pacific Ocean. He's still working on that time-box of his and claims he has it just about perfected."

"I thought he had given up on that years and years ago." Roscoe leaned forward on the sofa.

"No, he's still at it just like he's still writing music and sending it all over the place. Well, he's finally figured out a way to get the voices of the past into this box—sounds like some new kind of a radio the way he describes it. He claims he can bring back words from outer space, that words are energy that never gets absorbed. They just move up, out, and away into space."

Irwin frowned. "This is news to me. How in hell can he do that?"

"You forgot that your brother is a downhome genius," Baby Sister said. "It started one day when he was mad at Daddy, I don't remember what for, but he asked Daddy what happened to words after they were spoken. Daddy looked at him and, to tell you the truth, I don't know whether he was going to laugh or cry. So he told Tyrone that he didn't know—I thought the world was going to end that very second!—and told him to study up on it in school. Well, y'all know how all through high school and college he would read up on his history and build all those funny gadgets. Now he's claimed he's got the gadget that can take the sound energy, gather it from space, and bring it back. He's claimed he's heard Frederick Douglass talking with John Brown and heard a little of Denmark Vesey, too, before the static drowned it out."

"There's a lot of conversations to pick from," Roscoe said. "From the caveman on up. How can he pick just two out of millions and millions and millions?"

"That's where you got me, Roscoe. He explained it to me, something about intensity levels and color codes. You'll have to ask him about that."

The brothers sat stunned, the thought slowly sinking in. Why, he might even tune in the first remembered Americus! Together they wondered how those voices sounded. Jesus with a gravelly voice? Harriet Tubman cursing as she brought slaves through black woods? And could you hear Nat Turner talking in tongues, and what did Joe Louis say to his manager just before he left the dressing room for the second Schmelling fight? Televisions would grow cobwebs while people sat around Tyrone's box tuning in past conversations. Moses' voice with a flick of the switch. Roscoe saw it all! The world unveiling would be at the North Star Café with Cha-Cha as master of ceremonies.

Roscoe was shaking his head. "Go-ud damn, Sis! Tyrone perfect something like that, and white folks will be jamming money and prizes in his hip pocket."

"Or try to steal the idea," she said. "But it's only a matter of time with him. He's going to get off that boat and attract a whole lot of attention one of these days."

"Well, let's hope he gets off next summer," Irwin put in. "And I hope folk are ready for him when he does come back."

Baby Sister looked off. The Americuses would gather in the bright spring with lovers or spouses, and they'd talk and watch one another closely to gauge what time and love had done—as the three of them did that evening. An urgency was growing.

"Let's settle it then. I'm not letting you two out of my house until we agree on this thing. Next spring, OK? We've got almost a year."

Three days later Irwin left on a plane heading west into a bank of white billowy clouds. Before he left, he had visited briefly with Charlotte and the girls.

"They're doing fine, Ros," he said, as they walked toward the terminal. "They miss you, too. Charlotte didn't say that, of course, but I could tell. The girls can't wait for you to take them out this weekend. And happy birthday. You getting up there in age, bro. Don't you be no fool now." He gave Roscoe an expensive gold watch as a gift.

Roscoe drove him past the old house, two families of strangers as tenants now. Although he screened the tenants as carefully as possible, they were all simply passing through. The house needed a fresh coat of paint, several window screens needed patching.

The car stopped in front, the motor still running. "A week of work and it would look as good as it did years ago," Irwin said. "What's the inside like?"

Roscoe shrugged. "About as good as you could expect. Every

three months a toilet is stopped up or something else falls apart. Besides that, it's holding up well."

For a long moment they were silent as they listened for shouts and running steps twenty years old. They saw the ancient maple from which Irwin had once fallen and broken his collarbone. Gone was the front door of three glass panels through which Chris, an old sheet as his cape, had run through when he attempted to take flight as Superman. Gone was his blood from the porch, gone was Baby Sister's hopscotch ladder on the front sidewalk, gone was the yellow glider, gone were the rose bushes that grew so wildly at the side of the house. A thin woman in pink mules had waved from the porch and Roscoe waved back. Then they sped off to the airport.

Walking from the terminal now, Roscoe remembered Irwin standing in the doorway of the plane and talking smack to the stewardess while others shifted restlessly behind him. He would have her phone number before the plane started its descent toward Chicago. Irwin, the late starter, making up for all the lost time he had spent being respectable. Roscoe chuckled. And him with the nerve to talk about age and being a fool!

Roscoe turned back to finishing the dirty work of clearing the land, because he thought it the least he could do. The land case was settled in a few days, as expected. The county sheriff and real estate agent gave the squatters three days to get off the land. There was no fight, no frontier ambush. The squatters were gone in two days. No one knew where they went, as no one knew where they came from. Eastern Kentucky was what one of the sheriff's men said. Tennessee, another had put in. It was dirty work for the deputies to chase off a poor white family so a black dentist from Chicago could buy land and claim it as his own. So Roscoe said little to them, just watching and listening while they went about their duty. Roscoe talked three men into helping him clear away a shack. The lumber and little bit of metal that was the house were sold at the junkyard, and Roscoe let his helpers split the money three ways. He fought the small pity coming on for the squatters, telling himself that it was his brother's land, after all. Irwin's legal right, though Irwin would never return home to live on it. A tax shelter, an excuse to get home every two years, good land for hunting? The Okies would find another corner of someone's land to plant. Besides Roscoe had convinced himself that Caudill had been sired by "paterollers" and lynchers. Therefore, it was easier to wish him and his family eternal pilgrimages around the Middle West, haunting the backwoods and the gloomy banks of rivers.

LINE 3

THE LOVES AND LIVES of the daddies of daddies of daddies. New blood in those extensions as they drive through their lives. On his fortieth birthday, Roscoe, Sr., had walked into the kitchen, pushed his hat far back on his head, relit a stub of a cigar, and spoken to his four sons gathered restlessly at the kitchen table.

"Cut that playing out now." Then he had settled back in a chair, stroking his belly upward. That was the signal. Roscoe, Jr., stopped cuffing his brothers on the sides of their heads. Irwin snatched a wandering marble from under the table and straightened up.

"You boys young now. Or at least you pretend you young. But I know you got sense. You lived in this house long enough for you to have good sense. So believe me when I tell you that you only as young as you feel. A lot of folks say that, but only a few live by it. You can do anything you want if you decide to. Anything, that is, except act too mannish and cross me and your mama. Especially your mama. If you cross me, you'll get stripes across your butts, just a whippin. But if you cross your Mama, you in for a stone beatin. You'll look worse than a zebra. But I'm not here to scare you this day, just here to tell you that I feel like a million dollars, and when y'all get to be forty years old just remember what your old man was like on this day. And that he announced that he would never die."

Looks were traded all around. Except that it was afternoon and he was home with the family, he looked OK. There was no madness burning brightly in the eyes, no nervous high-voltage wringing of the hands. These were the only cues the boys knew, picked up from watching Mr. Otis Sparks whom everyone called crazy. Sparks was a man who walked the back alleys at night, crying, groaning, chanting to himself. Nutty as a fruitcake, neighbors had whispered about him. But, no, there was nothing like that about their father. And he said that he would live forever!

They shrugged and watched him go tenderly among his gifts. The can of cheap cigars was Emmanuel's idea. The shirts in brilliant geometric designs were Irwin's. Irwin would be a whiz with triangles and trigonometry. The checkered ties to balance the shirts were Chris's gift, Irwin was just a kid after all. Roscoe, Sr., would wear those shirts and those ties, not together, however, but wear them just the same, for he would rather risk the teases of gin-drinking poker players than the disappointment of his sons.

And after the thank-yous and the bearhugs, the older boys would notice him slipping two fingers of bourbon into his tea. That afternoon, forty in the shade of his kitchen, he would sip from the cup, lean dangerously back in the chair, and tell them what they had heard only a few times before. About family and blood and time. About how the family was so tight and never took any mess from anything or anybody. He would lead them through the maze of family history, the broken line of steel mills, of stinking slaughterhouses, and the Ohio River, of Georgia pine forests. The end was the beginning, and a huge man and a town in Georgia— Georgia where the root ends were warmed at the fiery core. Of family of blood of time.

BUT, DADDY

And it was 1834, that end which was the beginning, and the lie of Major Riley. No one knew where the "major" part came from except, perhaps, that the old man was continually waiting around for a war to prove his courage. Such a war would never come, at least enough for him to recognize the daily struggles of men as war. The man died in 1859, mad, wrestling death in a shameful way, much like an old hound, its throat slashed, yet still closing in on a cornered racoon.

But in 1834 his tall slave Caesar, the best blacksmith in south-central Georgia, bought his freedom. Was given a note from the courage-keeping major. "Return this boy to me." Caesar couldn't read, and thought the scribbling was sure enough freedom papers, a sign of mutual honor among men. He started north on a useless swaybacked horse that the major sold him. Only once did he bother to show that note. That one time was almost his undoing. He showed it to a kind-faced bank clerk who was riding out to a plantation to confirm some figures. The man greeted Caesar and summoned enough nerve to ask for the freedom paper. He read it, then rode down the road a piece with Caesar. When they came upon three paterollers, he turned Caesar over to them. Caesar was only five miles from Riley's plantation and somehow hoping that the North, the Ohio River, would be just over the next ridge. Tennessee as an acre, Kentucky as a backyard of his new life.

The three men led him back to the Major, the long-gone clerk done read them the note because they couldn't read either. They were grizzled men in tatters, "dirt-eaters" they used to call them. Well, they rode back a couple miles before Caesar took and slapped away the rifle of one of the men, slammed a right to the face of another man, crushing bone, and urged the broken-down horse toward the trees. A ball whizzed past his head. Another. He dug his heels into that horse's ribs. They got to the woods, crossed a stream, then headed for thicker cover. Whatever that horse was, he seemed to take to the forest, wasn't scared of the darkness and the trees, whatsoever. Caesar slapped that horse on, and they followed the stream away from Riley's plantation. Yells, curses, screams behind them. Were they a mile away from the paterollers? Were the men just at his ear? He didn't bother to look back, just pushing that horse on, knowing that it would fall out sooner or later from being so tired and from surprise that it could run so fast.

And away, away he rode, not knowing where except that it was away from the plantations. He rode for what seemed like hours until that horse slowed down and stopped. Caesar cursed and kicked that horse, then realized that it had done the best it could do. It needed rest. "Can you see him now, boys? Can you see him in those strange woods on foot?"

Roscoe, Sr., had stood, his hat cocked well over one eye by then, fists raised. Then he removed his hat and ran his thumb across his forehead. From the front of the house came their mother's humming, the insistent hum that's never noticed until it stops. The boys didn't dare move, didn't dare speak.

"You must see him lead that horse out of the woods and look across a road to a big field of cotton. There must have been a dozen or so folk in the field, and every once in a while one of them would straighten up and half-scream, half-chant his way through a song. Like young Job who screamed like a woman and called that singing. Then down the road came a wagon. The driver was sitting up there with his head down, shoulders rocking slowly to the corner of his mouth, a large floppy hat draped low, shadowing his eyes. Caesar greeted the man, scaring him half to death. The driver looked around to see if the overseer was around.

"What do you want?" that driver must have asked.

"I want somebody to write a note for me." As he fanned flies, he explained all to the driver, trusting him. The man glanced again to the woods, to the broken-down horse nibbling brush at the wood's edge, to the big man standing in front of the wagon. Then he scratched his throat.

"Only person I know can write is back there about a mile. Name is Ola. But you better not try to see her. She in the house." He must have explained that the owner of the plantation was away, but that the head overseer was around. "You wait here off the road, back up in the piney woods. I'll take you to her."

"How long will that be?" Caesar asked. Any second now he expected the white trash to come busting out of those woods.

"I don't know. Just do like I say if you want me to help you."

Why should he trust that man he had never seen before? Just because they were the same color? He was never going back to Riley's plantation. Never. He faded into the trees, looking behind, around him, searching out sound, then watched the road. Again, the screamchant from the field.

And it seemed like hours before that wagon came back along the road, moving just as slow as it did before. Looking straight ahead as the wagon came up, the driver said, "Climb in back there and get under that blanket. And keep still if you don't want one hundred lashes."

"To hell with lashes," I can hear Caesar saying. "I take lashes off no man."

55

"Just hush up and get in back." Caesar could hear the man talking as that wagon started moving. He told Caesar about three men who stopped him three miles down the road. They asked him whether he had seen a big man on an ugly gray horse. The driver said that he had and pointed off in another direction. They lit out, not even bothering to thank him.

"Their horses looked a little tired. We don't have much time. They might come back trying to find me."

Yet Caesar still wondered at his faith. Suppose this man driving the wagon had told them otherwise? Suppose they were waiting up the road to take him in? They'd give the driver a new coat for his treason. You often trusted those you suffered with, but then only a few of those could be trusted with your life. The wagon slowed, picked up speed, slowed again. Either the man or the horse couldn't make up its mind. Why was it taking so long? Caesar kept an eye out, watched the brownish red road snake from under the wagon and away. The wagon pulled inside a gate, then stopped. He heard voices.

"Stay here and don't move, son. I'm bringing Ola for you."

The afternoon sun baked him under the scratchy cover. Flies discovered the smell of his sweat from the small opening he kept in order to breathe. Flies as traitors, the enemy that sun. And he waited, not moving, just the fingers still propping the cover to keep the air coming in, though it was as if a hand had been clapped over his nose and mouth. Then footsteps, a woman's voice shushed quiet.

"I got somebody here who can write. Tell her what you want. Just stay like you is."

Caesar could see only the gray cotton skirt draped over thin hips, an elbow with dry skin at the joint.

"Sho is hot, Cle," the voice said. Then she asked Caesar what he wanted her to write. He told her, watching her arm move. "Not so fast." She wrote on, the old man talking to himself about the weather, about fishing. Then several pieces of paper dropped past the opening. She pushed two pieces under the cover and picked up the others.

"Clumsy, ain't I?" she giggled.

"Thank you, girl. We'll see you later."

The gray dress moved away. Caesar heard the man climb in the wagon. They were moving again, turning in a circle.

"You going back to your horse and them piney woods now. Ola gave you two papers. You might lose one. You never know."

They moved on the bumpy road, and Caesar tried to make out the writing. He couldn't read, only judge script. But it was too dark to judge. He pushed the paper into the light.

"Put that paper back in! The woods got eyes, that cotton field got eyes. Them crows can spread secrets just as sure as I'm sitting here. Ain't you lived long enough to know that?"

Then soon the wagon stopped. "There's yo' hoss yonder. He should be good and rested by now. There's something for him in this here bucket. When you finish with the bucket leave it by the big bush over there. Walk back in the woods and wait until dark. Ain't too long now 'fore dark. Then y'all start north. Them po' trash will probably stop somewhere and get drunk come dark. You follow the north star, son. Just follow the star."

A HOME, WHERE?

Then Chris had shifted, Emmanuel shifted. The name, Daddy. Tell us about the name.

Sons, we here as testimony of Caesar's faith in the old man and his courage getting through woods at night. South Georgia was evil in them days, the devil's playground. If I could find you boys another word for it, I would tell it to you. But evil is the best I can do now 'cause your Mama in the next room half-listenin' and she don't want me introducin' y'all to cuss words . . .

His mind was on the North. On Canada and the snow. Somebody probably told him about cutting east to Savannah and catching a ship bound for Philadelphia or someplace like that. But Caesar was not excited about getting out on anybody's ocean, so he took his chances on land. Chance those paterollers, those mountains in Tennessee, past those caves in Kentucky that could hide a hundred bears, past those Indians in Ohio who caught and boiled runaway slaves for stew—that's what they used to tell them in those days, you know. He knew the dangers, though not the vastness of the land. Can you ride with him awhile?

Two days after he left the plantation with his new papers, he stopped just above a small town and rested under some big ol' pine trees. They probably smelled like turpentine. By now those things like slave catchers and Indians didn't bother him. Now it was his name that bothered him. He had told himself that he would take the Major's last name whenever he went free. That was before the Major tried to trick him back into slavery. No, he'd never call himself Riley.

He lay beneath that tree thinking, must have. It was nice there and he rested and the horse rested, and he knew that somewhere he would have to leave that horse and get another one. Gotta leave the best of your helpers sometimes. That town was quiet and peaceful, and somewhere he heard a bell ringing. He must have thought again about the North. If he had to stay in the woods, would there be plenty of fish in the creeks, plenty rabbits in the woods just like down there?

He decided just like that to take the name of that town because of that peaceful moment, nothing else. Somehow with the name he could always remember that moment of peace while struggling to get away. Americus was the name of the town. Americus was the name he took. Caesar Americus. (Years later somebody would tell him how the town got its name. It was named after the richest, powerfulest, and drunkest man around. The man used to claim that he was 'a merry ole cuss' and so named his town after his ways. Some white folks got strange ways of makin' jokes, sons.)

He never told how he got from central Georgia. And to me that was always the part I wanted to hear about. Did he go west to the Mississippi and catch a boat going up past Memphis, St. Louis, and Cairo, Illinois? did he get in with a free black family riding North in a wagon? We don't know, except three months later this warm-weather man done crossed the Ohio River and is working in Cincinnati. It was October and turning cold already. The first chill made him give up thinking about Canada for awhile.

He worked on the river. After all, it wasn't the ocean and you could always see the other side. You could make a lot of money working the river. In those days, river rats was what they called the men working on the barges. And he soon became the heart of legends as something of an imitator. Could solo at the head of crews doing them Irish songs. Out-Irish the Irish, he could. Could do the same with the German language, too. Plus he could out-drink them red-faced Germans who came to Cincinnati with their beer recipes and would make whole fortunes on beer, then later on sausages and hams. And he stayed on in that town which on warm evenings grew to stink of river and a little further up among its hills to smell of slaughtered cows and pigs.

In 1842 Caesar opened a bar on the levee, a bar which became the prime target of threats and hisses from the local chapter of the Colored Women's Temperance Society. A window was once broken by an enraged woman screaming about the evils of drink. She called Caesar the devil's helper and a scoundrel who gave the race a bad name. She aimed a rock at the shingle with his name over the door, NORTH STAR CAFE, C. AMERICUS, ESQ., PRO-PRIETOR. Missed. Then the others joined in the screaming, looking around for rocks. Caesar pleaded with them. Told them they were taking food from the mouths of his young wife and baby sons. He promised a healthy donation to the society, to close at a decent hour, to allow no man to drink himself into a blind stupor. He told them he would even take the "bones" from the fists of the river rats. All this he told them, hating himself for having to say it. All this to save his North Star Café, a testimony to faith.

BUT, DADDY, WHERE IS HOME IN THIS STRANGE LAND?

The bar would be passed down, battle-tried, standing squat there near the alley in Bucktown. From Caesar's oldest son Stewart to Stewart's oldest son Asbury to his second son Leo because Asbury's oldest, Theodore, my Daddy, had died in France in 1918. It stopped with Uncle Leo, who wasn't too interested in running a café. The family café died out until I come up here and opened up my little place over the B & O tracks. But it ain't good enough yet to call a real café in the way the family used to have. One of these days it will be.

But let me get back to Caesar. The business was his life, though he raised big strapping sons who worked the river. One went clear to Oberlin to hear the great Frederick Douglass and shake his hand. There were the two who fought for the Union, the same two who begged their father, fifty-year-old Caesar, to stay at the café and keep it open. Folks would need that kind of place to talk, lean back in their chairs, back into their lives. Although he could still floor a bull with one punch, they thought him too old to do anything else. He resigned himself to an uneasy peace of sheltering countless frightened families who crossed over from Kentucky, content to feed them hot meals and let the men sample his homemade whiskey.

He kept the bar open for blue-suited men who would limp in, their pants baggy, thinning in the seat and at the knees, and coats too tight. An army of men. They would sit long into the winter nights, and they would talk of battles along hills and rivers named after Indians. The men pointed to scars and said that they never wanted to see war again. When Caesar died, these same scarred men rode through the night to make one of the largest funerals ever held in Cincinnati.

Let me tell y'all right quick about the end of the North Star Café in that town. It was 1918, a little before the war ended. Leo, bless his soul, wasn't too good a manager. He thought the bar could run itself on its past history, I guess. So when he saw it was about to go under, he sold it to an Irishman named Gilligan. Didn't check with none of the family, just up and sold the place. Well, I was mad at him for that, stayed mad at him for that, stayed mad at him for years. I hung around town working in the stockyards and in a foundry for five or six years before I came up here. Heard that the steel and paper mills were hiring like crazy. When I got up here, I walked into the rolling mill office, and the man gave me a shovel and asked me if I could start that day. Worked long hours and made real good money, too. Then later on I fell in with a man named Herschel Evans, and old Herschel had him a truck. On weekends we'd drive down to the coal mines, right along the Ohio River below Portsmouth. We'd leave before the sun came up, get down there, and load that truck skyhigh with coal, buy some large jars of moonshine, and bring all that back here. We'd sell the coal and moonshine in one day, try to get some sleep, and then be back in the mill the next day. By and by I had enough money so that I could open me up an after-hours joint. Right where it is now at the B & O overpass. All these years I've wanted to buy another place, but it's never worked out that way. The depression came along and stopped everything. Settled over this town like a mean and suffocating fog.

It took until after the war for me to really recover. Started fish fries on Friday nights and chicken fries on Saturdays. Your Mama did most of the cooking. They were fighting to get in here then, so many of them. I painted the windows black out of respect for the church folk and had to pay a little side-money to Officer Starkey to keep them quiet downtown at police headquarters. There were four of y'all already. Bedrooms had to be added on and the kitchen needed new plumbing. Well, it got so we kept it open four nights a week.

AND DADDY WHAT MORE, EVEN NOW FROM BEYOND DEATH, WHAT MORE?

And still what more of the birth, of work, of death of the fathers? The deaths were quick. Caesar died in the café, a loud laugh going to a rattling cough. He fell to the floor behind the bar. Stewart died just as suddenly, while breaking up an argument between two teamsters. Asbury died of pneumonia, the result of working in the rain while helping to put up a YMCA building. Dazed from gas, Theodore stepped on a mine in central France. But Roscoe, Sr.'s death was the cruelest of all.

61

By his fiftieth birthday, Roscoe, Sr., the Old Man, as the boys had begun to call him, could afford to drive a red Buick Dynaflow. He wore another dark hat, greying already along the brim, cocked to one side of his large head. There was always a half-smoked cigar in one corner of his mouth. On that fiftieth birthday he leaned back on a chair in the bright kitchen as he had done ten years before.

"Sons, gather close to you the ones you love and protect them if you can." That before the history.

Strange about the murderers of giants in this world—the thinness of their rage, their unforgivable isolation. It was snagga-toothed Jake Mays who did it. Few folks respected Mays and it wasn't just because of his weakness. A weak man can be tolerated and even loved by some. But Mays's weakness willed ugliness. He'd smack a woman or a child for show, but he never touched a man who insulted him.

It started, if it is ever clear when anything starts, when Mays lost his first ten fights as a child, when his father looked at him in pity, frowning at his fistless son. Or was it simply the day after the night Jake lost one hundred dollars in an American Legion crap game? That morning he was on his way to Robinson's Café for a cup of coffee. To tease the new big-legged waitress, maybe, and let any stray smile from her soothe his sense of hurt. Tyrone was playing touch football in the street with a gang of other boys. Quarterback for one of the teams, Tyrone faded back, as he had heard Otto Graham do, and fired a long pass to one of his men. The ball missed the outstretched arms of the receiver by a few yards and hit slow-moving Jake square in the face. The players leaned on fences, cars, on each other, snickering. Looked at Mays's hurt face and laughed some more. Tyrone ran to gather the ball and mumbled something about being sorry. But it was those grins and laughs that Mays saw and heard. He limped closer to Tyrone and smacked him hard. Once. No one moved. Then, as Mays moved away, Tyrone searched for a rock, a pop bottle, to throw. Whatever he found and threw missed. Mays turned around, stared at the boy, then walked on more quickly, looking back twice.

When Roscoe heard about it, he walked out of the house. He found Mays at Robinson's, hunched over coffee. He called Mays outside, and without a word he whipped Mays like a child. The few people in the café crowded in the door to watch, the slaps sounding like dull shots. Then Roscoe let him drop to the pavement, bleeding from a busted lip.

"Don't ever touch one of my boys again. Nobody touches my sons except me." Then he turned and walked away, wiping his hands as if he had touched something filthy.

But there is even a pride in cowardice, a desperate and nervous pride. Near dawn, with a knife and slipping up on the Old Man as he was closing up, Mays found a desperate strength to strike once, twice. Surprised at what he had done, he covered his opened mouth with both hands and ran. Another man, rushing to catch a hand in the last poker game, found Roscoe near the door trying to crawl inside. The knife lay only a few feet away. This man cried his way to a phone and called an ambulance. Then he called Roscoe's home. The sons beat the ambulance there. Beat the 6:30 freight train that rumbled past every morning, heading south, shaking the old blackeyed building.

By the time of the funeral it was decided between Roscoe and Emmanuel that they would have to catch Mays, that he would have to die. He already had a four-day headstart. The question was who. Roscoe, Jr., was finishing his freshman year at Ohio State, and the boys argued that he should go back to school. When Earline overheard them, she tried to stop such talk. After all, there was a law, and to harm the worthless Mays would be two crimes committed. They told her that justice was a sometime thing if you didn't perform it yourself.

And Emmanuel packed a bag after talking with old Silas, a man who roomed in the same house with Mays. Silas, with the all-seeing eye, said Mays was in Chicago. Emmanuel left without saying good-bye to anyone, and by the next morning he was winding through Indiana, feeding a quart of oil to his old Ford every three hundred miles, a revolver resting beneath the front seat. No one heard from him for a month. And no one expected Emmanuel to return without Mays. Emmanuel, the quiet one who sang in the church choir and rarely had fights while growing up. But when he did fight he hurt others so badly. Didn't know where to stop, this Emmanuel, whose intensity silenced the agitators and forced them to look around for someone to stop these few fights.

Then the scribbled letters started coming and kept coming, one about every other month for the next three years. At first Earline would read the letters silently, then refold them. She hid them away, and all they knew were the names of the towns. "Your brother is in Battle Creek, Wyoming, now." After she died a letter mysteriously came to Baby Sister once a year. Baby Sister also found the earlier ones and shared them with Roscoe and any other brother who happened to visit her. All those tortured letters with no return addresses.

One letter said he had missed Mays by three days in St. Paul, Minnesota. When a letter came from Lincoln, Nebraska, the brothers figured Mays's time was up. In a place like that Mays should stick out like a rabbit against the snow. But then the letters came from Denver, Salt Lake City, Cheyenne. Denver again. Places Roscoe had never been, could barely imagine except as towns where cowboys shot up bars on Saturday nights.

Earline went to work in a container plant and raised her children. She was too old to start factory work, but they needed the money. Factory work paid much better than domestic work. A sympathetic foreman understood and gave her the lightest job on the line. The boys helped her run the after-hours club on weekends. Baby Sister ran the house.

Earline had talked less and less about Emmanuel before she died, as she talked less and less about the law and justice. Her husband had died at the hands of a miserable and lonely man, and no matter how senseless and enraging the fact, nothing would ever bring the big man back home. Emmanuel would come back one day, and she had hoped to live to see that day. She hoped that when he did return he could still smile, that he could live again, that everything in his life had not been wasted.

On the morning of his fortieth birthday, Roscoe, Jr., stopped his car in front of the house where until two months ago he had lived. As if on cue, his two daughters rushed to the car, appearing as if they wanted to run, but were held in check by that shadow behind the front door. Roscoe waved to the shadow of his wife, then opened the door for his children.

"Give me a little of that good sugar," he begged them. "Thataway, thataway." Then he pulled them down and announced that he was taking them to the zoo. They clapped their hands, did mean shimmies in their gratitude. Real showboats, his girls. Real class. They presented him with a boldly striped silk tie, and he made a mighty fuss over it. Then he let them roll the window down partially, but not too much, he scolded, because once they would get on the expressway, the wind might just reach in and pull them out.

"Then we could fly?" asked Grace, the daughter with Roscoe's mouth and forehead.

Mayisha giggled. "The way you eat, Grace, you'd be too heavy to fly." Mayisha, with her mother's face, who would be very tall. Roscoe remembered the slouch of her shoulders as she walked to the car. Teach a tall woman to keep high her head and shoulders. Teach her to move like a natural queen. He would teach her not to deny nature's gift of elegant motions. Ever. It only made for stunted beauty.

The girls talked of approaching summer, of swimming lessons they looked forward to, of Bible school they wanted to avoid. Roscoe was relieved that they were still too young for boys. What would he do then? What will he do then? What will he do now? All that he knew for sure was that he was taking his two daughters out for a summer's day and nothing else—the bar, the insatiable Everjean, spiteful Charlotte—nothing else mattered.

Grace curled up next to him. "Daddy, when are we going to King's Point like you promised?"

"How come you're asking Daddy?" Mayisha asked. "You're scared of all the rides anyway."

"Well, let's just see how things turn out today, huh? Today is the zoo."

And the zoo was a hot round of cages with Roscoe coaxing the girls back to see the lions twice. Cotton candy, peanuts, and popcorn. He loved the zoo as much as they did. Zoos and circuses had always been weaknesses of his. Some people remembered cities by the weather or money made or lost there, by lovers. Roscoe remembered places by the food, the bars, and most important, the zoos. There were Washington and Cleveland and St. Louis and San Diego and the Bronx, good zoos in all those places. As he watched the lions for the second time, the girls fidgeted and hummed songs. He considered other places, other times.

Once into a time the air was much chillier, no leaves on the trees. For seven hours he held his wife's hands in the labor room of a hospital. Her lips dry, her eyes frequently opening in the stunned surprise of the cycle of pain. Roscoe held her hands and tried to think of the greatest pain he had known. The twisted knee in the Michigan game? The cracked rib much earlier in high school? None of the bumps, few of the smashes of bone against his muscle gave him pain great beyond the moment. Few caused hours of agony. As he looked at his wife he was a little embarrassed that there was a mystery about her pain that he could never know. Was it a ripple of pain moving wavelike across her belly? A sharp stab? Later in the waiting room after she had been wheeled into delivery, he studied the afternoon. Outside it was partly sunny with the temperature near freezing. He could hear the steady rhythm of a heavy wire against the flagpole in front of the hospital. The traffic flowed in the fitful movement of his luck. It would be a boy this time, he knew. A big healthy fat-cheeked baby boy to carry the family name. Then he thought again to the pain, though his wife would be numbed from her stomach down. Again, to the pain he could only guess at.

"Daddy, how come we can't do this everyday?"

Grace. It was Grace talking through her mouthful of popcorn. Grace that afternoon, too.

"You'd like the zoo everyday, Grace?" asked Roscoe reaching to retie a ribbon around her hair.

"Well, not zoos all the time. Maybe parks, yeah, parks. Or swimming? Mama doesn't like to swim."

"Maybe your Mama gets a little tired sometime working around the house. You have to understand that."

"I understand," she said, taking another fistful of popcorn. "But I still like the parks and swimming and stuff like that."

He and Charlotte had agreed not to get back at one another through the girls, not to use them as weapons. They would tell them that, even though they were separated, they still loved each other and the girls very very much. The children would nod helplessly and they wouldn't understand. They could not understand what their parents could not understand.

"Hey, girl, you almost finished with that popcorn? Let's go back to the bears."

Mayisha had been quietly watching the morning crowd, the Cub Scout troops, the elderly folk with small bags of peanuts. Mayisha, the serene wise one. She'd be a painter, photographer, taking in all in the way she does. Roscoe knew that he'd screen the boys so roughly that only the most intelligent, the most aggressive would trouble themselves for her. After all, she wouldn't want to be bothered with idle chatter about clothes, cars, and dances. No, not his Mayisha.

With Roscoe holding his daughters' hands, they moved off through the bright afternoon. The times with his daughters were the best times. The lady days. Going home, he told them the funny animal stories his grandmother had once told him. One day he would tell them the family history.

Then in the speckled shade of an old maple tree in front of the house, Roscoe's ladies stepped grandly from the car. A finger lowered a slat in the front window venetian blinds. He was ready for the stare coming over it from the cool dark of the house he once

67

called home. The stare of those last days, the last nights that he slept on the couch. The girls lingered at the curb. After the hugs and kisses, they stood there wanting more, expecting more, needing more. But there was only his smile.

"Will we see you tomorrow, daddy?"

"I can't promise tomorrow, but I can promise you Saturday. Where do you want to go?"

"Fun Park, can we Daddy, huh? I want to try the roller coaster this time."

Roscoe nodded and waved. "Take care of your pretty selves. And your mother."

He pulled off from the shadow of the old tree and down the quiet street into the gloom of memory. Stared into the mirror.

"Well, Old Man, what do you think now? Am I less of a man because I didn't go inside and hold the woman I've loved for seven of the last twelve years?"

Then he caught himself, as he noticed Mrs. Patterson pausing to watch him from among her daffodils. He smiled at the elderly woman who once brought them spice cakes. Waved, this man Americus, this former husband, football and wrestling star—waved and drove to the other side of town.

LINE 4

AFTER IRWIN'S VISIT, after his birthday, Roscoe slipped on a banana-peel-of-a-day and fell square on his butt. That afternoon he mostly scowled as he sat in a front booth and read a newspaper. Then Wilson walked in.

"What is this, a bar or what?"

"Man, today I'm not really sure. It could be a bar, or a church. With you here it might be a circus. Take your pick. But remember that there's life in here and don't step on it."

"Well, I'll just sit here and figure it out."

"Inez will see that you get started off on the right track, might as well drink while you're figuring." Roscoe turned to the sports page. "What you doing out of uniform so early in the day, Wilson?"

"I'm off for a week. The supermarket is remodeling. They don't have to rent no guards while they remodel."

Roscoe nodded then lingered over the story of a pro running back negotiating a contract for the upcoming season. He had seen this same player smiling in TV commercials for aftershave lotions and Sears summer suits. He had also read that the player was considering a movie career.

"Go-ud damn, y'all," he announced to Inez and Wilson, to the dying street outside. "They just giving this dude money and he ain't no prettier than me. Shoot, I'm the one who should be in those ads, taking rich white folks' money and laughing all the way to the bank. This dude already got so much money he don't know what to do with it. Just bought his wife a Rolls for her birthday, the paper say. I can't understand it. They sit around in some office in New York figuring out ways to give this cat more money." Roscoe paused, shook his head. "Black folks done come a long way, y'all. Just think: they used to figure out ways to steal money from us. Now they throwing it at us."

"Don't say 'us,'" Wilson answered. "Him. The Superstar. That player is making somebody else besides himself a whole lot of money. You'd be on TV, too, if you could make somebody a whole lot of money."

Roscoe snorted, then refolded the paper. "I'm not whining about not being on television, you understand. I've been on television dozens of times. When I wrestled I used to holler, point, and shout into the camera. No, it's the gravy I'm talking about. It's just that things have changed a lot since 1964. You ever get the feeling you were made for a different time, that you belong to a different time? That you were born twenty years too early or twenty years too late?"

"Can't say I ever had that feeling," Wilson said. "I definitely wouldn't want to go way back to slavery times or the depression or the war, if you want to know the truth about it. And I don't know how it's going to be twenty years from now. Might not be no world, then where would I be? And I always did figure that things will get worse before they'll get better."

Roscoe sighed, got up, and walked to the jukebox. No imagination. If the man could sit there and imagine no other possibility for himself, then he's closed up inside, and I don't want to hear him whine and whine. Let him talk Inez' ears off.

He dropped in a quarter, punched Mary Wells's "My Guy," Little Willie John's "Fever," and Miles Davis' "Walkin." Strange how people wanted to dodge the horns of life rather than take those horns and snatch life anyway they wanted. Somewhere he had heard that there were three kinds of people: those that made things happen, those to whom things happened, and those who wondered what happened. For the past few years of his life he had been a "happened-to." Wilson only wondered.

In walked Holmes, a tall rangy fellow who had once played split end for Lincoln University in Missouri. Over the years Roscoe had played a lot of basketball in the park with him. Not much of a scorer for his height, this Holmes, but once in a while he would slap your jump shots off the court and into an alley.

"How you doing, Roscoe? You got a minute?"

"That's about all I got, Holmie. What's on your mind?"

"Well, you probably know about our team, the Bombers, right?

70

We're getting started early this year. A few of the fellows won't be able to come back this year, and we're trying to plug up some big gaps on the team. We're trying to get more folks to come out for the team." Roscoe looked up as the man hesitated. "I remember how you used to say you were thinking about a comeback. Well, I'm here to call you at your word and see whether or not you want to try out with us this year."

Roscoe snorted. "Man, do you realize that I have not played football in eighteen years?"

"I know that, but you stay in shape. You're probably in much better shape than half the dudes on the squad. Plus we need a line coach, somebody who knows what he's talking about. The other so-called line coach—you remember Tony, don't you—well, he done been transferred to Philly with his company. So you could be a player-coach."

Roscoe leaned back and laughed. "Look, how much could y'all pay me? I ain't gon' just jump up and run out there at my age for a freebee."

"You have to talk that over with King. He's the boss. As a matter of fact he would have been the one to mention all this to you, but since I was over this way I thought I'd run it down."

"You also know that King and I don't get along worth a damn."

Holmes frowned. "There you have it. It's not like getting a call from Don Shula in the middle of the middle of the night, but it's there all the same. Y'all don't have to love each other. Plus, the league is getting better. They're adding three new teams this year."

Roscoe yawned. "I'm flattered, man, but I'll have to think about it for awhile. Tell that to King, too, so he won't run in here trying to put the hard sell on me." Holmes smiled and left. Roscoe fingered the newspaper, chuckling to himself.

"Hear that, Wilson? They want me to play on the Bombers this year."

"What you going to be, the Satchel Paige of football?"

"I didn't tell them I'd play or anything. I might just coach a little. Those jitterbugs need help with the fundamentals of the game. I've watched them plenty of times."

71

Inez looked up from her nails and snickered. "We know you're going to play. Who you trying to fool? Wilson, he been talking about a comeback so much, he even got his jersey number all picked out."

"Well, they have been after me for years," Roscoe said. "When I first got back in town there was a raggedy team that wanted me to play with them. They they folded and the Bombers came along and they been after me for the longest, like I say. But I got to think about it this time, I really do."

The next day while jogging, all those glorious moments of past games crowded his thoughts. He had played and replayed those games so much he had forgotten what had been real and what was embellishment to spice up the reruns. He never grew bored with those memories.

What if he plunged on and the comeback failed? What if he had lost it all and what about the knee? Nothing would suffer except his pride. And he could lay to rest this itch to get the cheers from the crowd again, to test himself against the younger players, to be in the arena again, and not on the sidelines complaining about the morning rains of his thinning hair, the flesh slowly growing at his waist.

For the next month, he accelerated his training program, picking up the pace of his morning run. He started to lift weights at the YMCA, hoping to tone up some of the bulk in his arms, thighs, and chest. Even if he were to forget the offer to try out, come to his senses, finally, and admit that at some stage of his life *too late* became a simple truth and not a fear, he would still be better for it. He only dreaded making a fool of himself. Accepting the invitation to play and coach was one thing, but to go back to playing and look sorry was inexcusable. What the crowd thought wasn't as important as meeting the standard he set for himself. Crowds are fickle, changing in seconds from applauses to boos, from kisses to tomato throwing. Whole careers are spent learning this, as if applause were as steady as the sun, the air, the grass. Some careers foundered on the rocks of vanity, others remained hooked to the cliffs of self-pity. And there was always the horror of the fall, the long dizzying fall.

"Say, man, you trying to go up against Ali or what?" It was Newhouse who asked the question when Roscoe rushed into the Y locker room. Already dressed for the workout, Newhouse had spent the last five years lifting weights and trying to put on enough weight to present himself as a football player.

"A man's pride is his body," Roscoe said.

"You might have a point there, Big Man."

After loosening up, they started their routine, grunting as they worked their way up in weights. From time to time, each would pause to catch sight of himself in the full-length wall mirror. Flab melted before their very eyes, and flesh hardened, strength sprouting in seconds. It was drudgery, this building of the body beautiful, this nourishing of pride. Might some shrewd scientist make it all simpler one day with a pill? Drop a pill and make up for all one's sins—drink yourself blind, eat yourself soft, but a pill will make it all right again.

Roscoe saw himself in the Olympics, a super heavyweight, up against a big-bellied Russian. Snatching a ton above his head like a grinning John Henry. Machines, let alone a Russian, wouldn't stand a chance. Dead lifts were the halves of small cars lifted two feet from the floor, back muscles straining, the hamstrings and the backs of the thighs straining, forcing the center of gravity to the ass, all the crud collecting there, about to explode there. Would all that strain gather together years later to haunt him, hammering his shoulders forward and down into a permanent stoop, slamming pain up and down the spine when he tried to walk?

He set the weight down, and he felt suddenly as if he had just run another three miles.

"Good lift, Ros," Newhouse praised. "You keep at it and you'll be ready for the AAU championships."

Roscoe grinned and went to a full-length mirror. He smiled at himself, then patted the top of his head. Damned hair still coming out. He hadn't told anyone about his trips to a hair clinic during the winter. In a seedy fifth-floor office downtown, he had been hypnotized by the smile of the pretty receptionist, by her legs, which she crossed as she took down information on a file card. He was whisked to an office where a grave man in a long white coat met him and shook his hand. The man was bearded and thickly afroed in some new, curlier style, kept smoothing his hair as he talked gravely. On the walls were hung cross sections of the human scalp in vivid colors. The man moved to one side of the room and grunted over vials in a cabinet. Then he tested a few drops on Roscoe's scalp and grunted again.

"You can be helped," the man said triumphantly. He added that patience and five hundred dollars were necessary to work the miracle. Roscoe screamed at the five hundred and told the magician to forget it. He was entitled to a free scalp treatment, however. Despite the gentle fingers of the receptionist moving over his scalp—she doubled as a masseuse—and her soft talk into his ear, he left the place with no new hope. He bought three bottles of brightly colored potions (snake oil?) and applied them through the winter. His scalp grew nothing but funny smells. When he called back to complain, a recorded voice told him that the clinic's phone had been disconnected. His secret.

Now he listened to Newhouse huff and puff behind him. One day that man might make it. Meanwhile what kept driving him here? The roar from invisible crowds? In the mirror, Roscoe watched the man hold the weight over his head, his arms trembling, a fierce scowl on his face. Two seconds, three seconds the man held it.

"Right on, House." Five seconds of wild trembling in both arms, the weight pushing House to the right in a stagger. He dropped it, jumping back and raised his hands high overhead. The invisible crowd roared once again and Roscoe was among them. Newhouse was whole again and smiling, both hands high with the victory sign.

"Some days I don't have it, some days I do."

Roscoe turned. "You're doing fine, House. You're going after two hundred now?"

"Might as well." Roscoe helped him add weight to the bars,

74

then stepped to the side. Newhouse chalked his hands, then stepped up to the bar, the bar touched low on his shins. He breathed deeply, closed his eyes. Roscoe smiled. Dramatic, this Newhouse.

Then bending at the knees, butt high, he gripped the bar, and began breathing harder. He dropped his butt quickly then went to the lift. First there was the jerk of the head, the stiffening of the neck muscles, their stretching to taut cords. The feet set. He grunted and the weight rose in slow motion above his knees and waist to his chest. Quickly his legs scissored outward and he brought the bar to his shoulders. Gathering himself and still grunting and blowing hard as he must have seen them do on the broadcasts from the Olympic Games, he paused for a few seconds. Roscoe wondered what he would do were Newhouse to collapse under shock. The man had never "cleaned" that much weight before. But, Newhouse brought the weight over his head, then, cheeks bulged, he brought his feet together. He held the weight steady for a few seconds then dropped it arrogantly as if he were the greatest in the world and as if the world, his audience, had held its last breath, captive until he had the weight overhead and steady.

Roscoe slapped palms with Newhouse. "Next thing I know you'll be doubling your weight, House, and I won't be able to do nothing with you then."

Roscoe went to lift his own body's weight, then, shaking, cleared three hundred pounds, thirty pounds over his body weight. "Let's call it a day," he pronounced. "It's important to know when to stop, too."

So everyday for that week, those two champions lifted weights as if their goals were so specific, so tangible, that they washed the dullness from the routines. And after four weeks Roscoe decided to play football again.

The team workouts began in late July, and, as player-coach, Roscoe met with King a few days early to iron out strategy, to learn the new system. He found the offense a little flamboyant for his taste, a little too complicated for a semipro team that would probably need to spend an enormous amount of time on fundamentals. Only a handful of men had played college ball, though all had played on high school teams. One player had learned the game in prison. With the median age of twenty-five, most hadn't played organized ball for seven years.

"They'll be in good shape if nothing else," King said as they sat in one of the back booths in the bar. "I believe in thorough conditioning. We ain't had much problem in the past getting it together. It's been the timing in the offensive backfield, for one thing. Our quarterback and halfbacks colliding on handoffs, stuff like that. Then our zone switchoffs have been pretty messed up, too. On some plays a free safety will be standing, looking around as people whiz by him. We've got to shore up in those areas."

Roscoe winced as King went on.

"We've always done OK. Nothing to write home about, you understand, and nothing to bring the Pittsburgh Steelers scouts over to take a look. We break even—win four, lose four, but we've never won the league in the five years we've been in it. We're getting some tough fellows this year, Roscoe, with you being the main one. We gon' have our first championship at the end of this year. Watch what I say."

"I don't doubt that, King. I figure there's no sense spending a lot of time on the game if you're not winning."

"Hell yes," said King, looking off. "When they hear that we got Roscoe Americus, *the* all-time Mr. America, they'll pee on themselves they be so scared."

So, their pact signed and sealed, King and Roscoe soon met with two other coaches. Roscoe had serious doubts about their knowledge of the game, but with them deferring to him in most cases, he could help them make a motley group of men into a team.

July's heat was an inferno. The heat stammered at the backs of heads, sent the less committed scurrying for the shade of the trees at the top of the hills where others watched. Their first exhibition game was scheduled at the end of two weeks of practice.

At the end of the first week, Roscoe had lost ten pounds and had begun to remember many of the fundamentals and tricks he thought he had lost. He was getting the jump on the younger lineman who played him nose-to-nose. Each day he came off the ball quicker and quicker. In college, he had drawn a number of penalty flags because most officials could not believe that he or anyone else could move so quickly off the snap. Some called him Big Cat then. Of course, he knew that he would never be that quick again—the reflexes were always the first to go. Yet the memory became the standard, so he suffered through the deep soreness in the hamstring muscles and in the lower back. He'd be the baddest forty-year-old tackle on the planet.

He was further gratified that on the goal line offensive drills, most of the running plays were run off his position. Which was as it should be: if they couldn't score off his block, they would never score at all. He remembered the three times against Indiana. The second half of the game began in a blizzard, and the yard lines were impossible to see by the end of the third quarter. They managed to get down to the eight-yard line of a long march. First and goal. The quarterback called the same play three times in succession. The last time the hole was wide enough for a tank to rumble through. A newspaper photographer at the back of the end zone claimed later that one of the Indiana linebackers was knocked through the end zone by one of Roscoe's forearm smashes. The photographer had the picture to prove it.

Roscoe drove the linemen in practice. They would drill and run run run as if they were offensive backs.

"OK, you lardasses, move!" Well before he first coached at the high school, he had been curious about what it took to mold a few dozen men into a precision unit. It was still a mystery, though for four years he had watched Woody Hayes do it well. At the high school Roscoe had reasonable success: his linemen were rated the best in the league during the two years he coached.

But now his players were older, though perhaps no less hungry. Too many were out of shape, many of them ignorant of the basics. When a few complained that the last six windsprints after practice were unnecessary, Roscoe snapped, "You want a democracy or you want to win? The time we take to vote on every little thing could be spent getting into shape."

"You pushing them a little hard, ain't you, Ros?" one of the other assistant coaches asked one day.

"I'm not asking them to do what I won't try to do. If you and King want the best, I'm here to give it to you. Just make sure you got a quarterback who can throw and got the smarts to call plays, and make sure you got some backs who can run the ball. Everything else will be taken care of."

"We got the horses, Big Man,"

"That's all I wanted to hear."

In their first exhibition game, the Bombers rolled up a big score in the first half and held on in the second to win by two touchdowns. Roscoe's play was awesome for three quarters. On some plays he cleaned out his hole, got up, and hustled down field to hurl downfield blocks at fleeing defensive backs. By the fourth quarter he had slowed considerably, lagging on screen plays. The men opposite him began to even things up then, beating Roscoe one out of every three plays. The younger players seemed to grow stronger and, though wheezing themselves, began to taunt Roscoe with "You ain't getting tired now, are you, Old Man?" and "You ought to be home with your grandkids." Their taunts inspired Roscoe to force one last effort or to remember a dirty trick, and he sent the other men to the sideline gasping for breath, clutching at their bellies. The Bombers won the game, and both he and the team had taken their first running steps to glory.

In the shower afterwards, he daydreamed they would win the league. Then in a few years, maybe barnstorm, playing exhibition games with the pro teams, Canadian or American, it made no difference. He would go on to talk shows, then maybe endorse Fords or toothpaste. They'd make a movie on them, and everything—his past, the present, the bustups of his life—would be vindicated. Roscoe Americus, Jr.:

All-American, '60, '61
North American Heavyweight Wrestling Champion
'63, '64
Superstar '80–

REFRAIN

IN SEPTEMBER, if it had to take that long, he would sweat through central Kansas, and, as he gained higher ground near Oakley, face the chill of Colorado. Somewhere on the other side of the curtain of rock would be his brother. He would drive on into Denver, find a moderately priced motel, and rest awhile. There would be no rush. Over twenty years had already passed since he had seen Emmanuel, and an hour's nap would not matter much. Time wasn't the problem.

The next morning a muscular Chicano would ask him whether he was looking for work. The airport was hiring men to work on the construction of its new wing. Just show up and ask for a Mr. Marks. How could the man know he was looking for anything? Something in the hunch of his shoulders as he ate his pancakes? The way he held his steaming coffee, cup to his mouth, watching all over its top?

"No, thank you. I'm not looking for work, but thank you."

In front of the restaurant he would watch a woman beat her child for no reason worth remembering. The world would be sad for minutes. But only then. There was a lost brother to be found.

Then he would drive past construction sites, union halls, rooming houses where janitors sported huge tattoos on their skinny arms. Already certain, he would be, that Emmanuel was somewhere farther west still going in tighter and tighter circles . . .

The next outposts would be Laramie and Cheyenne after you left Denver and were afraid to take US 40 through the mountains that time of year. US 40 was tricky enough in good weather when the clear mountain air hosted vision. Roscoe remembered a long-ago late September there, well beyond Berthoud Pass and nearing Steamboat Springs, the town he remembered for the bells tolling at dusk and the sound carrying for miles. The rich colors of the leaves in the valleys—the brilliant yellows, oranges, and browns—and he wondered how long he could last in a place like

79

that after the newness wore off. A month? A year? Years, like his brother? After Steamboat Springs he had wrestled that night and beaten a short wiry man from the Missouri Ozarks, who posed as a mystic Russian. The man invoked the stars before each match by rubbing his hands in vodka, rolling his eyes, and chanting loudly in gutteral bursts. The crowd, of course, was inspired by the act.

But somewhere in Wyoming a big woman would stand in front of a motel and ask him inside to the bar for a drink, and she would ask him to spend a little time with her. She would tell him that she owned her own one hundred acres, that she was a widow who didn't come to town much, and could he keep a lonely woman warm that night? He would want to say that he couldn't, that he had a search to complete, but he wouldn't say that. He and the hot-blooded woman would enter her room and search desperately for pleasure treasures.

Along the way he'd kid with occasional Shoshones who pumped gas. One might shade his eyes and point to a distant mountain in answer to Roscoe's question. "The tip of that mountain is as flat as a table, that's why they call it Tabletop. But you can't tell that much under all that snow. You can see the top only three months out of the year." The Shoshone would like him, tell him to stay over that night and drink at the Horseshoe Bar. The cowboys would be in, a sheepherder or two, and the women. And the Indian would wink. But he would move on, hoping to make Salt Lake City before winter's early darkness was total.

By the time he reached Salt Lake City he would conclude that those wide-open spaces spawned mythmakers, lonely souls with long, long stories to tell. He would listen to only a few. All of them had known a Big Black Man somewhere in their lives and had shut him in a closet of their minds with dirty army uniforms, empty whiskey bottles, dusty photographs from visits to the old eastern cities. These phantoms were familiar, but none were Emmanuel.

In that city, the next night, a grizzled white man shivering in a wool shirt would draw out a knife and hold the blade near Roscoe's navel. The man would try to smile.

"Big Man, you look strong enough to slap down a bullet and hard enough to break this here blade on my knife. So spare a poor soul embarrassment and loan me a quarter." The knife was really rubber, and the man, a pathetic joker who smelled of wine. Roscoe wouldn't like the forced humor and therefore walk on, leaving the man on the pavement where he nursed his cracked ribs.

How many poor souls had Emmanuel run into out here? What if one were more frightened or desperate than the last man? A man like Mays, say? What if Emmanuel had been robbed or killed, the trusting soul, by a pack of grizzled panhandlers and buried two feet, if that deep, into the frozen earth near the base of one of those mountains? Near those clumps of shrubs, off the road as you descend into the city? After all, the last letter to Baby Sister was a year old.

The sudden thought of the possibility of his brother's death brought up the taste of bile.

VERSE

─────

VIGIL

LINE 1

GLOOMY THURSDAY EVENING and the rain threatening for a half hour or so. Tornado watch. Roscoe and Inez were chuckling over Romeo and Juliet in the corner booth, loving it up with their backs to the world. Out of boredom Roscoe had pumped quarters into the jukebox for most of the afternoon, and he moved now to drop in two more. He glanced again at the couple. It was stupid to overdo the teasing bit, since in their dirty clothes and shameless loving Romeo and Juliet somehow kept a promise alive that both Roscoe and Inez had long considered burying.

Roscoe paused in the doorway leading to the back. The poolroom was doing its typical middle-of-the-week trade. In their work clothes, steel workers played and drank beer, and with each beer the balls grew fuzzier, smaller, and lopsided. Their slow surprise at this forced shrillness into their voices. Occasionally one of them would order a sandwich, and Inez would grumble as she fixed it. But mostly they tripped to the front for chips and peanuts to help the beer along, or to tease Roscoe about the slow business that time of the day. He shook his head slowly and went back to sit behind the bar.

Inez was still hypnotized by Romeo and Juliet. "How do you think they do it, Roscoe?" she asked. "I've never seen anything like them. Makes me wonder what went wrong with me and my man."

Roscoe threw up his hands. "Don't look at me, I just live in this town. They've been like that for years, and I still haven't quite figured them out. All they need is one another and their wine. A lot of folks call them nasty or say that the cheap wine makes them so crazy they'll do anything, anytime, anywhere. Those same folks would be better off if they just admit they don't know what keeps Nora and Teddy getting it on like that. On top of that, they be better off asking themselves if they can do it that strong with whoever they got."

Inez nodded. "Course I only been back a short while, but don't

85

much get by me. I notice Romeo and Juliet the only people you let come in here and sit without buying liquor."

Roscoe shrugged. "They ain't hurting nothing."

Inez flashed a grin, then began to move restlessly from one end of the bar to the other, from time to time peeking through the blinds at the darkening sky. She would shake her head and suck her teeth. Thunder rumbled and, while watching her, Roscoe suddenly imagined the bar's roof torn off and whirling away, the walls collapsing and crushing those who huddled inside. They said that a tornado sounded like a hundred locomotives roaring through the sudden tunnels of fear. Would the bar folks have a chance to do anything except trade looks of horror and pity, to plea to their gods for forgiveness as the wind's fury even blasted their prayers to silence? No way they could make it across the street to the musty basement below the barbershop, even if they wanted to. And who would take their places?

"Go on and take the afternoon off, Inez. When the tornado comes, I don't want to look up and see you hiding under one of those tables the way you did when that thunderstorm hit last week."

She waved her hand. "I'm staying, man. I sign up for forty hours and I put in forty hours. And that's that." She convinced no one.

"It's just that these things have always scared the hell out of me, Roscoe. I remember when I was young, my mama made us turn off all the electricity—radio, television, fans—everything. Then we'd sit still in the quiet, hot house while all that thunder and lightning and rain raised hell outdoors. She used to think the storm could hear something plugged in and would aim right for it. Staying quiet didn't do us no good, though, because it always seemed like the storm was right over our heads and shook our little house until it couldn't shake no more."

Roscoe snickered. "It wasn't much different at our place, I tell you. But this one doesn't look like it's going to raise much sand. It'll just wet the street a little bit and give the farmers across the river something to jump up and down about. Every time the sky gets dark around here, some joker right out of college try to scare the people with tornado talk. We've only had three tornadoes in this town that I can remember, and those hit the white folks' side of town."

Inez was not impressed. "Humph, but they keep gettin' closer and closer, don't they? The last one hit about a mile from here. That was the year before I left to go to Detroit. But anyway, now that I got your word that it won't tear up anything this afternoon, I'll be sure to stay." For the third time, Inez called Miss Hester, the elderly woman who sat with her two children while she worked.

Finally, inevitably, the rain came, chasing the idlers from the corner outside to someone's front porch, washing the schemes and off-the-wall conversation along the gutters with the twigs, papers, and cigarette butts. In the bar fear melted slightly, talk picking up. This storm would not last long. In an hour its anger would be spent, and the clouds would lift, the lowest ones showing pink in the western sky.

Iron Man Hawkins and Rufus Bridgewater had raced into the bar during the height of the storm. Iron Man was a short twisted wire of a man. Wise folks regarded Iron Man the way they regarded a poised rattler: they didn't mess with him. Said he sopped his gravy with steel wool. They learned to take his unfunny jokes in stride. It was said that he had killed a man in another town and had spent a few years in jail. Usually he talked a lot, but this afternoon he was quiet, letting Rufus do most of the talking.

Rufus was in his latest uniform—knit skullcap, faded dungaree suit with dried sweat stains under the arms, at the edges of the sleeves. The same age as Roscoe, balding Rufus kept his hat on these days.

"Hey, Big Man, can a thirsty man get a drink around here?" Rufus asked.

Roscoe turned from the window. "That depends on what the man is drinking. If it's soda pop, he might have to wait awhile."

"I'm drinking what I always drink, bourbon and water. Go light on the water, 'cause it's bad on my kidneys, heh-heh."

"Inez, fix the man a drink. I can't stand to see a grown man cry."

"Ha, Roscoe you a mess. Look here, when you gon' cut me in

on this place? I bet you making so much money, you need help gettin' to the bank."

"I'll cut you in when times get worse, Rufus. And the way things going around here you might not have too long to wait."

Rufus shook his head, then tasted his drink. "Man, what you say? I heard a boy say the other day that out at the mill they standing in line just to apply for work. Can you imagine that? Just to apply for a job they got to stand in line? And I heard one line was so long up in Detroit that they started a riot because they had to wait outdoors all day. It ain't been that bad in years. There might be a depression coming on and all of us gon' have to get back to white beans, fatback, and cornbread for breakfast, lunch, and dinner."

"I ain't never stopped eating them," kidded Inez.

Rufus went on after another sip. "Hell, look at me. I been at the mill for twelve years, and they done cut back so far they got me, too. Thank God, the unemployment check coming in. I mean, here I am with all this seniority, and I get knocked off the job like I'm some kid who's been on twelve days. It just ain't right, man. It just ain't right."

"You'll be back in no time, Rufus," Roscoe said. He settled onto his stool behind the bar. He had never been without a job and could not conceive of it. There was always something, whether wrestling, coaching kids, or selling beer. Something. The real challenge was to find good work and keep it good. He was his father's son, and the Old Man never kept still. But what could he tell this man who needed just any work?

"Yeah, man, come August you'll be back at the mill working like a Georgia mule and making enough money to keep yourself, your wife, and me happy."

Then Roscoe noticed that the rain was only silently streaking the windows now. Just as he thought, a lightweight rainstorm, nothing at all to get alarmed about. Inez relaxed at the end of the bar and started to read an old copy of *Ebony* in the dim light. Rufus and Iron Man had started to trade lies, and Romeo and Juliet were smiling about something or other.

When the rainstorm died out, Pretty Kenny bebopped through

the room, looked in the back, then idled to the bar and ordered a beer. His motions collected the gloom.

"Y'all heard about the shooting awhile ago?"

"We ain't heard nothin' except rain and Roscoe's mouth," Rufus said.

"This happened before the rain, down on the highway at that bar next to Brown's Burger place. Some white dude got hit, messing with a carload of young bloods. Blown away with a shotgun."

"Killed him?" Inez asked.

Kenny nodded. Inez shook her head and went back to the magazine. Such is the way of the world, her casualness proclaimed. Life, divorce, death. Rufus finished his drink and nodded to Roscoe for another.

"Who was in the car, Kenny?" Roscoe asked.

"Poon-Tang, Stone, Early, and, yeah, Jesse. That's what they tell me. Of course, I wasn't there, you understand."

"Well, how did you know who was in the car?" Roscoe was standing now.

"Big Man, bad news outrun lightning in this town. You know that. I got the news from Fat Daddy, John Henry's brother. He was there at the restaurant eating a hamburger, he claim. He don't know who shot the white boy. He said he just heard some shooting and saw a couple cars tear out of there. But he seen them four boys when they first pulled up."

"Did he say there was a lot of shooting or what?"

Kenny shook his head. "He didn't say nothing about that. He just heard one gun sounding off like a shotgun. At first he thought they were a couple big firecrackers, but when he heard the last one and saw them running, that's when he knew something was up. Then, like I said, he saw two cars tearing out of there."

"Two cars?" Roscoe asked.

"Yeah, there was another car, but he couldn't tell who was in it or what it was doing there."

Roscoe looked around the bar. The others were half-listening, Inez looking up from her magazine from time to time. He struggled to stay calm. That Stone, that bad-luck Stone!

"So nobody's been picked up yet?"

Kenny shrugged. "I figure like this. The whole thing happened just before the storm started, about one hour ago. Wow, if I was those cats I'd have been on the first bus out of town, but knowing the way scared-ass jitterbugs be thinking, they're probably in somebody's basement somewhere trying to figure out what to do. So let's figure somebody got the license plate numbers and figure, too, that before sundown one or two of them will be downtown at the jailhouse getting a headwhipping."

Rufus snorted loudly and turned back to his beer. Iron Man got up, patted his belly, and headed for the restroom. Roscoe frowned as Kenny eased to the jukebox to play a few songs. He was hoping that Kenny was wrong this time. His grapevine was generally good, though once in awhile there had been slip ups—like the time Kenny said it was Roger and not Mitch who tipped from the Myers woman's house one dawn, her husband in Cleveland with the Prince Hall Mason's Convention. Roger was threatened when word leaked to Myers. He hid from Myers for a whole year before the lie was straightened out, though the truth was never known. Most of the time, yes, Kenny was right about such matters.

The rain had started up again and could be heard against the window now, the fury of a new storm quickly building. A few more men risked the weather to get to the bar and Roscoe let Inez wait on them. He would nod at their greetings and touch the peaks and valleys of their conversations with an occasional "is that right?" But, otherwise, his thoughts were on Everjean's Stone and rows of cold prison cells painted dull brown and stretching to forever. What was Stone doing in that car anyway? That boy could get into trouble just walking down the street, it seemed. Once eight boys stole fruit in a supermarket, and, with cans of soda pop, they trooped loudly to the check-out lane. Only Stone's pocket burst when they walked past the cashier. The others ran but Stone was left there.

Everjean hoped he would finish high school without too many scrapes; he could then volunteer for the Navy. That was what Lank had done, except he had joined the Marines. Everjean had thought a different branch of military services might bring different luck to the family. Stone could learn a trade there and, later, with a job at least stay out of trouble. But Roscoe had long figured that Stone and trouble were the best of friends, and a separation, however desired, would confuse the boy.

Roscoe was not his father, only the man who shared his mother's bed three mornings a week. A real father would storm the jailhouse, were his son to be jailed, would steal a factory blind, fence the goods, to make bail for his son. He hoped desperately that Stone was not near the scene of the shooting and that Kenny, the keeper of the town's secrets, the instant relay, had missed a connection.

He tried to call Everjean now, but there was no answer. Couldn't she ever stay home? Where could she be in this thunderstorm? Maybe she was still buying up the town with what little money she had, anticipating the trip to Niagara Falls now scheduled for Labor Day. Maybe. He struggled with the thought that maybe she could be seeing someone else. Things had not been going that smoothly lately. They had promised to keep their options open, they were merely welcome stations in the uncharted wilds of their lonelinesses. Nothing more, they confessed, and so be it. Yet he knew that his jealousy shrouded even his most casual possessions, as if any loss, however minor, would leave him that much more alone.

Perhaps he should have gotten to know other women, the few available ones there were. Most of them were either too young or too tired to think new thoughts, aside from fabricating gossip with the help of gin. After all, he and Everjean went back a long, long way. He was troubled that he could even feel the birth of jealousy for another woman so soon after leaving his own wife. Stay free.

He shifted on the stool, looked around the room. His thoughts kept sweeping him miles away from this place. From some distant land, he watched a few people come in, one or two leave. There was Kenny whooping it up with two would-be pool hustlers. Kenny. Eight years before, Kenny had stepped off a Greyhound bus with a battered suitcase and didn't know a soul in town. Later he would explain that he liked the look of the town, as simple

91

as that, and told the bus driver to let him off. He had been on his way from Sylacauga, Alabama, where he was born and grew up, to Grand Rapids, Michigan, where an uncle lived and where better job prospects waited.

That first day he found a room at the YMCA, and his second night in town he came into the bar, passing shyly through to the poolroom. He stood around watching the games before some slick, nobody remembers exactly who now, invited him to try his hand at eight ball. Kenny lost the first game, but asked to play a second. When asked where he was from he said Sylacauga as if it were the name of a girl friend. The slicks in the big floppy hats snickered at the flat music of his drawl. He lost the second game, too, and that's when the boy he was playing asked him whether he cared to put a small bet on the game. Kenny said, "No big thing. Ain't nothin' but a sport." The boy winked at his friends and lost the next three games. Ever since, Kenny was something of a free-floating hero to the younger fellows who hung out around the poolroom. He made lots of money shooting pool in other, larger towns. He later tired of it, got a job with a construction company. Some said that he sold a little marijuana on the side, but no one seemed to know for sure. At least not Roscoe, who would have marched him to the door by the nape of his neck had he been certain.

One of Kenny's friends came in to whisper to him. With difficulty Roscoe recognized Preach, Sam Baker's son, in the floppy hat and wondered at how tall the boy had grown since he last saw him and how he had fallen in with Kenny. Then Kenny shook his head and came back to the bar, Preach at his heels.

"They got four of them a few minutes ago, Roscoe. Preach here claim they got two of them who was in the car and grabbed two more who was standing under the roof right there where you go into the swimming pool. They just happened to be there playing cards or something to keep dry. But you know how it goes with the law, any nigga will do."

"Who did they pick up, Preach?" Roscoe asked.

"Rodney and Lafayette. They grabbed Steebo and Puddin' just on a humble, see what I'm sayin'?"

Roscoe left them to take a seat on his stool again. The dizziness was the feeling he had the first night he showed up at Everjean's door, shuffling there when Stone answered the door and said nothing, just eyed him coldly. ("What's happening?" Roscoe had asked, trying to swagger off the uneasiness.) Stone must have seen him those afternoons driving Charlotte and the girls around the pool or picnicking in the park. He must have seen other men do the same with their families, too, before they made tracks to his mother's door. Those first times Stone would either smile a crooked smile or grunt for greeting when he answered the door or passed the couch where Roscoe and Jean sat. Everjean saw the coldness and scolded her son for not speaking when spoken to. But Stone found a better way; he stayed away when he could and slipped into his bedroom through the window if he knew Roscoe was in the house.

Once in Everjean's backyard, a yard barely large enough for a decent vegetable garden, Roscoe had watched Stone burn, sheet by sheet, some drawings his eight-year-old sister had made. This was his sudden revenge for her telling on him as he was about to sneak off and join his friends in the park. Roscoe stood up from the back porch where he had been sitting, waiting for Everjean to come out with two beers.

"Stone, what are you doing that for? She didn't mean no harm."

Stone looked at him evenly, a lighted match in one hand, a drawing balled up in the other. Without malice, without anything, he had said, "You can't talk to me. You ain't my Daddy."

Roscoe shifted on his stool again. When Inez came over to holler out an order, he crooked a finger.

"I'm going to run out in a little bit, sugar. I'll be back before closing time."

Inez nodded.

"Looks like we'll live, after all," Roscoe added, pointing toward the windows where the rain drops again slid along in silent streaks.

"Oh, I wasn't worried," Inez lied. "Just trying to kid y'all."

Apparently tiring, Romeo and Juliet were getting up on shakey legs. Roscoe waved back at them as he left.

He drove to Everjean's. Inside, Stone sat in the small dining room at the chipped, scarred table, twirling his hat on a finger. He didn't look up when Roscoe walked in. Everjean was puffy-eyed, looked tired. As she stood near her son, her shoulders drooped. Roscoe had never seen her look so helpless before. The room was dim. When would she ever replace those two burned-out bulbs in the lamp over her head?

"I guess you heard about it?" she asked. "That you who called? I just didn't feel like answering no phone." She tilted her head from one side to the other. Roscoe had nodded, and she saw that as some signal to launch into a sermon.

"He claim none of the boys in the car had a gun. But, Roscoe, he had no business in the world running around with them boys in the first place. I been trying to talk this boy into acting right since the day he come into the world, but it don't seem to make no difference. He don't listen. He try to act so grown."

"Take it easy, Jean." Roscoe went into the tiny dining room and sat down next to Stone who was trying to hum a song.

"I came by because I heard about what happened down on the highway, yeah. I got all of that from somebody who wasn't even there. So what I heard is thirdhand." He looked directly at Stone. "I don't trust that kind of talk. I want to know from you what happened and why y'all were there in the first place."

Stone stopped the hat. "Mr. Roscoe, we were down there because these white boys kept messing with us. Nobody wanted no shooting or nothing like that."

"Who had the gun?"

He twirled the hat once or twice more. "Nobody had a gun. We had a tire iron and I think maybe somebody had a baseball bat or something like that. Oh yeah, and Jesse had a knife. Ain't nobody had a gun, though."

"Stone, who shot the boy?" Roscoe asked, leaning closer.

"I don't know." Stone avoided Roscoe's eyes. He looked frightened, and Roscoe remembered too many other young boys, men-about-to-be, with that same look, as if life had dealt them a dirty losing hand, would always deal them a dirty losing hand, and heavy pep talks or nods at one's own ancient misfortunes could not ease that same hunch in the shoulders, that falling away behind the eyes where no one could reach. Such was Stone in that instant, and Roscoe realized that if the boy were telling the truth and if nothing came of this incident, he would be back to fear a month or two or six later.

He shook his head and repeated. "I swear 'fo' God, Mr. Roscoe, I don't know who killed that boy. I didn't even know he was dead. Some other dudes, older dudes, pulled up alongside of us down there. It might have been one of them. Everything happened so fast. We heard the gun and saw the boy fall. Then all of us ran to the car and got out of there."

"Who was in that other car?"

"All I know was Jeffrey, Red-Eye, and Willie. We call him Wild Willie. There were one or two more, but I couldn't see them too good."

"What happened after y'all left?" Roscoe asked.

"We just drove around a little. Everybody was kind of shook up, you know? We weren't going to back down from a fight, but at the same time we didn't mean for anybody to get hurt bad either. First we drove to the swimming pool, but when it started to rain we got Poon-tang to take us home."

"And you've been home ever since?"

Stone nodded. "They can't do nothing to us, 'cause we didn't do nothing."

"I hope not, Stone, but they might try."

Roscoe looked at Everjean, who closed her eyes as if to blank it all out. Then he squeezed Stone's shoulder, feeling the boy stiffen, and walked over to sit next to Jean.

"I believe the boy, Jean. But others might not. The main thing is that you keep yourself together. You've got to be ready no matter what happens. The boy might need a lawyer before this is all over. I only know of one downtown. I went to school with him."

95

"Roscoe, you know I don't know the first thing about hiring no lawyer. And plus you know I ain't got that kind of money."

"It'll be OK, Jean. It might not even get that far. But you have to be ready if something do break out. As far as the money thing is concerned, I can help out a little."

She frowned. "Uh-uh, Roscoe. I don't want that. Stone is Lank's and my boy. We the ones who have to get him through."

Roscoe decided not to push it. He recalled an earlier conversation they had had. Everjean told him about the last time she took money from a man and how a gift of cash can stay between a man and woman and make a friendship seem a bribe. That last man figured that he had bought her, that he could drop over anytime.

The silence stretched, then snapped. "Well, the first thing is for all of you to try to get some rest tonight," Roscoe said. "I ain't saying that it will be easy, but it would help."

Everjean began patting her thigh. "Roscoe, you really think they caught the one who shot the boy?"

He shrugged. "I don't know. Somebody might have gotten the license number off the car or something."

"If they could get it off the guilty boy's car, they could get it off the car Stone was riding in just as easy. Then they pick up one of those boys, scare him half to death, and he tell everybody's name he ever knew in his life to keep them off of him."

He couldn't answer that one. Wouldn't try. He stayed a little longer with them, and for an awkward moment when Jean carried her daughter to bed, he and Stone were alone. Roscoe asked him about his basketball, but Stone only grunted, his eyes staring ahead as if into a hypnotic flame. Roscoe wanted to touch him, reassure him, protect him. But the touch was impossible; the hope of protection, a cup handled by stiff fingers, slipping away, crashing into a thousand pieces never to be whole again. Then Stone looked up and they watched each other's eyes for a moment. Stone finally stood and went off to his room.

Later, on the couch, Roscoe held Jean and told her that it would all blow over, that no one could make a solid case against Stone. "What have they got, huh? OK, he was there at the scene, but they can't prove that they set out to kill that boy. There's no weapon. What have they got?" He was such a poor liar. At least to others. There might be hidden passages in the structure of the law that might seal Stone off from them forever. Roscoe fidgeted, stuttered, topped one lie with another in his efforts to prop her spirits. Finally he kissed Jean, reassured her that everything would be all right, then fled desperately to the relief of the muggy night.

But he barely slept. He might have been better off had he stayed with Everjean and Stone. The first hours back he brooded over the possibility of Stone being picked up. He knew, too, that neither Everjean nor Stone would get much sleep that night. She would start in telling the boy about how hard she worked to raise him right so he wouldn't be in and out of jail all his life. She would chainsmoke, watch television for a few minutes, then go back to his room with more words. Stone would lie in bed, looking away from her. Silent.

Roscoe looked out of his window to the street, glistening and peacesoaked after the rain. He wondered whether Everjean had called Lank. She had told him that since the separation Lank had rarely seen his son. Only by accident, they'd run into one another in hot Sunday afternoon crowds watching baseball or basketball games in the park. Every Christmas he would send her a check for fifty dollars to cover the children's gifts.

"Hell, these days I can't exactly buy out the shopping center with fifty dollars."

The last time Roscoe had seen Lank was only a year before. Lank had walked into the bar with one of his gambling friends, a short man who leaned to the left as if carrying a bucket of lead bricks in his left hand. The two men found seats at one end of the bar to knock out double shots of bourbon. They carried on with Inez every time she walked past. All the while, Lank's eyes would drift back to Roscoe, settling somewhere around Roscoe's throat, never meeting his look straight on. Of course, he had known about Roscoe and Jean before he married her. The whole town knew that. Now that he had left her, Lank might figure that Roscoe was seeing her again, might have been seeing her all the time they were together. Probably piling lie on top of lie in his imagination, he granted Roscoe a power over Everjean that he never had. That night Roscoe wanted to say something to the man, but anything he said would be twisted, he figured. If he commented on the weather, Lank might have taken it as an insult. If he commented on sports, Lank might have taken the comment as a jab. Everjean was between them. Despite it all Roscoe could sympathize with the man, this eternal stranger and enemy. Could he himself be a buddy, talk civilly to a man taking out his own Charlotte, were they to divorce? No, the past was never a dead thing for him, and his own jealousy was a net that grew tighter with time. Lank had played one of Roscoe's favorite records and smiled. At least the man recognized good music.

Yet, like two heavy-footed boxers, he and Lank circled one another that night, laughing too loud at Inez' jokes, going to their corners at the bell.

He jerked up, started. He had fallen asleep in a chair at the window, the light blazing, his clothes stiff and sweaty. The radio was still on, crackling static where music had been earlier. Had that awakened him? No, the phone. It rang again and as he reached for it he glanced over at the clock on the stove. Four-thirty.

It was Jean. "Roscoe, they just came to pick up Stone. They done left with my baby."

He rubbed his eyes, then reached for the back of his head. "When, Jean? They still there?"

"Naw, they just left the house. They claim they were taking him downtown to ask him a few questions. But they gon' try to beat him, I know they is."

"I'll be right over." He pushed through the night. It took him only a few minutes to get there, creeping through the red lights since he was the only one out at that hour, perhaps the only one out in the world. Except for the cops and Stone. At Everjean's he softly closed the door behind him. She was puffing a cigarette, her hair still in curlers. Wanda was sitting on the couch, her face showing the stunned surprise of waking suddenly deep in the night. She rubbed the corners of her eyes with her knuckles and tried to curl up against one arm of the couch, still not sure what was going on.

"Stone never did try to go to sleep. He still had his clothes on when they came for him and was sitting in the dining room like he expected them all the time. After the door bell rang, I heard him open the door, and by the time I got to the front room I heard them asking him 'You wanna come downtown with us?' Can you get to *that*, Roscoe? Three of them about to lock my baby up and they come asking in a voice the way the movie usher asks 'you wanna follow me?' So I stood in front of Stone, squeezed in front of him and saw that the eyes of those men were nowhere near as soft as their voices. They said they wanted to ask him a few questions. I told them they could ask him the questions there in front of me. They showed me a paper and said it was a warrant for his arrest. Any other time, seeing that paper would have knocked me to my knees. I was past that. I was strong like you told me, but I couldn't fight those three men. I just wanted them to know that there was folks on his side and that they'd better not mess with him. Then the only one with a uniform on took him to the car."

"He's going to need a lawyer for sure now," Roscoe said.

"I ain't finished yet." She sipped from a cup and started shaking her head. "They showed me a search warrant and said they were looking for a gun."

"A gun?"

"They said they were looking for a gun. I didn't want them to go through my house tearing it up. I told them that the only gun I had was the little one you gave me, Roscoe. I knew they'd find that real easy because I keep it in the top drawer of my chifforobe. So I got the gun for them. I had took the clip out and hid it some place a long time ago. You always hear about kids finding some gun and shooting themselves by accident. Anyway, they looked at the gun and started whispering something, then one of them asked me for the clip. He claim they were taking the gun downtown for tests. So I had to go and get the clip, too."

"Damn," Roscoe said softly. "We'll get a lawyer this morning."

"Well, I called Reverend Whitmore right after you left last night.

I started thinking and thinking and remembered how the church helped that Mitchell boy out of trouble that time. But I felt funny calling him at first 'cause I ain't been to church in so long. Anyway he told me to call Lonnie Bryant in case they do pick up Stone."

"I forgot about Lonnie. I heard he's working with one of the best around here."

Jean shook her head. "'Course he did grow up in town and everything, but I don't know that much about how good he is. Reverend Whitmore claims he's pretty good."

"He better be." He glanced around the room, almost helplessly. "You try to reach anybody else last night?"

"You mean, Lank? No. I guess I should, huh? I'll call him in an hour or so." She stroked her daughter's hair a minute, then stood to carry her to bed. "Wanda need her sleep."

Alone, Roscoe turned to the window and watched the confused colors of dawn creep low across the sky, among rooftops, the gathering light welcomed by the insistent birdsongs. A light or two came on in other houses along the street. Roscoe wondered how he had become so involved. Boys had fallen into trouble all around him before, and, though there was the concern on his part, he didn't lose sleep over it. It wasn't just a matter of whether or not he knew them well. The town simply wasn't that big. If he did not know the boy, then he certainly knew the father or a brother or an uncle.

Jean. He knew that after he stripped all the covers away he would get back to Jean. He had only planned a short affair. They were both clear-eyed about their involvement. He wanted no arrangement where he would be left brooding over her problems—which were many—or her family's. After all, he had a family of his own.

That morning they drank coffee together and watched the day grow fitfully to life: the milk and newspaper trucks going past, the laborers speeding to make the seven o'clock shift.

"I called Lank while I was in back," Jean said. "He said he would take off and come down this morning."

Roscoe nodded. "It'll be OK, Jean. I got a feeling that this will

100

pass. That boy'll be home eating your fried chicken tonight. Just watch and see didn't I tell you. In two weeks we'll be at Niagara Falls, the way we planned, you hear? We'll be standing there at the rail in front of the tall tower on the Canadian side, and you'll feel that spray come from those big ol' falls. You'll watch that water fall so slow and so white you'll forget it was water and think it was smoke going downhill. We'll spend a day or two there, then on to Toronto or maybe even Montreal, depending on how we feel." She smiled weakly. He continued.

"You figure you can handle all that excitement on the trip? 'Course the biggest excitement come when we're back in the room."

She ignored this, closed her eyes for a moment. "You know, I been ready for that trip ever since you first mentioned it back in May. I never have traveled much. Just once to Georgia when my grandmother died. After that, it's just been me, the babies, and bad luck in this little town."

"We'll get that boy home, Jean. That's the first thing. Then you and me got a lot of travelling to do." She tried to fix a smile before they kissed and she was still struggling with the smile as he turned to leave.

The door to the bar swung in and Inez entered. "Hey, big brown-eyed man, what you know good today?" She was in a mood to match the brightness of the day outside, a brightness that was overshadowed in the bar's brief noon. A lone swath of light cut through one window.

"I don't know nothing except we're going to make some big money today."

She laughed her high-pitched laugh and set her purse under the bar. As they set up, Roscoe told her about Stone's arrest and Everjean's confusion.

"I'd be the same way myself if my baby got arrested for something he didn't do. Or just arrested, period. I just know I would. What time she go down this morning?"

101

"I don't know exactly. She was going down with Lank some time this morning. I'll give her a call around noon."

"Um-um, that's a crying shame the way they messing over that boy already."

And Roscoe was sluggish by now, dragging a ball and chain on each leg. He had jogged earlier, right after he left Everjean's. He thought the run would bring him fully to life. But he had put in only two miles, wheezing and sputtering through the last two hundred yards. That awful hot pressure in the lungs. Good thing that the Baker boys weren't around that early; they would have laughed themselves into bad health. After a shower and short nap, he felt no better. The hamstring muscles were sore and his shoulders drooped as if carrying around a two hundred and fifty pound brute disguised as a wrestler. Fortunately, the Bombers were not practicing that evening. He hoped Inez would pick up the cue and give him some slack until he got himself together.

"Hey, we got the poetry reading this afternoon," she said. "Think we'll pack the place?"

"Who can tell? I just hope the word got out to enough folks. Otherwise it'll just be you and me here."

In the riot of the emotions surrounding all the events up to Stone's arrest, he had nearly forgotten his latest invention: a coffee-shop session with live poetry readings. A jam session of words. He must warm up to the idea as the day passed, so remote was it now.

Two mailmen came in with their heavy bags. Laughing Elbert and the bearded one everybody called simply Mailman. They dipped their shoulders, sliding the bags off them.

"I hope you fellows have passed most of your mail now," Roscoe said, serving them their usual beers. "Otherwise your bossman will come here and blame me if y'all deliver mail to the wrong houses. Somebody was in here the other night talking about how one of y'all was delivering mail at night, scaring all the dogs awake, staggering around and knocking over porch chairs. Cat called you all sorts of nasty names."

Both mailmen chuckled over that and reached for their mugs.

102

"That was Elbert," Mailman said. "Don't I look like I got more sense than to do something that goofy?"

"Well, I don't know about that now," Roscoe said looking from one man to the other. "Now that you mentioned looks, I just don't know. It seems to me that in a looks contest you and Elbert here would run about neck-and-neck."

"The hell you say!" Mailman said, faking rage. "I'm not talking about that. I'm talking about good sense. Who look like the one with good sense?"

Roscoe clapped his hands. "I don't want to get into that one. I want to keep getting my mail."

Elbert took a long swallow from the beer mug, then reached into his bag and handed Roscoe a stack of mail. Roscoe leafed through the envelopes quickly, reading the return addresses under his breath. All he ever got these days were bills. Except for a few Christmas cards, birthday cards, and a rare postcard from a former teammate, he hadn't received a personal letter in years. He tossed them on the counter near the cash register.

"Damn, Elbert, if all you gon' bring me is bills, I better cut you loose anyway." Roscoe plugged in the jukebox and punched out his selections.

Pretty Kenny walked in on the swath of noon light. Preach hovered near his shoulder. Both had studied too many gangster movies or the night moves of too many "popcorn" hustlers. Roscoe guessed that Kenny had more news. After waving to everyone else in the bar, Kenny sat at the bar with the bored expression of a palm reader on a slow day. He fished for a toothpick. Once he had explained, "Folks think I'm called Pretty because I'm handsome. Naw, man, it's because my ways is pretty."

But Roscoe would force the issue. "Big-time Kenny, when you going to take that fellow sitting next to you and find him a job?"

Preach turned away and muttered something to an invisible listener.

"Roscoe, you just have to understand Preach, that's all. He's my lawyer if he ain't never won a case. Plus he my very best hoss, if he ain't never won a race!"

103

"Save your tired poems for later. I expect both of you no-rappin dudes to be at the poetry reading this afternoon."

"How come you got to come down so hard, Big Man?" Smiling, Pretty Kenny leaned closer. "I got something that you might be interested in. I heard the Turrentine boy was sent out of town last night."

"Which Turrentine boy? They're more Turrentines in this town than the white man got lies."

"Spencer, T. J.'s boy. T. J. put him on a plane going somewhere. Boston, I think, because they got a lot of kinfolks up that way."

"So what? Was he in the car with Stone and them?"

"Naw, but I would lay big money that getting him out of town so fast got something to do with that shooting. It's for sure that trifling boy ain't going up there for a vacation. The other thing is that everybody know by now that shotgun hit that white boy. There wasn't no shotgun in Early's car. Maybe a badshootin' .22 or something small like that, but no shotgun."

"So why the police messing with the boys in Early's car then? How come they don't go after the shotgun?"

Kenny glanced at him, then away, trying to move his shoulders to the music. Must have known the question was one Roscoe already knew the answer to.

"Well, they done picked up everybody in the first car now. Maybe they figure that's all they need. But, look, I saw Jessie before they picked him up last night. He say there was only one person in the car that he knew for sure had a gun. It wasn't no shotgun and it wasn't even loaded. But Roscoe, he claim Stone had that gun."

Giant vultures of gloom settled to Roscoe's shoulders, perched there. "Oh, hell, man, how do you know Jessie's not just putting something on Stone?"

"I don't. I'm just telling you what the boy said. Sometimes it's good to get yourself ready for the worst."

There was a moment's silence between them filled with the strains of Motown music and the lies swapped among Inez and the two mailmen. Roscoe knew that the police would try to frighten the hell out of the four boys, force them to say anything to stop

104

the pressure. They'd separate them and compare the stories. Sooner or later one of them would crack and tell them a name, and all they needed for a lynching was a name.

"He got a lawyer, Roscoe?"

"Probably Lonnie."

Kenny whistled. "Well, Lonnie might have a big one. I hope he's good. I don't know that much about him, though I remember everybody used to tell me when I first got here that he was going to be the first black governor in this state."

"I guess he's good. He's working with one of the best criminal lawyers around. They got that Mitchell boy, Teddy, off last year. Everybody knew Teddy was supposed to be sent up for killing that white boy in self-defense."

"Well, the homeboy better be good because if they slap this jive on the fellas they gon' need Perry Mason and . . ."

"They can't slap a damn thing on them if they can't find a weapon."

"Well, I don't know that much about the law. Me myself, I just try to avoid the muthafucka, know what I mean? But you might be right. Anyway, somebody said that Tyree might know something about the shotgun, but you know Tyree don't talk too much. Say, Ros, how about a beer? Give Preach one, too."

Roscoe plunged both hands into the cooler. Why would Stone not mention the gun? Why would he need it? From what Roscoe could gather, there was a simple argument among a handful of boys. A little name-calling, a few curses, and fear and pride took over. In his own coming-up days in that small town, pride was in the fists. You hit quickly and cleanly, trying not to get hit, send the other guy running or crying for mercy at the sight of his own blood. Dance like a Sugar Ray, maybe, to lend elegance to it all. If the boys were white, you felt superior, armed with the myth that their natural fear would paralyze them. This held true, except for a few of the big cow-tossing sons of farmers who lived across the river. Some of them could go toe-to-toe with you. Force you to search around for large rocks to help make your point.

Roscoe had never had such a problem. His size forced most close-quarter arguments to mellow out, persuaded any enemy to cuss him from the sanctuary of a fast-moving car. Yes, fists, rocks, baseball bats, and words were the noble weapons of the time. Few bothered with knives or razors, and guns were almost unheard of. You gathered the effect, the blood, on your fingers. You felt bone crack under your knuckles or felt the impact of a solid hit ripple up your arm to the shoulder. Guns were the cheapest equality. But where did all this leave Stone and those boys? Inez was talking louder, and the mailmen were belching on their second beers. They all had had enough of Kenny for an afternoon.

"Yeah, I tell y'all I'm glad that the mothers don't spare telling their daughters the truth these days," Inez said. "My grandma raised me, you know, and the only thing she told me was to stay away from boys. Said if you got close enough to one and he stuck a finger in your eye, you would come up pregnant. Woosh! Just like that. You never know how many nights I spent thinking about how something could happen so easy. And I stayed away from boys except to throw rocks at them for trying to peek at my panties when I climbed up the monkey bars. Well, one day I got in a fight with this skinny-headed boy named Delano, and he was just swinging trying to knock my head off. Had arms long as an octopus. Once in awhile he'd try to sneak in a kick to my stomach. I guess he figured a girl supposed to cry if she got kicked in the stomach. So I'm moving around trying to keep him from kicking more, and he's falling down and all his friends laughing at him and agitating for not being able to hit me. I keep one eye covered so he can't jug a finger in there and make me pregnant, but my other hand steady slapping him upside his long, skinny head. Pi-yow! Pi-yow! Finally he got in one good lick and that's when I found a stick and took out after his ass. He got me on the forehead and that's the closest I ever come to getting pregnant before I got married to my first boyfriend."

All the men leaned back and laughed long and rumbling laughs. For an instant they were all busy in the hot summer playgrounds of their youth, bullying a sassy little girl in pigtails. They fled to such bullying days when low pay, divorce, and jails were the mean

106

tricks of middle-age luck. But Roscoe relaxed on his stool, not smiling, and waiting for late afternoon.

In Roscoe's town new ideas were as rare as easy money. Which is one reason he brooded so much over how to make the Coffeeshop Hour a success. He remembered the small clubs on High Street in Columbus where glassy-eyed men in beards and long-haired women in black leotards read their poetry to eery flute accompaniment. The audiences were generally small, most listeners staring intently at the dirty ceiling during the readings. Roscoe was first dragged to the readings by a girl he met in his psychology class, and he would follow her around campus just to be able to make five minutes of conversation. Those stuttering five-minute sessions added up to nothing in the end, and he forgot the girl. He did remember those evenings in the coffeeshops, however, and from time to time, maybe to impress a new girlfriend, he would wind up there, staring at the ceiling. On one occasion he even read some of his own poetry, consisting mostly of a string of one-liners stolen from popular records of the day, and was applauded politely.

So to help things along that afternoon he cut the price in half for all drinks. At four, several people gathered at the bar to guzzle down the cheap drinks. Roscoe was braced for disappointment, however. He would give the idea three chances, hoping that the third try would show the genius of this new move. He turned off the jukebox, but the people at the bar went right on talking as if nothing had changed. These early ones were clearly the lookers, the waiters, and the agitating amen corner. As conversations died out, nervous looks were exchanged. Elbows nudged sides. Roscoe went to the small platform, where Sandy danced two nights a week, and announced that now was the time for the master-rappers, the poets-who-didn't-know-it, the word magicians to do their thing.

"If we can make this go, we will do it on a regular basis. You never know, there might be another Langston Hughes among us. We might get so good here that we will put the churches out of business and bring folks here to get happy."

A couple of steelworkers applauded as Roscoe stepped down.

From the back could be heard the soft clacking of poolballs as a few men went on with their serious games of eight-ball. Roscoe went to the back to announce that as soon as they finished their games, the poolroom would close for two hours. Only Ripple seemed to like the idea. And a few minutes later, as they crowded into the bar, it was Ripple, the rackman, who broke the ice. "All y'all stop running your damn mouths and gather 'round. I got some sho nuff juju to lay on the wind." He read from several scraps of paper about shooting pool, young and old fools, and being cool. He stepped down to a shower of applause and whistles. Another man dug paper from his pocket, and in a hoarse voice, the poem broken by his nervous coughs, he recited about the bad times on his job and foremen who wanted to be slave drivers.

> Mr. Bossman, Mr. Bossman
> You think this time is gone with the Wind
> But I'm here to tell you
> That I'm as free as you and your kin.

There was much applause and head-nodding. The man, rolling his shoulders and bobbing his head, went on to another poem, this one committed to memory. It was a poem on women, about how a good woman was so hard to find in these times.

> So I'll keep looking high and low for
> that woman who'll love me true.
> People I tell you, I got to keep looking
> for that woman who'll love me true
> My money's been too funny and my lovin been overdue.

The pool players slapped palms on this one, and the whole room lit up. Roscoe relaxed for a moment. He saw big crowds every week, lines wrapped around the block as men and women stood waiting, rehearsing their lines. The bar would expand, sweep in the barbershop that was connected to the back poolroom by a wall. Maybe he'd start a chain of North Star Café franchises around the state. Was there a limit to such a good thing? Let's see those other rundown honky-tonks mess with this!

Inez got the spirit and recited a long and rambling tale about men problems and calling a lonely woman's life the center of a donut. One man told her afterwards that she hadn't done a poem because the words didn't rhyme.

"It don't have to rhyme to be true," she countered. But the man was not convinced, and there followed a lengthy fingershaking argument on whether the truth or the form of her poem was more important. This was cut short by a man who read a poem in which he compared life to a huge jellyroll filled with pleasant surprises, and all the men howled with delight and sent free beers in the man's direction. A college dropout working in a foundry read his testimony to the smooth thighs of the many women he had known. A few in the crowd could be heard to whisper that he was lying, that they couldn't recall ever seeing that man with a woman. Someone came in with a bongo drum and played behind a few of the readers.

"Next time we have to get some women in here," Inez said, during a slow moment. "Y'all men act like y'all got the last word on this stuff."

"I see what you're saying, Inez," Roscoe said, "but you think the ladies in this town got that much soul?"

"Problem is, most of them got to stay home and cook y'all's dinner. They got to do their poetry between that and changing diapers."

"Well, we don't want excuses. We just want the poetry."

"Don't you worry none about that, sugar. I'll get enough of them here to set the record straight." She was enjoying herself, and it was one of the few times Roscoe had seen her laugh so freely.

A few men did stand-up comedy routines, none of them funny, and the crowd was quick to let them know. "Y'all better do some more practicin'."

And finally Roscoe allowed on a man who did a sermon disguised as a poem. Then, figuring things were winding down, he called a halt to the fun.

He stood on the platform, gesturing grandly. "Next week. Same time, same place. Tell everybody that the North Star Café is where it's happening. We call it Jubilee Wednesday, so set your clocks to our time."

Into the early evening Roscoe was patting himself on the back, proud of his second new and successful idea in four months. He wondered how the Old Man would have enjoyed himself that afternoon. He wouldn't have expected praise from the Old Man, though. His father hardly ever praised the sons, took their achievements with about as much surprise as he took the weather.

Inez called him to the phone, intruding on his reverie. "It's Jean," she said.

He frowned, so engrossed in receiving backslaps he hadn't heard the phone.

"How did it go, Jean?" Roscoe asked, moving right to the point.

Everjean was crying. "They trying to send my baby to prison! They trying to say he killed that white boy, Roscoe. He wouldn't hurt a fly, and now they saying he the one killed somebody. Stone ain't done nothing like that."

"What did Lonnie do, Jean?"

"Nothing much he could do. They holding Stone and those boys on $50,000 bond. Lonnie say we got to raise that money, and that the cops don't have a case. What am I going to do Roscoe? Reverend Whitmore been over, and he said the church will try to help out, but Lord knows they don't have that kind of money either."

"Maybe there are a few folks around who might have it. Anybody talk with Doc Patterson?"

"No, not yet. Roscoe, I don't know no rich people here. How you know they gone want to help out?"

"They'll help, Jean," he said. "Lank there?"

"Uh-uh. He's out right now, but he'll be back later on. He want to stay in town tonight. But not here in my house. He's got friends around, you know." Roscoe said nothing, looked around the good-time bar where the folk were still enjoying themselves. "Call me tonight, Roscoe. Can you come by after you close up? I don't know which way to turn."

"Yeah, I'll be there."

Then he went to the jukebox to play a few more tunes, then some happy, uptempo songs: Bill Doggett's "Honky Tonk" and a couple by the Temptations. He needed a quick pickup. He sat behind the bar, occasionally stabbing at a hot sausage or pickled pig's foot to serve up to someone. He thought about the next Jubilee Wednesday and wondered whether someone would ever put together the right words in the right order to free an innocent boy from a jail.

The church could not raise enough money to meet the bond. And the few "rich" blacks could only give so much. Stone was too bad a risk, they would whisper. These were only the first disappointments in those three days after Stone and the others were first arrested. Because of their ages, they were transferred to the county juvenile detention center. A lineup was quickly scheduled for the next morning, and two witnesses, two friends of the dead boy, were brought down by the prosecutors to identify the murderers. As it turned out, none of the four boys were recognized by the witnesses. But, as Everjean would tell Roscoe, there's no hiding place once bad luck has marked you.

After the lineup the boys stood outside the courthouse, a detective with them. They were handcuffed together, and waited for a patrol car to take them back to the center. With one of the prosecutors, one of the witnesses stepped out of the courthouse, just as the car pulled up.

"That's the one right there in the purple shirt!"

The boy would later claim in court that Stone's shirt, loose-fitting and silky, appeared a different color under the lights in the lineup room but the pale sunlight revealed its true color. Stone was the one cursing and waving a pistol in the air, the boy was certain. The charges were promptly dropped against the other three.

Stone would be tried as an adult, and the trial date was scheduled in two months. With the coincidence of the boy recognizing Stone, Roscoe and Everjean seemed to feel that something inevitable and terrifying was now in motion, as if they were all on a doomed train, with no one in control. Stone was sealed off from them in another compartment, and there was no way to reach him so that they could all leap off together. Hurt they would be, but alive, at least.

The church, which had wasted no time taking collections for the bail, turned over nearly one thousand dollars to Everjean to help with the legal fees. The good church sisters had fanned out through town to beauty parlors and club meetings. Their pitch was the same: Stone could be one of your sons in a similar situation.

Lank had left town, but he would be down to Everjean's several nights a week until the trial. Even she was a little surprised. Roscoe would take her out, trying to get her mind off her son, but it did little good. In the middle of a movie she would break down, whimpering, then get up and rush to the rest room. She would come back twenty or so minutes later, looking off into dark space, only occasionally glancing at the screen.

He volunteered to drive her down to Stone's arraignment. When he stopped at her place that morning she met him with red eyes and only her robe on. She lit a cigarette and sat next to Roscoe on the couch.

"One helluva mother I've been, huh? Maybe if I had known more, stayed around the house more, talked to him like a real mother, maybe that would have made the difference . . ."

"You can't keep blaming yourself, Jean," he interrupted. "Come on, we want to get there on time."

"My mother was a real mother," she said, rocking back and forth as she spoke. "She kept our butts in line. After she died we went a little wild, I guess. Mable went to Detroit and married a gambler. Puddin been in Los Angeles and nobody's heard from him in all that time. And I marry a man who can't keep a job more than six months, whose luck was so bad he couldn't win for losing. Then we bust up and I try to raise these kids the best I know, but my best turned out to be pretty bad. I never did learn from my Mama. I just followed orders. Oh, she'd try to tell me things, but they'd go in one ear and out the other. I never thought there was any hurry to learn about raising children and being a wife. 'Cause I thought that it would be a long time coming for me anyway. I wanted to live and run and live some more.

"So I set out doing what everybody else do when they find out their life ain't going nowhere. I tried to teach the right way to my children. But if it didn't work for us, how do we expect it to work for them? And children today more hardheaded than we were. From the time Stone was five years old, everybody was telling me he take too much after Lank, tripping and falling all over the place, and staying into devilment. But I always saw it different, and I wanted him to be much more than his Daddy. But there was always something coming up, some bad luck steady on that boy's case . . ."

"Better get dressed, Jean. We don't have much time."

She sighed and stood up. "What do you wear to an arraignment, Roscoe? I've never been to one before." She had her compact case open and was dabbing at the tracks of her tears.

"It's not like a funeral, Jean. They just bring the charges, and Stone say either 'guilty' or 'not guilty' and that's that."

"That's all?" she asked, puzzled.

Roscoe nodded, feeling awkward, helpless, as she went to the back to finish dressing.

They went out to the car in the bright and muggy August morning. Roscoe had jogged earlier and had felt that he could have run forever. Just like he wanted to drive on and on this morning. He could have driven into Canada, say, into northern Ontario where the towns give out and there are just the two-lane bumpy roads that only the sportsmen and loggers know. It was the kind of day he would remember later for the smell of mint growing wild in someone's yard or the halfhearted wind that whirled paper down the sidewalk. But he could not share this with Everjean. He was taking her to a courthouse twenty miles away, a courthouse whose dull grayness assaulted the eyes. Perhaps such a day could be shared with only his daughters as he did many weeks ago at the zoo. He shook his head wearily at the sudden complications of his life, caught Everjean's glance, and faked cheeriness as he drove away from her house.

Everjean's friend, Delilah, rode with them to the arraignment. She was fond of calling Roscoe Babycakes and went in for loud, ambushing perfumes. The car would hold her smell for a week.

Later, inside the courthouse, they sat quietly in the back. When the guards brought in Stone, he looked so helpless, the fear hunching his shoulders, that Everjean broke down crying. Stone's look came up from the floor to watch her for a moment, then dropped again, away from the flat accusing eyes of the prosecution team.

"Not guilty," he said minutes later in answer to the charges. His voice was even.

Everjean was whimpering and Delilah comforted her. Roscoe watched the faces of the judge, of the lawyers, looking for a clue of doubt. But there was none. The gestures, the words, were methodical, precise. Even Lonnie's soft-voiced arguments to the judge. Stone was trying to force a smile toward his mother.

You ain't my daddy. Roscoe considered the actions in behalf of a bloodson. Would he snatch the prosecutor toward truth? Shake Lonnie from his dreams of becoming the first black governor of the state in order that he could see Stone in all his utter helplessness? Charge into the courtroom with a couple of automatic rifles and a hand grenade and demand blind justice rip off her veil and see the crime carried out in her name? *You ain't my daddy.* He did nothing now except blink away those images behind the eyes. Lonnie conferring with Stone and the boy nodding. People were filing out. Short and bittersweet, it had been. Stone waved a clenched fist to his mother as they walked him out.

Back in town Roscoe drove the women to the café. It was an hour before opening time. Everjean and Delilah sat next to a window, their table striped by the sunlight that would broaden and lengthen as the day went on. Roscoe busied himself fixing drinks as the women talked on about the impossibility of raising much more money for Lonnie's fees. He never drank so early in the day, but today's need was special. He would regret it during football practice later.

"You know Ruby who works for the judge?" Delilah asked. "Well, she claim she heard the judge say he gone get Stone." She raised her right hand. "I swear 'for God that's what she told somebody I know real well."

Roscoe wanted her to shut up. Even if the rumor were true, it didn't help Everjean at all.

But Delilah went on. "I tried to tell that to Lonnie, but ain't nothing much he can do unless he can get Ruby up on the stand or have her put it in writing. Which she won't 'cause if she do something like that, she'll never work another white house in this town. Ain't no sense of nobody calling himself a judge and he got his mind made up before the trial even start."

Roscoe brought their drinks over. "Well, we just have to be there everyday to show the judge that Stone ain't by himself."

"Will that do any good?" Everjean asked, absently stirring her drink. "I mean, really?"

"Right now we got to think that everything we do to get the boy free and to support him will do some good. Now look here, I want y'all to talk with the women at the churches, at the beauty parlors, wherever. You tell them to talk with their husbands. We want everybody who can get down there, to go. Everybody don't work the times the trial will be in session. I'll talk to the folk who come here. I'll check Ruby out to see how far she wants to go with that story. And I'm going to find out who really belongs up there on the stand in Stone's place."

Both women stared at him. In his look there was no room for surrender.

LINE 2

BEFORE THE TRIAL Roscoe saw and talked with Lonnie only twice. Both times Roscoe sought the glint of a warrior's steel in the eyes of the younger man. He remembered Lonnie from years ago when Lonnie tried to hang around the older fellows. He was a quiet boy and not exceptionally gifted as a rapper. Or as an athlete. Older boys were a little wary of him because of his good grades. They were also reluctant to bother him because his older brother Darnell was a Golden Gloves semifinalist. So they let him listen in on their conversations, this boy who always wanted to be older than what he was. After Roscoe went off to college, he did not see Lonnie again, even during the holidays home, and would remember him best as the runny-nosed boy bothering the older boys, innocently taking their crude messages to pretty girls passing through the park or past street corners, the little butt of their jokes. Yet Roscoe had heard of his plans, his ambitions, pronounced loudly to those who would listen.

Two days after the arraignment, he spotted Lonnie approaching on the crowded downtown street. From the way Lonnie moved Roscoe figured that he still wanted to be the first black governor of the state. His shoulders were pulled back, chin up. That bouncy stride and a cigar at the corner of his mouth. Roscoe felt pride because so few ever returned home moving like that. They slapped palms.

"Go-ud damn, Roscoe, you look like you could step on a football field right now and run a whole lot of dudes up into the stands."

"Just trying to keep the fat down."

"You look like you doing a helluva more than keeping the fat down. Somebody was telling me you're playing for the Bombers. Hard to get it out your blood, huh?"

"Yeah, they talked me into playing with them. Hell, I figure if a lot of those dudes like Marshall and Mean Joe could still get around the league at their age, I can limp around with a sandlot team. But, look here, you the man putting it all together, I understand. How you doing?"

Lonnie smiled. "I'm just out here scuffling, man." He stepped back and patted his obvious belly. "Except for putting on all this weight, just trying to make a living."

"Look like you make a pretty good living. Good steaks don't hurt."

Up close Lonnie's face was a little puffy. A steady diet of bourbon could work such magic. He was growing soft around the middle, a little butterball he was becoming. In ten years with a thicker cigar and a gray beat up hat tilted back on his head, Lonnie would be his father's twin. After thirty, men seemed to resemble their fathers in more ways than seemed possible earlier.

'Sip Bryant, Lonnie's father, had always been one of the few black men active in organized politics. There had been a small local Garveyite group that died out around 1950, and there had been those in and out of the local NAACP group. As far as organized politics, however—Republicans and Democrats—few sensed an urgency after Roosevelt, though there was a flurry of interest in the 1960 Kennedy–Nixon campaign. 'Sip had been a loyal Republican all these years. Perhaps he still waited for Lincoln's second coming, and unlike others had seen FDR as merely a slick card dealer. Lonnie echoed such feelings through his own time.

They walked to the town fountain, dirty and rust-streaked as ever, gushing water fitfully. A few suds were left in its pool where some joker had dumped a box of detergent a few days before.

"You know I got the Johnson boy's case?" Lonnie asked.

Roscoe nodded. Lonnie must have missed him at the arraignment the other day. Did he know about him and Everjean then? "A couple cats around the bar mentioned it. How does it look?"

"I think we have a damned good chance of getting the boy out."

Roscoe waited for more, wanted more from one of the town's few great hopes. Then a man passed, greeting both of them. He slapped Lonnie on the back and held him hard by the shoulder as he spoke, as older men will do when impressing a point upon the

117

prodigals. The man went on about his own son's interest in law school and whether Lonnie had any advice for the boy, and there were the no-good unions and working conditions at the mill. His complaints settled like soot. Nodding, Lonnie puffed on his cigar, slid a hand to his belly, and once more was his father's twin. Except that 'Sip would have been in boots whitened by plaster, stumping for Eisenhower between contracting jobs, and coming loudly to their house where the Old Man would give him a drink, then argue loudly with him. The Old Man rarely voted, but the arguments were good sparring sessions that kept both men sharp.

Roscoe stared into the pool as the man spoke on, remembering that the fountain had always been there, once gleaming, and thinking that it was a shame the way it had been allowed to run down.

The man moved on and Roscoe resumed his probing. "You say there's a good chance, Lonnie? You think the crackers in this town going to give the boy a fair trial?"

"They don't have much of a case, Roscoe. Just between you and me and this fountain, they know that boy didn't do any shooting. They want to get him on conspiracy on the one hand and want a lynching on the other. Keep all this under your hat."

Roscoe remembered the case of Bobbie Brown who was brought to trial with four others for beating up two boys after a football game. One of the victims was the son of one of the wealthiest merchants in town. They say that Bobbie's mother, a maid, knew the verdict and the length of the sentence a week before the start of the trial. She had served a party where the judge was a guest. He wasn't shy about making up his mind over drinks, and announcing verdicts to anyone who would listen. As he had already done with Stone this time, according to Ruby.

"You really have to have your stuff together to get by that judge, I hear."

"We'll have it all together by the time the trial rolls around, man."

Roscoe wanted to come at it from another direction. "Did you know Stone and Everjean when you were growing up here?"

"Man, who don't know Everjean?" Lonnie glanced around as if ready to spill other great secrets. "About half the dudes in this town grew up with a crush on her. Shoot, I remember how we used to get out on Wilson's street corner about 5:30 every evening just to see her get off the bus and walk by. Just her walk then caused a lot of men to leave their happy homes. Y'all used to be tight, didn't you, when you first got back in town?"

"For awhile, yeah."

"I never knew Stone that well. You know, he was just a baby when I was finishing college."

"Yeah, that's right. I should have remembered that. Only reason I brought it up is because I was wondering whether you knew what they were up against."

Again, Lonnie glanced around and this habit of his, as if seeking a larger audience, was beginning to irritate Roscoe. Aside from two elderly men on the other side of the fountain, they were the only ones standing at the center of town. "I'm not charging my full fee, man. I know how hard homefolks have to scuffle."

"And it ain't getting no easier for them, I can tell you that. Look, drop by the bar for a taste if you're going to be in town for awhile."

"I'll do that. I'm staying at my mother's a few days to find out what I can for the case. Keep everything I just said to yourself, OK?"

The second time Roscoe was to see Lonnie was the next night when Lonnie took Roscoe up on his invitation. He drank two bourbons on the house, then he went in back where he lost miserably in pool to old friends who had never left town. Lonnie soon came back to the front where he stared at the behinds of solitary women who wandered through, and he nodded at the ones who, according to Roscoe, were not there to meet someone else. He bought drinks for his friends and for one or two of the women. The talk with his friends would grow thin after they had relived their high school days and caught up on the gossip of all those who had never left town or stayed and somehow dropped out of circulation. Then they would float away, and Roscoe watched Lonnie move to the women, figuring that the man's suit and tie would

119

make most of the women wary. They indulged his talk, his teases, as they would the naughty whispers from a child. He didn't leave the bar with any and perhaps he didn't want to. Roscoe couldn't tell what he was doing. Picking up on some gossip that might help the case? Maybe he was simply trying to prove something to himself, trying to get back in touch with something. The stranger again, Lonnie was alone at the bar.

"Anything new in the works since yesterday?" Roscoe asked him.

"Nothing yet. You know, I was sitting here remembering how little I've gotten home over the years. It's good to keep your contacts clean here."

"I think I know what you're saying. Except that a lot of these young jokers around here ain't talking about too much, you know. Their conversation consists of lies about women, ignorance about sports, and cold-blooded nonsense about getting high off that dope."

"Well, they gon' always talk that talk. But, right now, I really don't know but it's something I feel needs to be stayed in contact with."

"Sound like you ready to move back," kidded Roscoe with a straight face.

"Naw, no way. I still have to eat, man. There probably wouldn't be enough business for me in this town. First, we scratch the white folks off the list. And the bloods figure that since I don't look like the judge, they will lose any case brought to me. I got this one by luck."

Roscoe burned, remembering that his first impulse was to recommend a white lawyer to Jean. Of course, Lonnie had slipped his mind, and he didn't know whether Lonnie even handled criminal cases. Yet his excuses didn't ease his guilt.

"What about politics, Lonnie? Still thinking about running for office some day?"

"Yeah, that's still in my blood. I got that from my old man, I guess. I used to follow him and work with him, and thought that, had his life gone down a little differently and if he were in a larger

120

town where they might appreciate him, he'd have been one hell of a politician."

"One tough dude, he was, anyway."

"Maybe in a couple years I'll make my move. Maybe the State House. But right now, I'm learning, man. Joe Vinson about the best lawyer around, and he has taught me more about the law than all my professors in law school. This is my biggest case and I don't plan to mess up. I got Joe looking over my shoulder and the politics to consider." He glanced around and leaned closer to Roscoe. "If I blow this one, I can hang it up. The town never would let me forget it. A whole bunch of folks—our own blood, Roscoe—would just love to see me fall on my face."

They were silent for awhile. Roscoe understood. There would be those who knew Lonnie but didn't like him, those who would smile at him and drink the liquor he'd buy them. Somehow they'd pin the frustration and prisons of their own lives on him, as if he had something to do with them. His confidence they would chalk up to being "cute" or being "saditty." Then, too, there were the town's movers and shakers, the rich white men, putting together the case against Stone and therefore Lonnie, amid cigar smoke and ice tinkling in glasses of sour mash whiskey. Both knew of the random violence between town blacks and whites over the years, though it appeared to be one of the most peacefully integrated towns in the state. Both could share common memories of events far less dramatic: of the Smith boy's three draws with a white girl for first place in a history contest sponsored by the Daughters of the American Revolution, of Stewart Mack's return home to give a high school commencement address one spring and forewarned by a fidgeting high school principal to steer clear of any references to race, of men who threw up their hands after years of shoveling slag and turned down for all the trainee programs, men who left the town to retrace their paths south in order to start all over again.

"How about another drink?" Roscoe said. "One more for the road."

"One more and I'll pass out right here and you'll have to get somebody to carry me home. By tomorrow morning the judge will hear about that. Unh-Unh. I might holler at the women, but I'm keeping my nose clean while this case is on."

He paused for a moment. "Roscoe, I did learn something else after I talked with you. I didn't know you were seeing Jean again. I really put my foot in my mouth."

"No big thing."

"I didn't know about you and Charlotte either. I hate to hear about y'all splitting up."

"Things like that go down." He searched for something to do behind the bar. "You married yet?"

"Not yet. It probably won't be too long before this girl in the city ties me down, though."

"Well, it's more than a notion. You probably already know that."

"It helps to hear it. It helps me keep running from it."

They both laughed. "But tell Everjean to relax before she worry herself crazy, OK?"

"I've only told her that forty-'leven times already."

Lonnie shook his head and drifted to the jukebox. He made his selections, then moved around the room at the edges of conversations to the video games. People stayed clear of him, not out of hostility, but because of their own nervousness that neither he nor they could quite dissolve.

Wilson was a little late. "Hey, Big Man, this don't look like much of a bar."

"Watch your mouth, Wilson. There's life in here. It might not look like it's worth much, but it's life all the same."

Wilson chuckled for the thousandth time over their customary greeting and squatted on a stool as Roscoe pushed a beer toward him. "Say, Superstar, ain't that Lonnie over there? What he doing in here with the lowlifers? That boy ought to be home right now getting all the rest he can 'stead of hanging out in a bar. When's the trial? Next week or something, ain't it? Shoot, crackers gon' try to run him stone crazy. Watch and see ain't I'm talking true. He and Stone both gon' need all the help they can get."

"You got that right. 'Course if anybody can get him off it's got to be Vinson, but he just looking over Lonnie's shoulder, from what Lonnie said. I figure like this, unless the student is piss-poor, he shouldn't lose with the master right there with him. You coming to the trial, Wilson?"

"Uh-uh. Courthouses is bad luck for niggas. It's best to stay out from 'round them."

"Look, fool, they need all the support, all our support. I've never known you to be superstitious."

Wilson scratched his jaw. "I ain't usually superstitious worth a damn. Ain't scared of nothing neither. But I know what's for real and what ain't. By the way, who you callin' 'fool'"?

"Just your knowing it won't help Stone."

"The way they got it hung on him now, the only thing that would do him any good is a fast plane out of the state. But what you mean callin . . .?"

"Ah, man, you talking silly."

Roscoe ignored Wilson's raised eyebrows and went to the other end of the bar, pretending to dump ash trays and wipe off the counter. Sissies. All of them sissies protecting their sorry chick-enshit selves.

The news of Billy Africa's return had reached the bar three days before he got to town. Billy had no choice but come by the café. Roscoe's place was one of the few places around here where you could catch up on everything missed while away from home. So Roscoe would wait for this boy he hadn't seen in thirteen years but who had grown into legend due to the letters written back to his brother, Poochie. Poochie related that Billy had left town the first time to register black voters in Lowndes County, Alabama, that he had been shot at with the other SNCC workers, jailed with King and Shuttlesworth, and his car run off the road and into a cornfield in deepest Mississippi. Over beers, Poochie would lean back in a booth and announce that Billy would have been the righthand man to King if he wanted to, but he had begun to change his mind about nonviolence. He fell in with Stokely next. Poochie had photographs of his brother with King and Carmichael and pushed them under the noses of skeptics. Billy later left rural Alabama for Atlanta, where he stayed until 1968. Then on to Washington, D.C. for two more years where he changed his last name from McQuinn to Africa. After that, no one knew where he was for three years—VietNam? Tanzania? college?—until Poochie got a letter informing him that Billy was in Denver. By day he worked with computers. As it turned out, he had finished his college degree out there and done night work picking up special skills in computer programming. By night he led an army of vigilantes, young black and Chicano men and women who were fighting to keep drugs out of their communities. Poochie would relate the last as if questioning it himself, as if straining to conjure up a picture of Billy and others stealing quietly in the night up to the apartments of big-hatted coke dealers (*snowmen* as Billy called them).

The story that sealed the legend was that Billy and the vigilantes had caught one of the major snowmen in the area and, in an open field north of the city, they chopped off his hand. A lie? A wild tale? Um-um, said Poochie.

"The truth as sure as I'm sitting here. He even sent a picture of the hand chopped at the wrist. Big rings on the fingers of that hand, too. I might have copped those rings myself. But I don't have those pictures with me to show you, man. All I can say is that my brother don't lie when it comes to his politics."

Yet few would take Poochie's word for anything, and he would never deliver the pictures of the hand for the barflies to gape at. So there were the stories, which few minded since all the drinkers at Roscoe's bar liked a good story, whether fact or not. After all he was smart, had gone to college, and had no real right to mess up his life. When was he going to settle down and make something out of himself, anyway, they would wonder. Sooner or later he would have to outgrow hunting down dope dealers.

Billy walked into the café on his second night in town. He wore the uniform of no army, just dungarees and faded longsleeved shirt with the sleeves rolled up to the elbows. He looked as if he had just come off work from Turner's Drug Store where he worked in high school. Up on his toes, Billy moved easily and looked as shifty as he did when he played guard on the high school basketball team. Though slightly over thirty, his hair seemed much thinner than that of Poochie, who was fifteen years older. There was a patch of gray already prominent above the widow's peak.

Roscoe had not seen him since that day during the Christmas holiday when they talked briefly about basketball and Billy's plans for college. Shy then, he had seemed honored to talk with Roscoe. Now Billy found a stool at the bar.

"Well, well, it's been a long time, blood," Roscoe said.

"That's right, Roscoe." They shook hands.

"What you drinking these days, Billy? Don't tell me you're still in training."

Billy laughed and ordered a bourbon on the rocks. After serving him and dropping more coins in the jukebox, Roscoe settled once more behind the bar. "How long you back for?"

Billy shrugged. "Maybe a week. I came back to see the family. Mama, mainly. You probably already know she's not doing too well. But what's changed around town, man? I see a lot of new buildings up and a lot of old buildings turned into parking lots."

"Nothing's changed. Folks still slipping around telling the same old lies, a few new folks in town telling new-style lies that grow old as quickly as milk go sour in the summertime."

Smiling Billy looked around the bar. More customers crowded into the booths. Most had already eaten dinner, then showered, and, their lotions and colognes alive, come back to the bar for the night round. Roscoe glanced at Billy who seemed content, not withdrawn. Certainly not fanatical, as Poochie could make him sound. Poochie lying as usual.

Billy turned back to Roscoe, nodding. "Well, a lot of things can change even though they remain the same. Change down deep, I mean. So deep that you'd never expect, and it works itself up so slow that one day you look at it, then look away, and look at it again and say 'God-dam, I'm seeing something different that I didn't see before.' But it was there all the time." He looked at Roscoe. Then, as if embarrassed, he managed a smile. "I guess I'm telling you what I've learned."

"Well, I hope you're right in what you say, Billy. But I swear I don't see that change yet. Everybody done come back here from a place they thought was worse. And once they here, they seemed relieved and they work and screw and go to sleep. Some call that living."

Billy sipped his beer. Unsmiling Billy now, in from the cold of unfamiliar places. The places he'd known and seen since leaving the South were places known only through TV westerns, through infamous pro football teams that lost to Cleveland and Cincinnati, spaces driven through enroute to visits with relatives in California. Places to blink at in one's impatience, places stolid brothers would live or glide through during the best years of their lives, cut off from home by private missions. Roscoe had known those places, had once been a hero in such strangenesses.

Roscoe imagined Billy meeting Emmanuel somewhere and Emmanuel nodding at the younger man's ideals, not clear on the specifics maybe, but sure of the need. Meanwhile, Emmanuel had his father's killer to find, and a larger idealism would be something he might pick up in a quieter time. But he must dream. At least, Roscoe guessed that his brother must dream of a time when there would be no sorry coward to chase. He would have to be storing up some plans for a life untouched by his obsession. Roscoe realized that he was staring at the younger man, that he was shuffling faces, and wanted to touch his brother's arm and tell him to stay inside out of the cold.

"Well, I'll try to give the town a chance the little while I plan to stay. You never know when you can learn something. It'd be good for me to come home and learn something."

But Roscoe went after the stuff of legends. "What's this Poochie talking about you being death on dope dealers out there?"

"Poochie's always saying something to make it sound a lot bigger than it is," Billy said, with a faint smile. He looked off for a brief moment, seemed to shift to look at the large photo of Roscoe behind the bar. Then back to Roscoe. "Dope kills, man. Nobody needs to lynch anymore. It's too crude. Dope is a quieter style, messes up the mind with less social backlash, if you can see where I'm coming from. Well, out there we decided to do something about it. And we discovered that's all you have to do—*decide* to do. Of course, there were some in the group we thought a little more extreme than others. They were the first ones to catch the pushers and take them into the mountains to cool them out. But that was only logical, I suppose. The cops wouldn't do it, especially the few of them who made big money helping to push the dope themselves. We were simply trying to clean up the town a little, to chase out some of them killers. Then we could go after the bigger oppressors, the large companies and corporations. But we thought we were fair. I mean, we just didn't leap in grabbing pushers off the street. We sent out a warning to all the pushers first. A few of them slowed down their activities just to see what we were all about, but most of them went on as if nothing was happening."

Billy sipped from his glass and leaned closer. "So we moved on those who were thickheaded. We took one guy, there were three of us, we took this cat up by the stockyards and made our warning a little more blunt. We didn't hit him or anything; we just told him if he didn't stop messing up we would cut off his hands. The law of the desert, man. He figured we were bluffing, called us jive. But we let him go anyway. The idea was still new to us. Maybe we were bluffing at first, too, I don't know. We knew we would have to get him again, and a month later we found him again, hustling around the high schools to the bloods and poor Chicanos. So one night we separated him from the bodyguard he had rented, stripped the pusher of his guns and while two of them held him down, I took a shorthandled axe and chopped off his hand."

Roscoe tried not to gasp. Involuntarily he had balled his own hand into a fist and flexed it open. "You dudes don't play, hunh?"

"Nobody else is playing either. At least, the pushers ain't. We got to clean up the places where we live, or we'll simply feed off one another. In the sixties I was in the South with crackers firing away at bloods, and some of the bloods make it to the North to fear one another on the street. That's one of the coldest shots. Eventually, we'll get to those big cats, as I say, but we need all the muscle possible, and it's hard to keep your muscle when it's doped up and sky-high. You know for yourself how lazy you feel when you're out of shape and that one laziness is the excuse for further laziness."

Roscoe nodded. "I think I see what you mean. I don't even let the thugs in my bar. But as far as going after the riff-raff here— well, that's a little different. It wouldn't work."

"Anybody ever try?" Billy asked.

"Well, no . . ."

They were interrupted by someone who recognized Billy. After the handshakes and backslaps, after Billy's few questions of the whereabouts of old friends, the conversation lapsed into a fitful silence. Roscoe remembered the identical experience of Lonnie only a few days earlier. The acquaintance would get up and say that he had to run an errand and that he would return in a half hour. Strangers and alone.

Roscoe returned to Billy's end of the bar. "Billy, have you heard about the big case we've got in town now?"

"The Johnson boy? Yeah, Poochie told me about it. He said that nobody think the boy did it, that he just got stuck with the rap."

"That's about the size of it."

"Anybody doing anything about it?" Billy asked. "Who's his lawyer?"

"Lonnie's working on the case for him. You remember Lonnie Bryant?" Roscoe wasn't sure how much Billy could remember after twelve years away.

"Yeah, you know he was just three–four years ahead of me in school, Roscoe. I remember he always wanted to be a lawyer. Are the folks backing him?"

"Well, the church is raising money to help out with the fees. We couldn't raise enough bail because nobody wanted to take a chance on him, though they knew deep down that he was innocent. Besides that, a few go down just about everyday to see him."

128

Billy was silent, drumming his fingers against his glass. Then he sighed. "Anybody know who did it?"

"No, just some wild guesses, that's all. Every night there'll be somebody come in here and claim they know who did it and where the gun at."

"Anybody try to find out who did it?"

Roscoe shook his head. There was another pause as the bass guitar from a song throbbed like a pulse through the floor, through their feet and up. "I think I'll go see him," Billy said.

"You know where he is then. Where they always send them?"

"Uh-huh. I don't know him. Like I say, he was just a young dude when I was coming along. But I do know what they can do to him. And I know he needs all the support he can get."

Roscoe nodded. Shame was the hot splash across the chest, up the neck. He had not brought himself to visit the boy in jail. He knew he would get only silence, even though by now Stone would probably welcome anybody. Roscoe had driven Jean down a few times, but sat in the car, going up to meet Jean on the steps when she walked out. Both times she started crying, must have been crying before she pushed open the heavy, glass door to come out. He sat in the car, guessing that a greeting to Stone would be met by a look that would knife at the root of his own helplessness. Roscoe imagined the worst: How come you're with my mother when you know you don't really give a damn about her? You're a stranger in your own home and a stranger in ours. What do you want from us? From yourself? We ain't got nothing to give you, and you ain't got nothing to give us.

Maybe it didn't have to be as bad as he imagined. Everjean could not understand why he didn't want to talk with her son. ("Come on in, Roscoe. You don't have to sit out here in this hot car.")

Billy stood. "Right now I'd better get out of here and get home to eat. Mama already claims I've lost so much weight she's ready to commit *me* to the hospital, get me a room right next to hers. Look, man, I'll be back before I leave. OK? It was good rapping."

They shook hands again and Roscoe watched him leave. Billy's bounce. If this man could wander so widely in search for the new land, surely he, Roscoe—older, more wise?—could take a stand in this place, this home. Time was running out on all of them, he felt, and stances had to be taken even if in quicksand. But he didn't move that day or the next to see Stone. Everyday he would phone Jean for the latest news and offer to take her down to see her son. She seemed to prefer the bus or Lank or a girl friend, and he really didn't know why. ("You've got a business to run, Ros. I don't want to take up all your time.") But he thought of Billy Africa going back to his camp at the base of the mountains, of Emmanuel standing on a plateau and sniffing the wind, one hand cupped to his ear. But what did he, Roscoe Superstar, have to find? Have to give?

For the next week he managed the bar and practiced with the team, thinking and thinking, until Ruby presented herself. Perhaps everything that came later started with Ruby when she walked in that slow night with her girl friends, Jackie and Cleo. All three of them were bent on having a good time. Ruby never came to the bar without them. Her husband Turbine was a steady customer, sometimes taking his dinner there: two ham sandwiches, french fries, all washed down with beer. The women usually had a couple of drinks apiece and a lot of laughs before leaving.

The sudden tug of Kenny's words yesterday: "Ruby told me that she heard that sawed-off judge say he gon' get Stone if it's the last thing he do. Heard him tell his wife and a couple of his drinking buddies that."

When Inez moved past to serve the women their second round, Roscoe whispered to her to shoo Jackie and Cleo away, that he had business with Ruby. When Inez smiled, Roscoe had to explain. "Just some information. Get the others to Pac-man or maybe in back on the pool table for fifteen minutes or so. You know how to do." Then he started for Ruby and her friends.

"How're you young ladies doing this evening? I hope the rich white folks ain't working y'all too hard these days."

"Uh-uh," Ruby said, "I wouldn't let them do that to me. I got to take care of myself."

After a minute of small talk, Inez interrupted with their drinks and their change. "Y'all come on with me. Ruby, chile, you just finish your drink. I know you don't like shooting pool much no-how." Ruby shrugged.

Roscoe smiled at the tired woman with the gold tooth, the large breasts, and the peeling polish on her fingernails. She reminded him of that maid in Boston whom Mack, the tenor player, talked about the last time he came through town. Her name was Della; she was the type that ran the house, maid or not. Tough smack-talking women who cleaned the Big Houses and looked after the young and old brats there.

Ruby's husband was called *mean* by the church folk. It was rumored that Turbine beat Ruby on occasion, though this rumor had died out over the years. Ruby looked like she could take care of herself. Yeah, that must have been only loose gossip from the past. The present was her on this night out, enjoying herself, and glancing over her shoulder at her friends giggling as they walked back to the pool tables. Here. The present was also the hanging judge. Was Stone. Was the mob.

"Ain't seen y'all come through here in quite awhile," he lied. Two weeks was a decade.

"Naw, we don't get out as much as we would like to. You know how you mens is. But I tell you this much, your place is about the only one in town where there ain't all that rowdyism and stuff. A woman go to the Legion or Elks Club these days, and she don't get no respect at all." She leaned closer. "But I done heard something about you, Roscoe."

"Me?" Was it all over town now, his crusade?

"Yeah, I done heard about you bringing that girl in here to dance with half her clothes off. Luke's girl, ain't it?"

Roscoe laughed. "She don't have half her clothes off."

"That ain't the way I heard it. They tell me she ain't got hardly nothing covering her little titties and a piece of cloth no bigger than a half dollar stuck there between her legs. The mens be coming to the house telling Turbine about it."

"Well, Ruby, you're just going to have to come down and see for yourself. You can't believe everything people tell you."

"Well, maybe . . ." She sipped her beer.

"Shame about that Johnson boy, huh?" Roscoe said. Later for tact.

"You mean Stone? Sure is. I know Everjean probably worrying herself to death over it right now."

He knew that she was probably playing right now, that she probably knew about Everjean and him seeing each other. But he plodded on. "You work for the judge, don't you, Ruby?"

"Uh-uh. I work for his best friends, the Curtises. They get together a lot for dinner and stuff. But I tell you I don't like the little squirt. Look too much like George Wallace in the face for me, anyway."

"I see."

"That judge drink like a fish, too. Hah, you ought to see him! You know, you was talking about Stone. One night not too long back after he found out the trial was coming down to him, he tell Mr. Curtis that Stone don't have a leg to stand on. He say that they gon' get him."

"I'll be damned," Roscoe said, now leaning forward with both elbows on the bar. "That boy ain't got a chance."

"Naw, it don't look that way. 'Course the judge done lost a few before. One smart lawyer even had him disqualified."

"Well, the lawyers need proof. Hold tight just a minute, Ruby." Another customer had come in, the silent C. C. in dirty coveralls. Roscoe served him a beer and a pickled pig's foot without smiling. He went back to Ruby, wiping along the bar as he walked. He hoped his comment about proof was sinking in.

"Suppose Lonnie came up to you and told you they could disqualify the judge this time if you take the stand at a hearing. What would you do?"

She thought for a moment. Apparently the move had never crossed her mind. "Well, I'd probably say 'no.'"

"Even if it could save the boy's life?"

"If I told on the judge, I'd never work again in this town." Her look was steady.

The phone rang, but he ignored it. Inez would pick it up in back. "Well, now, I don't know about that. I mean, you could work here. Help out Inez, maybe. I don't know how much you making now, but I think I could match it."

She was frowning in disbelief. Then she shook her head. "I ain't gon' be nobody's hero, Roscoe." She looked over her shoulder again. "Thanks for the job offer, but no thanks."

She picked up her glass and left to join her friends. Roscoe was left at the bar with C. C., who was no doubt already planning new and bad poems for the walls of the john. He shook his head. Had he made an enemy by simply asking Ruby that question? It upset her, he could see that. But what was there to worry about? He'd pay her to tell the truth. She could sit home if she wanted. Then, too, plenty of women made much better money working out of town, commuting twenty miles in car pools. What was she afraid of?

"You get all your talking done?" It was Inez who had just hung up the phone. Roscoe nodded. "That's good because it was hell getting them started back there on the table. At first, they didn't want to shoot pool. Too mannish, they claim. Now, look at them! They don't want to quit. By the way, Roscoe, that was your wife who just called. She want you to call her back." He nodded.

When the women finished in back, they returned to the juke-box. They soon tired of dropping quarters in the jukebox and rolling their shoulders to the rhythm, no willing dance partners around. Ruby announced that they were leaving. She avoided Roscoe's eyes.

"Y'all come back now, you hear?" Roscoe said. "Somebody claim the ladies don't like the idea of a girl in here dancing on Friday nights. Well, I'm open to all suggestions. Matter of fact, I've been doing some heavy thinking, and come up with something for the ladies. How about a man up there dancing?"

The women traded looks and giggled. "Roscoe, you a mess," said Cleo, touching the stiff ends of her hair.

"I might even break down and do a little dancing up there my-self." And he cut a little step behind the bar, rolling his shoulders. "'Course I don't want to excite the women too much. Might break up their happy homes."

Inez waved her hand at him. "Shoot, if you get up there dancing, we would pack the place with folk just trying to figure out the dance you'd be doing. The Camel Walk been out of style."

The women laughed and left. Roscoe hoped that Ruby would be back again, that she'd think it through. Meanwhile, he would follow the maze of rumors to track down other truths. He could have been a detective, he thought.

"Thanks for the favor, Inez."

"No big thing. Just put it on my next check." He snorted drily. If they ever ran him out of town, Inez would be the one he'd stand at the fork in the road to point the posse into the trees. They would split the gold later.

Red-eyed Roger Turrentine, the Best Body Man in Town, sat on the grass next to Roscoe. The town's semipro baseball team was warming up for their last game of the season. They had lost as many games as they had won, but their fans were loyal, sitting five-deep along the hill that paralleled the first-base line. New bleachers were two years overdue.

Turrentine was a squat short man built along the lines of Ruby's husband, Turbine. His facial features were similar to those of Joe Frazier, one of Roscoe's favorite boxers. A good-sized pulling guard Roger would have been, too, leading sweeps around end, ahead of a fast back. Roger had gone to Kentucky State for a semester and had hoped to play ball there. Got into trouble with a bad crowd, went one story. Got a girl pregnant, went another. At any rate he came home on a bus during the middle of the second semester and married a hometown girl six months later. And the man had been a loyal fan of Roscoe's when he played at Ohio State. He had brought carloads of "homeboys" to Columbus during the last two seasons.

"Roscoe, this team they're playing today couldn't whip their way out of a paper bag. Clowns be striking out like it's going out of style. They everybody's patsies. All Willie have to do is rear back and fire his fastball. Maybe a slow curve every once in awhile to keep them honest. But that's all he got to do today. Them turkeys will be slicing air." He chuckled. Roger never missed a game, any kind of game, if he could help it. For example, after a long day of pulling out dents or replacing fenders, he was known to root wildly at the pee-wee league games and even at the girls' volleyball practices.

As if snapping a jab, he passed his brown bag over and Roscoe took a long swallow of warm beer. They stretched out on the hill. It was Sunday afternoon, the kind of afternoon he'd given to his family a summer ago.

He glanced at Roger. Roscoe would have to ask him about his son and his connection to the murder on the highway. For two days he had thought about his approach, but nothing was any clearer now. Was this whole idea a mistake?

"Look at that, will you!" Roger nodded behind them half-turning. Two girls pedaled bicycles past them and the men's looks lingered on their smooth legs, on the tautness of their thighs as they pushed down, at their behinds as they pedaled away.

Roger shook his head. "Roscoe, I need to be younger."

"It ain't got nothing to do with age."

"Shit. Something young as them would give me a heart attack at my age. But you can believe I'd go out grinning. Hee-hee."

Roscoe cleared his throat and turned back to the game. "R. T., the way Willie warming up I don't know whether you right about how this game's going to turn out. It might come out a helluva lot closer than we think. Look to me like something's wrong with his shoulder the way he keep hunching it up when he throws. Plus he looks as sluggish as a pregnant cow. He should be, too, the way he was guzzling Jack Daniels the other night in the bar. I had to pull the fool away and remind him that I had a bet on the game today. I'd rather lose money in the bar than lose a bundle out here, I told him. But I figure if he can't control himself when he's got a game coming up, he's a sorry-assed athlete."

"You always control yourself the night before a game?" Turrentine asked. He appeared genuinely curious. Yawning, Roscoe stretched out on his back again.

"Well, it only took me one time to figure my limits. I used to know some of the players who tried and tried, slipping a little wine here, a cigarette there. But Woody got hip to all that and kept us out of town the nights of the game. Claimed it helped our concentration along. We'd watch cowboy or war movies all night long, and the coaches would take roll call to make sure all the players were down there in the motel TV room. Well, at one of the away games, I think it was Iowa—yeah, yeah Iowa—there was this girl there I wanted to see. She used to go to O State, and she was one of the ones I dug hanging out at the coffeeshop there. So I gave her a call when we first got to town, and she asked me to come over. She had her own apartment and everything, jim. I told her about curfew and all, and she said that that was my problem and that if I figured out a way to get away she'd be home all night.

"So I got to thinking and made up a lie about homework. One of the coaches bought it and told me to stay in my room and study, that I could miss the John Wayne flick that night. Well, I slipped out and got to her apartment. It wasn't no time after we had talked over old times that we're in the bedroom, and I'm dealing and she's moaning and going on, and I'm trying to concentrate and not think about the game, my scholarship, how the fellows would laugh their butts off if I'm caught sneaking back in, and this fine woman throwing at me all the good, slow loving I could ever hope to handle, and it's beautiful, man. The team plus the coaches plus the Marines couldn't have dragged me from that woman that night. I got back about two in the morning. Now one thing I can say, it relaxed me. Before a game I'm all jittery, about to throw up and everything. But that game I wasn't. The problem was, I was sluggish as hell! 'Bout like Willie is out there now. He probably had some last night. But anyway, about the second quarter I get caught on the mouth with an elbow, and I wind up sucking blood the rest of the game. And I looked so bad in the films. I learned my lesson. Celebrate after the game, not before. Lots of these youngbloods out here don't understand that."

Turrentine had thrown his head back in loud long laughter, purple gums showing. "Man, you crazy. Here I was thinking all you dudes up there was indestructible. Could work an eight-hour shift in a coal mine or stay up and run women until dawn, then go out and beat Michigan."

"Well, now you know different. That's how come I'm not drink-

136

ing anything strong now. Been off for a couple months now. I have to do that if I want to make my comeback."

"Yeah, I heard about that. I guess at our age you don't let your mouth write no checks your body can't cash, hunh?"

It was nearing time for the game to start. Roscoe pulled out a five dollar bill and dropped it on the grass between them. "My money say the patsies win this game."

Turrentine eyed the money, then dug into his pocket. "Easy money is something I never turn away." His balled-up five bounced next to Roscoe's.

Roscoe shrugged and they were silent as the teams took the field. He wondered how braced Turrentine would be. Was his lonely crusade all over town by now? ("Watch out for Roscoe, y'all. He trying to start trouble.") Well, he'd just have to try. Too many lives here were already run by rumors and whispers, by averted eyes, and quiet actions not taken.

"Where's Spencer, R. T.? Don't he usually like these games?"

"He's in New York, visiting his cousins," Roger said, not taking his eyes off the field.

"Oh, yeah? How he liking it up there?"

"He's crazy about it. He even called back and say he might want to stay up there and go to school."

"What do you think about that?" Roscoe asked, starting to shell peanuts.

"Huh?"

"About him wanting to stay in New York?"

"I don't like it. As much trouble and devilment he keep raising at home, though, he ought to stay somewhere else. But New York won't be good for him."

"Yeah, probably get into a helluva lot more in New York than he could here, from what they say about things up there now."

R. T. kept his eyes on the game. Pointed. "Ah-ha, see there! Willie throwing nothing but smoke. He's gon' wear out that poor catcher's mitt by the fifth inning."

"Well, we'll see about that. Say, speaking of devilment, I know you've heard about Everjean's boy Stone."

"Who ain't heard about that? Everybody in town done heard

137

about that. I hope Lonnie can get the kid off, man. I really do."

"Yeah, I hope he can, too. A few folks around the bar say that there are a few boys who might know some things that might help Stone out. Lonnie needs some witnesses, some help, in getting his case together. Some of them claim Spencer could help."

Roger turned to him this time and raised up. "Well, they a goddam lie. How can Spencer help? He in New York. Been in New York." A few heads turned as Roger's voice grew louder.

"Was he in New York the day of the shooting?" Roscoe asked.

Roger's look was ugly. "Naw, it just so happen that he left on the same day, I think. But what his leaving got to do with Stone? And who is spreading all these lies?"

"Nobody's spreading anything, Roger. Just be cool. OK? All I'm saying is that we need witnesses, people who can say that Stone didn't shoot that boy down on the highway."

"How do I know he didn't do it?"

"Oh, goddam it, because I say so! That boy couldn't harm a flea, and you're sitting here asking me if he could shoot somebody. Look, he had a little .22 and the boy was killed with a shotgun. OK? I'm saying to you what quite a few have said to me, and that is Spencer and a few others might be able to testify and get Stone off."

Roger was a bit calmer, shaking his head. "What you saying is that Spencer had something to do with it, huh? You just trying to say that on the sly, now ain't you?"

"You said that, I didn't."

"Yeah, I see now. You got me out here today to try to bring my boy back to stand trial for Stone. I see through your jive, Roscoe!"

Neither one moved. "You doing this because of Everjean, huh?" R. T. said.

"I'm just trying to bring an innocent boy home. I'd do it for anybody. I mean, we're sitting here on our asses while some innocent boy is in jail."

"I told you I feel for the boy, Roscoe."

Roscoe glanced around. The folks nearest them had taken their interest back to the baseball game. "Seems like they're just going to have to drag the river for that gun."

Roger stiffened. "What you mean?"

"I heard the gun is in the river. Somebody threw the gun in the river down near the dam."

"You sho find out a lot sitting over there in that bar, don't you?"

Kenny had been on the mark all the way. Roger was more excited than Roscoe had ever seen him. Short sniffs through the nostrils, lips tight together and pushed up toward the nose, as if curled by a rank smell. He kept sipping at the bottle that Roscoe had long known was empty.

"Who's going to drag a river because of what some drunk nigga probably told you in your bar?"

Roscoe chuckled. "You know how this town is, R. T. Don't too much go unseen or unheard."

"Well, all I got to say is that my boy ain't seen nothing and he's in New York. He ain't coming back here for no damned trial that he ain't got nothing to do with. The boy's going to go to school, learn a trade and make something out of himself. If he can't do it in New York, he'll go some place or even come back here. He thought once about going into tailoring. If he want to do that, I don't stand in his way, and I won't let nobody else stand in his way either. You see what I'm saying?"

Roscoe said nothing. He knew that he would hurt this man or that they might hurt one another on this Sunday afternoon in the park watching two mediocre baseball teams. They could destroy one another so easily over that son sent away. Hiding guilt, whisking it out of view, was going to destroy a lot of lives and dreams, anyway. No way around it, there would be pain. Was Roscoe to blame for that? They were all dooming themselves in their lies.

He looked again to the people behind him, all out to have a good time. Other girls in tight shorts skirted the hill, and the heads of older men turned in unison once more. Watching the game was something people did between lies.

"Roscoe, you know we could storm the jailhouse, put the redneck guards up against the wall, you know, and haul ol' Stone out of there. Huh, what about that? Look, you know he got the best lawyers. Ain't much more any of us can do."

"Conscience is a bitch, ain't it?" Roscoe said.

"Mine's clear. What you talking about?"

"And that blood there, too, on your hands. It's going to eat away at your son, too. It's like a slow poison, they tell me." Snatching his money, Roscoe stood up and wiped the seat of his pants and, without another word to Roger, left.

Sitting at the bar, Wilson jerked back and scratched his chin. "What do you mean you know where the shotgun is?"

"I know where it is and pretty good idea of who put it there."

"How come you telling me this? You need to tell Lonnie, though I don't know how much good it will do him."

Roscoe frowned. "What do you mean? It should do a lot of good."

"Superstar, do you think they're going to drag the whole god-dam river to find some beatup shotgun? Then if they do find it how do they know Stone didn't put it there? Maybe some drunk hunter tossed it in after missing rabbits all day. That river hold a lot of secrets. Hell, it probably got more secrets than Ft. Knox got gold. You got somebody to go on that stand and testify that they put that gun there? Or even better, somebody with so much conscience they will come out and confess and trade places with Stone in the jailhouse? You must done found Jesus, Roscoe, and you must done hid him some place good, 'cause I sure as hell haven't seen him yet in this town." Wilson looked around him, at the ceiling, under his beer glass. Jesus nowhere to be found.

"No, Wilson, it's not about finding Jesus to come to free Stone. Jesus probably gave up on this town a long time ago, anyway."

"That's what I say. That conscience jive should be left to the church. Anyway, folks right in this town have killed, lied, cheated, and done most everything else and sleep just as sound as a baby. Whereas somebody like you might stay up half the night worrying every time you beat your customers out of a couple hard-earned pennies. Some folks got a conscience, others ain't. Simple as that. Give me another beer."

Roscoe watched Wilson's adam's apple bob up and down as he guzzled his third beer. Wilson finished the long swallow, set his glass down, smothered a belch. His fingertips ran a silent riff down the side of the glass. "As you tell it, only two people can get Stone out of jail. The person who put the gun in the river and the boy who did the shooting. Three, if we add Ruby who heard the judge's own words. But let's scratch her off, because who around here is going to take a maid's word against a judge's? Hunh? Who? So we're back to two. The one who did the shooting and the one who ditched the gun, assuming they different people. All I know is what you tell me. But it all goes back to the one who did the shooting."

"Yeah, I guess you're right." Roscoe glanced at the huge photograph behind the bar. Each time he looked at the picture now he could feel the strain in his arms, the pull of the neck cords as he brought the man over his head, the trembling of his arms as he held him overhead, inviting the cameras' clickings, the taunts and screams from the bloodthirsty crowd. The conqueror. Mr. America kicking ass. He turned around.

"R. T. just about had a fit the other day when I told him to bring his trifling son back from New York."

"I guess he would," said Wilson. "If you had a boy, wouldn't you worry about saving his neck no matter how trifling he was?"

"Well, there is something called responsibility, Wilson. I would try to teach my boy something about that especially if it means someone else might get lynched for it."

"It's easy to say, Superstar. But they always tell me that blood is thicker than water."

"Well, they still say a lot of things that don't add up to *right*."

"Just don't expect no off-the-wall miracles. Besides you think that hardhead Lonnie will listen? He's probably figured out already how many votes he's won or lost on this case. You can still try to talk to him, though. It's your neck."

"Thanks for the pep talk, Wilson."

Just then, Sandy, the dancer, walked in. For two months, she had been a regular on weekends. Her first two times had gone over so well that the customers demanded that Roscoe keep her on. A few backed up their demands with threats to boycott, picket, and failing by those means, wrecking the place if he didn't bring her back. So on weekends his bar put a real whipping on the American Legion and Elks clubs. He was now thinking about really doing it up, having Sandy fancy-dance in a floor-to-ceiling cylinder of clear plastic, but Inez reminded him that the customers probably wouldn't want her caged up like that. Cages went out of style with bell-bottom pants. They wanted to keep alive the possibility of touching her. So aside from a platform, there was only a revolving light filter of bright colors over her head.

Sandy was grinning at Roscoe now. "You still don't have my special dressing room ready yet, Mr. Roscoe?"

"I'm working on it, sugar. Maybe in a week or two I can have one ready with a big gold star on the door."

Then they laughed together. As he watched her walk away, he cursed his questionable fortune of having these young women lean on him as if he were a father. Of course, he had never been able to convince Charlotte that there was nothing more to such motions. Did it have anything to do with his size? Did they see him as the strong, gentle type and admire his calmness in the face of crises? Was it too late to change his style?

Roscoe chuckled to himself as he remembered the second night she danced. Word had gotten out, and a few stood in front of her gawking and blocking the view of others at the bar and in booths along the walls. "Say, Slick, you got to drink to look," Roscoe had told them.

Sandy was a spellbinder, her skin as smooth as new satin. "Fine as wine and twice as mellow" chanted the oldtimers, scratching the backs of their hands.

The problem with these young pretty girls were their slow boyfriends. Jealous as hell they could be. Her boyfriend was big Junior who tossed around fifty-pound crates all day on a loading dock. Junior came in the first night with a friend and seemed very proud of his sweet-hipped girl friend, playing proud when her shimmies created delirium in the room, stiffly proud when a few overdone grinds left nothing to the imaginations of the mill men. When he. took her home that night, however, he must have told her to quit. Sandy hushed him when she showed the money Roscoe wisely advanced her in anticipation of Junior's response. After all, they were scuffling to save enough to get married and buy a small home. Every little bit helped.

"You and your bigtime ideas gonna have you run out of this town," Wilson kidded. "You going to have a mob of women come down here with axes, chopping your place down, and chasing their husbands home."

"Do, and they'll have a real fight on their hands."

He grew serious and talked more to himself than with Wilson. "Y'all wouldn't know what to do without me and the North Star Café here. I mean, you, yourself, would just go to pieces, Wilson."

"I got to admit you got a good place here, the best around. But people make adjustments. I'd just slide over to Chippie's and give him my money. There'll always be a place for good times. Now it might not have class, but it'll be a place all the same. I might even steal your ideas and open up a place myself."

"You would do that, wouldn't you?"

Sudden muted howls went up. Sandy came out in a gold bikini and knee-high white boots, the heels slightly worn, the toes a little scuffed. Someone fed the jukebox a coin and the Isley Brothers leaped out at them, a bass guitar fluttering madly, and Sandy, before even pausing to catch her breath, before even acknowledging the applause, went right to work.

She stepped right into the beat and shook and shimmied. She stepped right into the firebrand lust of the men except for Roscoe, who was fashioning a scene in which the Turrentine boy took the gun to Felton's barbershop. Spencer must have called Felton outside away from his customers, and he must have pleaded that Felton help him. The Turrentines and Tyrees had been close over the years, one family continually indebted to the other. It must have been the Tyrees' turn that day. Then Spencer went home, eventually blurting the story to the father, and Roger, having the boy pack a bag or two and after telling the mother to hush her crying, sped to the airport thirty miles away. New York-bound the boy was, where there would be kinfolks who knew the value of secrets, of blood-thicker-than-water. And he'd stay there until the

143

family wanted him back. His fate no longer his own, his fate managed by shadows, silent, hovering, just above and behind his shoulder. Yes, off went the guilty son, the always-in-trouble son, and left behind without the plane ticket and open-armed waiting kinfolks at the other end was Stone. Stone, the forever unlucky son in the stories of the old ones.

But, as Sandy danced—squatting slightly, hands to her thighs as she did a slow grind—other words tugged at Roscoe. Was it an African proverb he had read somewhere? Or was it something he had overheard on a Columbus, Ohio, bus? Or was it his mother pausing from her fruit canning and drying her hands on the faded plaid apron to make a point? Yes, it must have been Mama on one of those gray November afternoons with the kids underfoot, chili bubbling on one part of the stove, Mason jars boiling on another, the windows steamed up, Mama who said that when you turn your back on someone in trouble, you've killed them in your heart.

Roscoe walked to the end of the bar, closer to Sandy whose body moved ahead, behind, and on top of the beats. She sure had a future in front of her. Behind her, too. Then he saw the note Inez had scribbled and left on the cash register earlier. "Call your wife." He turned the slip of paper face down, then popped his fingers to help the music and fancy-dancing along.

Roscoe dialed long distance and waited. He hoped Lonnie was in his office. A receptionist answered and methodically transferred him to Lonnie's office.

"Lonnie? This is Roscoe. I took a chance, hoping you'd be there this late. What would you say if I told you I had something that might get Stone out of jail?"

"If it were anybody else but you, Roscoe, I might think he was bullshitting. What you got?"

"I think I know where the gun is that killed that white boy."

"Go on." Lonnie's voice was disturbingly calm.

"It's in the river, Lonnie. Somebody threw it in the river."

Roscoe heard him take a deep breath this time, blow out slowly. "Do you know who threw it in the river?"

144

"No, not exactly," he lied. "But I might get somebody to lead you to it."

"The gun won't do us much good. We need a statement from a witness or the person who put it there. Or we need a confession from the boy who did it. They're the only things that'll get Stone out. You realize he's in for conspiracy. They don't have to prove he did any shooting at all. I need you to bring one of those people to me or give me his name so I can go to him."

"You need a confession. Is that it, Lonnie?"

"Confessions, affidavits—anything that somebody will stand behind in a court of law. Rumors won't get it. I need more than that to have the river dragged."

"I don't go in for rumor either . . ."

"No, no, I wasn't talking about you, but the judge and jury, you know, need hard facts they can't blink away."

"So you're saying my sources have to put their faces on and come to court?"

"That's about the size of it."

Roscoe poured the cheap red wine into Dixie cups. Aside from the taste of it, the wine couldn't be good for him a week before his first regular-season game. Actually he hated the sweet sticky stuff, but he knew that Felton Tyree loved the wine like a bear loves honey. The barbershop had just closed, and they sat in the high chairs. Felton had his white smock unbuttoned at the shoulder. The other licensed black barber in town wore silk shirts, heavy gold chains around his neck, and designer jeans. That barber took care of the younger men and stayed in step with the newest styles. Felton stuck to his whites and the small but hard core of customers who had not deserted him.

"Barbering business ain't nothing no more, Roscoe. Folks used to come through and talk, drop off some numbers, or spread the latest jive. And if they sat around long enough, they might consider an edge-up, a moustache trim or even a shoeshine. But now we don't get those big crowds no more. We had to let Big Shorty go so he could try bootblacking someplace else, do a little freelancing. We got all those jitterbug bootleggers running around cutting hair in they basements now. They don't know nothing about no unions or going to school and getting a license." He shook his head and gulped his wine.

"You got to stay enterprising, Felton. I mean in business like yours and mine we have to stay one jump ahead of the competition or we look up and our joints are empty."

"I've thought about stealing one of your ideas, Roscoe. Put a foxy sister up in the window boogeying down. If that don't bring the brothers in to get haircuts, I don't know what will. Just the other day, I heard of a place in Chicago with the manicurists tipping around in tight red shorts, and they charging the bloods up there top dollar, but nobody seems to mind."

"There you go, Felton. Course you don't have to charge an arm and a leg here. Matter of fact, you can't. But you can give them a little imagination, something that no other shop, plus the bootleggers, can copy. They'll be lining up around the corner to get in. Shoot, you do it right and they'll be begging you to stay open."

Their chuckles bounced around the peach-painted room, and burst like bubbles above their heads.

"How are your people, man? Anybody heard from Emmanuel?" Felton was Emmanuel's age. If Emmanuel had stayed, he and Felton would have graduated in the same class.

"He'll be back next summer. We're getting together a family reunion for July, not a big thing, just all my brothers and my sisters. Emmanuel's married now and has a son and we haven't seen either of them yet."

"So he done gon' and tied up, huh? Old Emmanuel, hah, he used to be about the shyest dude around. Remember how chicks used to have to strong-arm the cat so he'd pay them some attention? And that wasn't no easy thing for them to do with your brother, the Baby Bull."

Not knowing why he had lied about Emmanuel's return and having a family, Roscoe sipped the last of the wine, winced, then poured himself another cupful. Never let it be said that he couldn't drink another man's drink. He vowed to slow down, however, because he wanted to be clearheaded when his point was being made. He could see himself in the small front mirror. He touched the thin spot at the top of his head.

"I guess you seen ol' Billy by now," Felton said. "He still call himself Billy Africa. Dude still ain't changed much, man. A beautiful cat like he was when he left here, but still out here trying to change the world."

"I don't know if he's trying to change the world, Felton. Maybe make the space where he's at a little better."

"Yeah, well, if that's how you see it. Me myself, I think the blood has a lot of potential, but if he want to spend his life fighting dope dealers and risking getting his head blown off by some cold-blooded fool who would sell his own mama, well . . . I don't know whether it's worth it."

"Got to start somewhere, Felton."

"For what? You sound like there's some kind of war going on, pardner."

"There damn might be. Wars going on everywhere all the time, big ones, little ones. Some even in our own backyards." Roscoe was holding his cup up to the light trying to recall what some wine expert on television had said about the aging of wine, its body, and character. He could not remember. He gave up and glanced at Felton guzzling the wine as if it were grape juice.

"Shame about Stone, ain't it?" Roscoe said.

"Damn straight, it is. They gon' try to send that boy straight to the slammer. Watch."

They finished their wine at the same time and Roscoe refilled the cups once more, then set back against the chair, head nestled against the headrest. "Yeah, it's like the way the old dudes described the mess down south. Lynch a dude without any proof, just because he's black."

"Un-huh."

"They ain't even found a gun yet. I mean a shotgun. From what I heard it's at the bottom of the river."

"You're right," Felton said calmly. "That's where it is."

Roscoe sat up in his chair. "Think anybody will ever find it?"

"I don't know how anybody would unless they were down there looking for old tires. And anybody taking a swim in that river gon' smell like shit when he come out. Heh-heh. Catfish and carp gave up on that river years ago."

"It's out that you threw the gun there, Felton."

"I did." The barber's tongue licked at the ends of-his long moustache.

"Lonnie ever talk with you about it? I mean, it seems like he would have heard about it, too."

"Lonnie? How come? Ain't no sense of him dragging somebody else into court. All he and his big-shot lawyer friends got to do is prove that Stone didn't do it or that they weren't down there with the intent of killing anybody. So what he got to talk with me about? I wouldn't tell him anything if he would ask me."

"What? You wouldn't tell him anything, Felton?" Roscoe braved another sip, trying to stay calm.

"Hell, no. The only thing they need me for is to tell them who gave me the gun to throw away."

"And you couldn't tell that either?" Felton shook his head. Roscoe felt the tightness of rage shoot from the pit of his stomach, the nape of his neck to the crown of his head. But he didn't want Felton in a corner, up on his hind legs, and ready to lash back. At least, not yet. The more the barber talked, however, the more Roscoe disliked him and remembered that there was a vague dislike that had kept them on merely social terms all these years.

"Even if you could get Stone out, you wouldn't talk?"

"Hey, man, how you sound? They'd have my ass for destroying evidence. With me in jail this shop would go to hell. And jail would drive me nuts, man. Besides none of these dudes here know how to run a shop. They'd be done turned it into a hotdog stand or something." Dry snicker and the grin fading quickly.

"Naw, Roscoe. That would be just trading one nigga—no, two—for one that's in jail now."

"Except that the one in jail now didn't do a damn thing except stand down on the highway and woof."

Felton finished his wine, then stared at Roscoe. "I don't under-

148

stand what you're saying. Hey, it's not my fault about the boy being sent to trial. I really feel sorry for the cat. Years ago my own uncle was sent up three years for something he didn't do. It's those lawyers who can't argue their way out of a paper bag that will stick it to you every time. They're the ones you ought to be trying to tighten up."

"Well, you're in it, Felton. No matter what, you're in it."

"I sleep pretty good at night, Roscoe."

"Look, I didn't come here to argue, man. Just to share a little wine and rap a bit, know what I mean?" He brought his cup up to the light again. "It's just that there's a boy out there who's innocent and got no business being in jail. If he gets out before he's dead, then it still won't do much good because it'll be too late. He'll be dead anyway."

"Sounds like you been going to church lately, man."

"It ain't got nothing to do with church. How come everybody want to bring up church? You know I never been big on church. It's got to do with helping somebody in trouble."

"That's all I did was to help somebody in trouble."

"Damn, Felton, you did more than that. You should have let that boy dump his own gun in the river, at least. Sooner or later he's going to have to stand up and face something. He stands behind a tree and shoots some hillbilly—I don't care anymore about that white boy than you do. The boy shoots him, spraying half his own friends with buckshot. Then he runs off."

"You got something against the Turrentines, ain't you? I remember your families never did get along too good. Something about Turrentine owing your old man a lot of money from a long time ago, right?"

Roscoe whistled drily. "I don't know anything about that one, and it wouldn't make any difference to me. That's some old mess you're bringing up. I'm here talking about you and me and Stone and Roger."

Felton sighed. "Roscoe, you remember how the old folks used to talk about the lynchings down South? How they would grab anybody off the street, then lynch them? You know, just because some hard-up whore with stringy hair said she had been raped or some poor dirt farmer dreamed about a black man humping his daughter? You know those stories, don't you? Well, after they lynched a man, do you think those black folks were going to raise a fuss looking for the right man, then say 'here, white folks, he the one who really did it'? They would lynch him, too, so there'd be two dead instead of one. And they might add one or two just out of spite."

"This is different, Felton. Stone's not dead yet. Look at it plain. There was a shooting and you know who did it and I know who did it. And if we let the wrong boy die for it, it's going to change something between you and me and all of us in this town."

"I don't see it that way, Home. A couple of minutes ago I thought you were jiving. I said to myself, ol' Roscoe over there playing with me. But I see you're serious as a heart attack. I don't know what's in it for you, but there's nothing I can do."

Roscoe balled his cup and tossed it at Felton. It bounced from his chest to the floor. They stared at one another, then the barber's eyes shifted to the razors under the mirror. Roscoe was too big for him to take on barehanded. Roscoe read his thoughts, smiled a weak smile. He could grab him now by the throat before Felton could blink and give him a couple backhands across the mouth. So easily, he could. Buy why? That shooting was working slow poison, killing the roots of all friendship, pushing them from the underground, and turning them ugly up into the air. Was he crazy to care so much about the case, to want to shuffle the faces the victim tossed to the mob? The mob didn't care about size, eye color, religion, or dreams. Just feed it. And in a week he had a comeback to make. He had a wife's calls to return. There was life ahead of him, enough troublesome life, without him trying to rescue everyone else.

"What the hell are we doing here, doing this to each other?" He walked wearily outside.

LINE 3

"A DIVORCE, Charlotte? Damn, you hide my girls at their grand-mother's and bring me over this morning to ask about that?"

She poured coffee for both of them, then lit a cigarette. "Well, Roscoe, you never returned my calls. I had to do something to get you over here. I'm sorry for lying. Mama will bring them back over at noon, but I wanted us to talk a little."

She looked at him, pursed her lips. "This . . . in-between stuff, I . . . I can't live like this. You're not coming back home. I think we both realize that by now."

He watched the thick threads of steam rising from his coffee. Perhaps it all should have been settled four months back when he first left. He was too much of a coward then, and she was too afraid of him to say anything, he supposed. He had talked with her only twice during the summer. The first time was to settle the days he would pick up his daughters every week. The second time was last night when he agreed to take the girls shopping for school clothes. There had been a weak moment or two when he had wanted to ask Charlotte out to dinner or to a movie. After-wards they could walk through familiar night streets, win-dowshop, or go dancing. But he had closed out such thoughts, as one lowers the shade against a painful and glaring light.

"It makes the most sense, Charlotte."

She nodded. After four months do you remember all the little cues—the frown starting downward from the right corner of the mouth, the dimple side, meaning a tentative disappointment? The slow, downward shift of the eyes as a warning of something about to be carefully slipped into the stream of their conversation? She was speaking, and he was wondering about the damage they had done to one another over the years. He quickly concluded that the score was about even.

". . . the children are used to it now. It's not as if it would be some big awful shock." She was looking toward the window. They were sitting at the kitchen table. On the refrigerator were taped

Mayisha's drawings: great snaggle-toothed houses and, standing outside them, their people as large lollipops with arms and legs.

"We'll need a lawyer, but first we get things straight between us. You know, who gets what."

"I know, I know," she said. "I wanted us to first agree on . . . divorce. We can deal with the rest quickly."

"Uh-hunh." He didn't want to talk anymore. Their decision had been calmly made. Inevitable. Yes, yes, yes.

But Charlotte looked up first. "It's a shame about that boy in jail, hunh? I mean especially since most everyone knows he didn't do it. Meanwhile, the bad ones running wild around here, breaking into houses while people are at work. Somebody even tried to break in here a few weeks ago. Mr. Wright up the street just happened to be walking past and saw two of them at the side door. They ran when he hollered. It used to be so different around here. The whole town is changing."

"It's just growing up, that's all," Roscoe said, stretching his legs beneath the table. "This town is big time now. It's studied the ways of Detroit and Chi-town and it wants to catch up."

"Big time, my foot! Folks here just as country as they ever were." When she looked at him again, he thought she was staring at his thinning hair. He touched the top of his head despite himself.

"They say you're helping Lonnie get the defense together for the trial." She would know that, would know about Everjean, would know all. Sharp ears and loose tongues everywhere. "You always wanted a son, didn't you?"

"What the hell are you talking about? I'm happy with the girls, Charlotte. I've grown out of that."

"I know you're happy with the girls and you're a good father to them. The best. But a son is different, would have been different, for you."

"It wouldn't have changed anything between us, if that's what you mean."

Her mouth tightened. "I didn't mean that. I don't know whether anything could ever been changed between us . . ."

"You're right, it's a little too late to blame. A little bit useless, too. It doesn't make any sense. The point is the divorce. That's what we need to get one another out of our systems. What we need to live again, really live again."

"You make it sound so easy, Roscoe. After all these months I don't know whether I've succeeded or not. It's just me and the kids. And this house." She smoked too quickly.

Roscoe got up to turn the radio up. It was the same one that he had bought at one of the many "sales" downtown, where he was robbed by smooth-talking salesmen. Charlotte would fume that he was not ever good at shopping, that he should leave such things to her. But he was only trying to please, he would argue. Only trying to please. He brought the subject back to Stone.

"The jury is all white, you know."

"I know."

Roscoe told her about the encounters with Ruby, Turrentine, and Felton. She watched him with growing amazement.

"You've really thrown yourself into this thing, haven't you? You were always throwing yourself into things. Like that no-singing group of kids you've been working with for the past two years. Then there was the softball team you got together three years ago and none of them showed up for practices, but they all wanted to play the games. Remember? Everybody else had given up and gone indoors, and you were still out there trying to put things together."

"Does that go for the marriage?" he asked.

She tried to smile, then shook her head. "Mr. Moonkiller . . ."

"Don't call me that."

"Well, you were drunk then. What else could I tell the girls and the damn nosey neighbors except that you were drunk and felt like shooting at the sky? I mean, it wasn't even New Year's Eve. That's the only time anybody around here ever . . ."

"I thought the subject this morning was the children," he said.

"It's all come back, hasn't it, that bad feeling? Here we go again blaming, blaming." Charlotte stood and went past him to lean back against the sink, her legs crossed at the ankles. "Hey, Mayisha got all A's on her last report card in June."

"She told me and I'll have to add something special in with the other school clothes. You sure you trust me buying their clothes? Remember when I used to buy you those dresses? You would take them back because you didn't like the style. Too sexy or something like that, and not befitting your schoolteacher's image."

"You always bought those things the teenagers were into—short tight skirts. I wasn't a teenager."

"The point is that you built fine, It's no sin to show off a little of what you got."

She laughed. "A little bit? You had the dresses so tight I thought I was going to bust out of them any second. And you the first one to get mad at some man for looking."

"I wanted them to look a little bit . . ."

"Make sense now. Do you look at your friends' wives? You know, really look at their behinds and stuff you men would like to do when your friends aren't watching?"

He laughed. "You're the finest thing around. I didn't have to bother looking at second-best."

They traded looks and his eyes strayed to the start of the valley between her breasts, the slope of her shoulders. She would snag him this morning and put something on his mind for him to ponder through the cold nights ahead. He saw it so suddenly, so clearly now. She had planned to give him this morning to take back to Everjean. To remember. Nothing would change the divorce or the coldness between them that cut so deeply. But they talked for well over an hour, while he sipped his lukewarm, too-sweet coffee. She was confessing her loneliness by degrees. Would he confess his? He thought of the long Sunday mornings during the earliest years of their marriage. He thought of the last time they had made love, months ago. Her cinnamon smell that March night when the last big snow of the year was falling. The hopeless tangle of the sheets.

When he stood to rinse out his cup, he brushed against her, saw close the plea in her eyes. She slipped her arms around him and was laughing and crying at the same time.

"I was afraid of this," she said. "I really didn't want this to happen and I know it's over between us. But let's erase that last night in May, OK? Please?"

He touched the back of her neck, stroked her across the shoulders and down. Kissed her forehead. Weak in the knees, Mr. America led his wife through the living room to the front bedroom. Outside he heard the roar of delivery trucks pulling up in front of the corner grocery store. From behind the closed blinds he heard the neighbors helloing loudly from their porches and recognized all those voices. That was Alma's laugh, Miss Clora's loud lead-in to gossip. As he watched her step from her gown, he wondered how many things would ever be final about their time, this place.

Afterwards, he could say that at least he got Charlotte to come to his first regular season game. She would never qualify as a football nut. On chilly autumn Sundays when they were together, she would often dress the girls, pack them in the car, and visit friends for the afternoon. Roscoe would then have the house to himself. He'd kick off his shoes, open a can of beer and there'd be just him and the Pittsburgh Steelers with any team suicidal enough to play them during their dynasty. So he was a little surprised that morning when she consented to see the Bombers play their first game. He chalked it up to good loving. A real miracle worker, he had long ago concluded.

In bed, he tried to tell her something about the comeback. "Well, I did it first on a dare. Then the idea come to me that I'm in as good a shape as the youngbloods who would be out there playing. And then I began to wonder why in the hell I should sit around reliving the good ole days in my head, when I could get up off my butt and make the good ole days come alive right now. Here. I mean, I could die. I thought a little about death and how some of the guys I played with in college are dropping like flies from heart attacks and stuff. And I asked myself if I wanted to go out, say, dropping off of a stool while trading lies in the bar. It would be better to go out sweating and grunting on the field or"—he smiled at his wife—"in bed with some fine woman."

Her elbow caught him sharply in the ribs. "You and your weird way of looking at things. At your age out there with those boys. I don't understand you."

"Yeah, everybody says they think I've lost my mind. But sometimes you've got to take things in your hands. Take your life the same way you'd take a lost new-born bird in your hand. You got to hold it just tight enough so that it won't try to fly and kill itself, but not too hard that you crush it. Most of all, you have to feel it there. Then one day soon you let it go, you let it seek its home."

Charlotte was trying to smile. He had opened up to her more than he wanted to. He could see in her attempt to listen that she was opening the door for him to come home, but not too far open for her to risk having her pride stepped on. But he didn't want to return. At least, not yet. Being away had been important and necessary to him, had started him on a course he wanted to ride out first. Maybe they both would be better off alone for a longer while.

"So, look, I'll pick you up around six. I have to get there early and all."

"OK, Roscoe. But can't I meet you there? The game isn't until 8:30."

"No, let's ride together," he said firmly and left. There would be much more to talk about.

But the game, what of the game? There wasn't much riding on it, he lied to himself. Nothing on it except his huge overblown pride. Forty minutes before the game, the team went out to warm up. Applause from the sparse early crowd came like the sound of distant small firecrackers on the wind. He assumed R. T. would be up there somewhere, hating him. Usually the bleachers would not fill, if at all, until the second quarter. The Bombers, led by Roscoe and Bo Witherspoon, jogged around the field, making enough noise for three teams. Roscoe spotted Charlotte in the stands sitting near a group of women. The wives and girl friends of the players always sat together in the center of the bleachers. He hoped that it would be a good night for her. For them.

By the time they had finished their jumping jacks, the other

156

team, the Columbus Crusaders, stormed out of their locker room in a blaze of red-and-gold glory.

"Hey, hey, bring on the turkeys!" Roscoe yelled, bringing his men alive again. They warmed up well, and Roscoe was surprised to enjoy the pregame calesthenics. He had always hated them, saw them as nervous shuffling of the feet. Minutes later his team jogged off the field.

Sweating lightly, swishing warm water around in his mouth, he waited on the sidelines for the coin toss. When one of the officials signaled that they had lost the toss and would be kicking off, he spat out the water and shouted, "OK, fellows, we know what we have to do. Just like practice. Make them cough it up on the kick-off and put a little fear in their hearts. Go!"

Then he led the defensive team onto the field. On the kickoff they charged downfield, Roscoe going three-quarter to keep his body under control. During the practices, he had realized that, though his mental reflexes were as sharp as ever, sometimes his body would not respond as quickly as he wanted it to. So when a stocky guard sprinted toward him and threw himself at his legs Kamikaze style, Roscoe's leap was a little too slow, and the man caught his ankles a foot off the ground. He cut Roscoe down the way a sickle cuts through tall grass. Roscoe popped back up, a little embarrassed, and wound up in the general area of the tackle.

When the other team broke its huddle for the first play, Roscoe sized up the man who played opposite him. The man was big, around 230 pounds, though Roscoe would still have thirty pounds on him. The fellow wore tape everywhere, wrists, fingers, shoes— the effect of watching the pros on Sunday afternoons.

"You sure you want this whipping I'm going to put on you to-night?" Roscoe asked, getting down in a three-point stance, his free hand resting across a knee. He heard the snicker of Tommy, the defensive end lined up next to him.

"You gon' have to bring it to get it," said the opposing tackle.

"Ain't nothing but a word," Roscoe snorted, and after the snap they collided like bulls. The play was to the other side, but Roscoe gave his man another bump before pursuing. He felt good about that initial contact on the line. The contact was solid, the connection had been made. Any butterflies left in his belly died sudden deaths. The game was on.

He would slip in and out of blind spots, out of memories. He concentrated play after play, but it was almost as if he had no idea whom he was playing against. Or who was winning. When it was time to change goals at the end of the quarter he was momentarily confused. But physically he felt fine, the legs were good, his wind was good. All that running during the summer was paying off.

Once again they were lining up. "Young blood, I asked you once before if you wanted all this whipping I'm putting on you. Young boy like you probably worried what he gon' be looking like after the game. You ought to look at yourself now. When I finish with you, your girl friend gon' trade you in."

"Old Man, I'm gonna retire you before the half," said the tackle, getting a true whipping but still game. Roscoe liked him for that reason: he could respect a man who could take a beating and never say die. Maybe he would ease up on him if the Bombers got ahead. At any rate he would have to reach into his bag of tricks and use some old ones by the fourth quarter. He knew that he'd be exhausted by then.

Roscoe managed two sacks of the quarterback before the half, exaggerated his growls as he slammed the quarterback down. On the second one, he stood over the downed player and raised both arms high. The small crowd went wild. Then he pulled the boy up and tapped him playfully on the butt.

"Lucky tackle, Big Man," said the quarterback. "Don't come back."

Roscoe snorted, told him how soon he would be back. At half time Roscoe's team led 6–0 and, trotting to the locker room, he was proud that here in his first football game in almost twenty years he had dished out more punishment than he had received.

In the locker room the older players tried to guard against overconfidence, since a one-touchdown lead was nothing to brag about. No one had known that much about the team they were playing.

"A scrappy bunch," was all that King had passed along. They might be second-half steamrollers.

Roscoe went through the room patting the backs of all the men who had played in the first half, even pausing with the second stringers and telling them to be ready and alert for action at any time. He suggested to his fellow linemen that they be ready for adjustments in their alignments during the second half. Roscoe guessed that the Crusaders might switch to a different offensive set to surprise them. He quizzed and requizzed them. He was satisifed that they were alert enough to make any shift. He had taught them well.

"Way to pop, fellas! But just remember it's a whole new ball-game this half. You got to play as though ain't nothing happen. First half don't mean doodley squat." King strutted back and forth, after they had settled on the benches. Second stringers sat at the far end of the room. The players sucked on oranges that had been sliced in quarters and kept cold in a bucket of ice.

King waved a finger. "They're going to try for some adjustments because we've stopped them pretty good so far. Bet you good money they'll start going to a few traps, screen passes, and draws. Plus any other tricky mess then can resort to. You defensive ends and outside linebackers keep your eyes open."

"On offense we've got to get that sweep going better. That's our bread and butter. Henderson, you've got to get your butt out there in front of the ball carrier. You been pulling like an ole lady 'bout lame in one hip and creeping arthritis in the other. You can do better. I know you can."

King finished with a flourish, telling the players how important the first victory was. Then he turned to Roscoe.

"You got anything to tell them, Ros?"

"Uh-uh, King. I've done my talking." Actually he hated trying to give a pep talk. Every time he had tried, and a speech fell limp at his feet.

"OK now, take a few more minutes to rest up. We're due back out soon."

Roscoe's memory drifted to other half-times when Woody would

159

have the Scarlet and Grey ready to charge out and wrestle dragons barehanded, tackle tornadoes, or throw cross-body blocks on big trailer rigs. There would be insane mutterings by boys who had escaped tiny mining towns along the Ohio River where it carved out West Virginia and Kentucky. If the Buckeyes happened to be behind at half-time, there would be faces in which red eyes burned, in which rockhard jaws showed the flutter of erratic nerves. The second stringers would sit erectly, quietly, as if in church. Assistant coaches standing on tables pleading with their troops to salvage their dignity and not make the world safe for sissies. Here the players slouched, no scholarships to protect, traded a joke or two, and slapped palms. The bush league.

In the third quarter, the Bombers scored the first time they got the ball, Ferguson banging over left tackle for the final six yards. In the end zone he did a dance he had practiced for three days and slammed the ball mercilessly to the turf as he had seen them do on television. The extra point was good.

"OK, defense, let's put the freeze on these chumps," Roscoe said.

After the kickoff, the Crusaders began to move methodically up the field, sweeping wide left and right, using crisp counters and reverses. In the defensive huddles, Roscoe hollered at his men to plug the holes, to stop the tide. But their opponents moved on across midfield into their territory. When they reached the thirty-yard line, Roscoe dug in and snorted.

"This is where y'all stop, youngblood. Ahmo hit you with something so hard you ain't gon' know whether to piss or go blind."

Mighty collision that measured six on the Richter scale. A two-yard gain, nonetheless.

They lined up again. "Junior, I'm the man you always wanted to be. I'm Roscoe Americus, Jr., the man who wrestles time."

Roscoe's forearm blow would have shaken the walls of ancient cities. The younger man groaned and kept moving. No gain on the play.

Nose to nose once more. "Junior, I'll give you my autograph after the game if you can still stand. I'll even let you carry my helmet. But you got to learn to respect your elders."

The younger man over him just chuckled, which upset Roscoe this time. He'd give him something to wipe that smile off his face. At the snap, his man blocked down on the guard. Roscoe was suddenly in the backfield with the play coming his way. He realized too late that he was in a trap. As he whirled to protect himself, he saw the pulling guard already off his feet and flying low. The guard slammed into Roscoe's knees, and the halfback cut sharply into what must have been a gaping hole. While he lay on his back, Roscoe counted a long time before he heard the whistle blow.

"Damn!" He got up catching up a handful of grass, but dropped back on the ground. And suddenly the pain, gathering force as if a ball of fire behind the knee, a ball of fire then exploding up his thigh. He tried to get up again, but fell with a loud groan. As he lay there with Patterson standing over him and asking if he were OK—he knew that it would be his last game for a long time.

King trotted out with Charlie, the trainer. "It's the knee," Roscoe said, "the goddam knee. I need help getting off the field."

With King and Charlie, each man under an arm, he limped off. He looked quickly to the stands to Charlotte and saw her standing, a hurt look on her face. He dropped to the bench and Charlie immediately taped a large pack of ice on the knee.

"Can you move it at all, Ros? I mean, try it real slow."

When Roscoe flexed the knee, the pain tore up again and he fell back, nearly losing his balance. The second stringers looked grim.

"How bad is it, Roscoe?" Charlotte suddenly just behind him.

He shrugged. "I don't know. A doctor will have to look at it. We don't have a team doctor here in the pros."

"Roscoe, it might be bad."

"It can wait. This ice'll keep down the swelling."

He turned away and she knew that it would be futile to argue with him. She took a seat on the first row behind the bench.

King came by. "You want Charlie to run you on out to emergency, Ros?"

"No, it can wait, man. I'm still one of the coaches out here, and the game ain't over yet."

King hesitated, then went back to pace along the sidelines. The

Crusaders were on the five now, and in two more plays, while King was shouting at the referees to distract and intimidate them, they scored. He threw down his hat and kicked it onto the field.

"OK, fellows, let's get it back."

Roscoe's replacement was a tall rangy fellow called the Octopus. He was neither particularly strong nor fast, but he was elusive, keeping his man away from his body and sliding up and down the line toward the play. One thing for sure, since the man didn't like contact, he'd never get trapped.

As Roscoe watched the game settle to a standoff at 13–7, the sweat drying on him, his shoulders drooped slowly. His eyes glazed. He was miles and years beyond the game now, this small event where his unpolished team of has-beens and never-weres—dreamers, all of them—were barely getting by another bunch of players who had far less finesse. He sat on the bench alone, having driven off anyone offering the gifts of sympathy no matter how crudely wrapped and gruffly presented. Alone, he was, on that hard bench, not sure where his career would now lead. That simple powerlessness knotted to a coldness at the base of the spine. He sat as if watching the world through a thick and clear glass, a glass upon which he could hammer his fists, behind which he could scream, and occasionally someone might pause to watch from the other side, amused at such strange gestures. And yet he was the baddest dude on two feet, who could whip cyclones and floods, who once bodyslammed three hundred young crackers from the Ozarks and put hammerlocks on the brains of their managers and the promoters. At forty, here he was, listening to the sweat dry on his face, feeling his face tighten, and knowing how the sweat would leave those white tracks in the wrinkles of his forehead, in the deep grooves at the corners of his mouth.

He sat while his team managed to hold off the other team through the last quarter. He wanted to stay on and celebrate with them, to feel victory with them, especially the linemen he had worked with so hard over the summer. As a player he would be a long, long time being able to share anything with them again.

"Take care of that leg, Roscoe," they all said, coming off the field, faces flushed with victory and the promise of after-the-game celebration with their women and friends. "We need you back, man."

He showered and dressed in great pain, then, after slapping a few more backs, went upstairs. Again he refused any help.

She was standing alone. She was always standing alone as far back as he could remember. She never made that many friends. He had known it was shyness after he had dismissed aloofness. But it was just her style. Of course, most others would whisper that she was stuck-up, being a schoolteacher and all. But they were wrong. That much he knew, that much he was sure of.

"You going to be OK, Roscoe?" It was Mary, Ernie-the-linebacker's wife.

"Uh-huh, just a little twist is all. I should be back for the next one."

Then he limped to the car ahead of Charlotte. "Sorry you had to see this. I was hoping my debut would be perfect."

"Don't worry about that. You were great. I remember what you told me about getting the quarterback and making them run their plays to the other side of the field. Away from you. But you have to get to a doctor now. Look, I'll drive."

He didn't want to argue this one, and he handed her the keys. The knee was swelling despite the ice, and the pain was electric now that his body temperature was back to normal. They rode most of the way in silence. Then the hospital, built on a hill and brightly lit, floated closer and closer to the car like a slow-moving cruise ship.

His wife spoke first. "I think you have a good team. You know I still don't know that much about football, but it seemed like they have a lot of spirit."

"It takes more than spirit to make a good team. Did you enjoy yourself? I mean it wasn't the Sugar Bowl or anything. Just some dumb guys with nothing better to do on a Saturday night."

"Don't be so hard on them and yourself . . ."

"Did you have a chance to talk with the girls? The wives and

163

girlfriends are the most loyal friends we have. I know you heard that crazy Louise."

"Oh, yeah. She kept everybody in the stands laughing about how bad the referees were."

He smiled at her valiant effort to sound excited over the game, the crowd. Him. Then they pulled into the hospital parking lot, just beyond the emergency entrance. On Saturday nights there would usually be a couple of gunshot wounds and maybe one or two knifings, he guessed. How many torn ligaments or twisted knees from washed-up greats?

"It might take a while," he told her, groaning as he tried to climb out of the car.

But she went with him, not knowing how to help him to the door. Inside, when he finally was led away by a nurse, he turned to see her finding a seat and waving. For the next hour he was X-rayed and chided by a doctor who looked much younger than himself. Roscoe said nothing, not even nodding when the doctor said something about how hard it was to do all the things at forty that one could do at twenty.

Later, when he emerged on crutches, his knee heavily wrapped, Charlotte rose, dropping a magazine, and she walked with him in silence to the car.

"Where do we go from here?" she asked.

"I go from here to take you home. Then I'm going home, you understand, pour me a big shot of whiskey, and cuss myself out."

"Cuss yourself out?" his wife asked. She was not amused.

"For being so stupid. I fell for the oldest trick in the book, something every high school player knows. I got carried away, I let my mind overrule my instincts. I mean, I was feeling too good, dealing like a champ and—bam!—here I am on crutches." He flagged a hand at the street, the large silent houses that ringed the hospital. "Never let your instincts down."

"You're going to blame yourself, Roscoe? Maybe it was a warning. Maybe you would have gotten hurt far worse later in the game or the next game or the next. You know how you used to always believe in signs. You used to look for a sign for everything, even to go to the bathroom."

"OK, be funny, huh?"

"I didn't mean it," she said shaking her head. "But try to look at another side."

"To hell with another side. I mean, there I was in the game raising sand and cut down by some dummie who wouldn't have been old enough to carry my cleats when I made all-American."

On they rode to home. Homes.

"What are you going to do?" his wife asked again, looking straight ahead.

"I thought that was settled," Roscoe said, reshaping her meaning. He leaned to adjust the radio dial. A voice advertising hair spray, as if on a wave, coming and going, clicks, static.

"No, we hadn't settled it," she said, her shoulders stiffening. "You're gone. That's the only fact. I mean, that's the only thing that's certain. You're gone and I'm raising the girls."

"Look, you're going to start the poormouthing again about how hard it is with the girls, right? And I'm supposed to feel sorry and come back, huh? To fulfill my duty as a husband and father?"

"I don't want you to feel pity for me. I don't want any man on those terms." She fished in her purse for a cigarette, then stabbed at the lighter near the radio.

"Doesn't work, remember?" Roscoe said. She dropped the cigarette back into the purse. "Well, if you don't want pity, you sure bring up the girls enough. They aren't the problem. It's you and me."

"Roscoe, I didn't want any of this tonight, you know? I came tonight because you invited me. Because the game seemed so important to you and all. You know I don't know anything about the game. I was excited because you were excited. And the other day, well, it seemed that something was possible again for us, that anything was possible."

He rolled down his window farther, he liked the touch of air coming in, its kiss along the side of his face, his neck. He sensed

165

the crutches, strange ugly things lying across the backseat. So fragile, that knee. Superstar gone, season gone, comeback and final glory so quickly gone.

He wanted to be alone, away from the storm brewing in the car. Nothing would be settled, nothing changed. He was not coming back.

He noticed that she was taking the long way. "You and my brother have a good talk when he came through?"

"Yeah. Sounds as if he's doing OK in Chicago. But I heard y'all had a little trouble with that land over there across the river."

"Nothing so big we couldn't take care of it."

"Well, anyway, I hear from your sister, too. She wants me to bring the girls up sometime."

Roscoe frowned. What was this, an army fighting him? She could charm his family all she wanted, but it wouldn't change his mind. They weren't married to her.

"He said all of you supposed to get together next year. A family reunion."

"Yeah, but I don't see how we're going to get all those hardheads together. Nobody knows where Emmanuel is. He may be half nuts by now, out there going in circles."

"Don't be hard on him. He's your brother."

"I know he's my brother. That's why I hate to see him wasting his life."

She started to speak but checked herself for a moment. She ballooned her cheeks, a finger tapping the wheel. Roscoe watched her, then settled back in his seat and tried to relax. Settled back, trying to ignore the pain in his leg that only eased to a dull ache if he kept still, trying to ignore the soreness in the hamstring muscles behind the thighs, soreness across the lower back, across the upper back, and he knew he would have to rub himself down with muscle rub when he got to his apartment, and he knew how much better it would be to lie under a woman's fingers kneading his back muscles, and he smiled in spite of himself and looked again at this woman, this wife he had left because love died the death of a voiceless suffering animal, this woman who was now driving herself home, his home, too, at one time, but she would leave him there in front with the motor running, and she would leave and he would slide under the wheel, and he was suddenly cold and shivering, and he thought to the chill in an early April night when he, Moonkiller, had almost killed her.

LINE 4

THERE WAS A TIME when Roscoe walked proudly past young bright-eyed boys with their fathers. They would pull at their fathers' coat sleeves and point to him. "Daddy, I want to be like him when I grow up." Great and mad dogs would cower and slink past him with averted eyes, their tails limp. Trucks would jackknife at intersections rather than run a red light and risk his forearm. That bad, Roscoe was.

But now he limped around town on crutches, certain that the magic was gone. If little boys still leaped into their fathers' arms and pointed, if German shepherds meowed, if truck drivers plowed their rigs into corner drugstores, he didn't notice. He had too much on his mind: his wife, and Everjean, who had predictably found out about Roscoe and Charlotte seeing one another again. Roscoe thought it strange that Jean would nearly let jealousy crowd out her anxiety over Stone's upcoming trial. He had avoided her after they had exchanged fire-breathing words over the phone. She got in the last words.

"You don't tapdance on my feelings, man. You better hurry up and make up your mind, because you ain't the only man out there, you hear?"

He moped around the bar for several days. Both Wilson and Inez knew enough to give him elbow room.

He cursed at idling pool players, told them to leave if they could do nothing more than watch others play.

"Let the doorknob hit you where some mangy dog should have bit you."

So they left, circling him. No use aggravating an already angry giant. You might get more than your feelings hurt. It was during this hateful spell that Roscoe confronted C. C., the long suspected poet of the rest-room walls.

"Why you keep writing that mess all over my walls?"

The man leaned back and frowned. "What you talking about, Roscoe?"

168

"Stop playing dumb, Passmore. I'm hip to you. You come in here everyday, drink two beers, then when you think I'm not looking you ease back there to the john and write all that goofy shit on the walls."

The man shook his head, no doubt aware of Roscoe's grumpiness. "How come I would write your bathroom walls? You must think I'm in pretty bad shape."

Roscoe hesitated. The man could just as easily have written on the johns at the mill. Roscoe had worked there and he remembered the hot, tedious work. He remembered how the work could knot his insides sometimes. Maybe C. C. did write there. And here, too. Maybe he assaulted every wall available. "All I'm saying is that I think you're the one who's been putting those two- and three-line poems on the wall for Ripple to wash off every week. Every time you come out of there, I find more stuff on the wall."

The man stared, seemingly bewildered. "Roscoe, do you sit here and check up on everybody using the bathroom?"

Stated that way, it did sound a little ridiculous. Roscoe tapped the floor with one of the crutches. "I'm saying that if you are the one doing the writing, cut it out. Or better, show up on Jubilee Wednesdays and go public."

"I don't have to hear this mess." C. C. banged his glass down and rushed out. Another enemy. But not for long. There was no other decent place for these folks to go. They couldn't just sit at home, they'd go batty. No, he wouldn't worry. The man would be back.

The trial was a blur of faces, a smear of nasal voices. The prosecutor was a big blond-haired man who, except for his long sideburns and thick moustache, reminded Roscoe of the army ROTC instructors around Ohio State. He walked around the courtroom as if he owned it, taking long strides ranging from the hip, as if slinging mud from his shoes. He was eager, hungry.

Lonnie looked confident, too, but moved around the room a little more slowly, never looking at the prosecutor or the crowd. Roscoe wanted real tension between them like two boxers about to square off. But he knew enough about their jobs to know that they could very easily have lunch together during the noon recesses. Yet for the first two days of the trial, at least, he wanted to think otherwise. He wanted to think that at any given dramatic moment in the trial the two of them would go to blows.

Late during the first morning, the long, long line of rehearsed stutters began. Called to the stand were white high school students who would get no farther than the steel mill or, at best, a stint in the army before returning home to settle down. Three or four of them came to the stand and talked about the racial confusion at the high school, about the fights after the football and basketball games, no matter whether the team won or lost. Then the bad feelings were carried away from the games to one of the drive-in restaurants at the south end of town where all the kids hung out. These places were the stuff of tradition: for years the students treated their girl friends to hamburgers or pizzas and Cokes, or a carload of boys would kill time over an order of french fries, would pass around bottles of cheap sweet wine, though more lately, tightly rolled joints or a little coke made the rounds. They moved their shoulders to the music leaping from the speakers.

Fights would spring up like brush fires at the edge of the parking lot. No one would know exactly why—an insult to someone's girl friend, perhaps—and no one seemed to care very much. There would be quick hits, a tire iron or two would appear, then a quick fade before the cops showed up. The next week there would be volleys of words between them passing in the school hallways. Late nights there would be shouting between carloads on the main streets of town.

On the stand the boys went on about how the situation grew worse and worse. Simple aggressiveness at that age? Their parents' bile spilling out in fierce relay? Nothing more to be gained than pride. And there was Stone among friends, all with fake ID's, standing outside the bar behind the drive-in and words were exchanged, words as knives tearing through the flesh to the brittle bone of pride.

The "colored boy" on somebody's case: "Say, Ugly Harold, who was that fine chick you were with last night? I didn't know you knew anything about talking to women."

Just a joke as it started out, but Harold, a husky football star, didn't laugh. His friend, just as big and in a hurry, pulled at his arm. "C'mon, Harold, Big Mike will go on duty soon. We ain't got all day."

Harold wanted to finish with the agitator who listened, grinning, until the big boy said something about knocking his teeth out. Perhaps they should have fought then. There would have been a few bumps and bruises, but little else. Instead there would be a showdown, asses would be kicked (as the promise went). Outside the bar they'd meet. A half hour later as the two white boys stood in the door, the few other bar patrons rising in curiosity, the "colored boy" and the others still stood in front, their stances cut in stone. As Harold stepped out of the door, there burst the hollow thunder of a shotgun, and Harold was knocked back inside. Blood spurting from his neck and upper shoulder. Some heard the car, for somehow there were suddenly two cars, maybe more, when before there was only one. The cars tore out of there, tires screaming, and there was just a lot of hollering and yelling going on, and it was just about the awfullest thing you ever wanted to see, sir.

"Did you see who killed Harold?"

"It was like . . . it happened so fast and all. I did see one of them with something. It looked like a long shiny object . . ."

"Is that person you saw in this room?" asked the prosecutor, turning away to scan the room.

"Yessir, he looked like Johnson over there."

"Are you positive it was Johnson?" asked the prosecutor.

"Pretty sure, sir."

"Thank you."

"You're welcome, sir."

And there was that terrible death that no one had figured on. From curse words in gym classes or in the hall, harmless playing really, you never know how that kind of thing turns out, but you don't want it to turn out where anybody gets hurt or killed, and if something like that happens you see yourself in something much

171

much bigger, like waking up in a river's rough rapids and trying to fight upstream to an island you vaguely remember from a dream. You wonder who those strangers were you've been talking to all along.

Roscoe glanced at the jury, all white. Two of them, a man and a woman, he knew. The man was a foreman at the mill and liked to talk football endlessly. Had a son in college and was disappointed that the boy could do no better than second-string split end his sophomore year. His chin tilted up, the man squinted at the witnesses as if trying to see the smallest bead of sweat on their noses. The woman was a clerk in a drugstore where Roscoe bought his cigars. Friendly with all the customers, she was. Eyes somehow flat, thin nervous hands as she handled the sales. Others looked intent, plainly dressed. One executive among the group. No doubt they would make him foreman of the jury. What would Roscoe say to them if he could say something now? Know this boy like I know him, see through his eyes, and you will know that he is not the one.

Another boy was on the stand now. The one who stood with Harold in the doorway, the one who tried to catch him falling.

"Harold was your best friend, wasn't he, Ronnie?"

"Yessir, I've been knowing Harold ever since his family moved to town eight years ago. We played basketball together, did everything together."

"Um-hum. Ronnie, I know how difficult it is for you to recall these tragic circumstances, but can you tell the court about the final half-hour of Harold's life?"

The boy cleared his throat, then swallowed. "Well, Harold, Larry, and me used to go down to Charlie's Big Boy place and sit around talking and joking with our friends. Everybody knows about Charlie's and everybody would come through there. Colored and the white. Everybody used to get along pretty good most of the time. Oh, there started to be a thing where the whites and colored might holler at one another from the cars, but that wasn't nothing serious and only happened every once in a while, you know? Except that it seemed more and more fights were going on . . ."

"Ronnie, my question was about the last thirty minutes or so."

"I'm trying to get to that, sir. Things weren't always that bad. Most blamed it on a few boys who called themselves 'militant,' but no one really knew for sure what was going on. Things just got different. Anyway, Harold and I were down there that day, and this one boy, I never seen the fellow, teases Harold about some girl he had seen him talking to. This didn't sit too well with Harold so he and the fellow exchanged a few words. Well, the next thing I know they're talking about fighting in a half hour and the colored boy warns Harold that he'll be back with some friends in a half hour and that we'd better be ready. He must have figured that there would be a whole army in the bar and that they'd help us out. But there were only two or three in there at that time of day. So me and Harold sat there trying to figure out what to do, and later Larry came in and we told him about it."

The boy shifted, coughed softly. "So they came back before we knew what to do, and they were standing out front and hollering. We could hear them through the screen door and could see that there were four or five of them. The bartender said not to worry about them, that the coloreds' bark is worse than their bite. Well, they kept calling for us to come out, so we figured that we would except we wouldn't get too close.

"I told Harold that I wanted to finish my beer first, so he laughed and said we could go settle whatever there was to settle and come back before my beer could get warm. I hopped up to follow behind him and Larry. But when he pushed open the door I heard the shot that knocked him back. At first he screamed, a kind of softlike scream. Then he fell right in front of me, the blood spreading . . ." The boy trembled after he stopped.

"Just take it easy, son." The prosecutor turned away, running a big freckled hand across the top of his head. In the silence he let the shriek, and the spreading pool of blood in the boy's story burn themselves into the jury's memory. He let silence seal it there.

Others came up with the same stories, and Lonnie, trying to break them down during cross-examination, could get no further than the fact that many high school students went to the bar even

173

though they were under age. He could make the bartender squirm a bit, but little else. And none of them saw the boy who shot their Harold. They would simply proceed to say that, except for a few troublemakers, they got along with the "colored."

"Would you explain to the court exactly what you mean by 'getting along with most of the colored,' Mr. Ratliff?" Lonnie asked.

"Well, it's just like I said. We all got along in the classes and everything. On the teams we all play together, but on the outside, we all went our separate ways. Then when all the fights started, it seemed like nothing we did before mattered. The fight became everything."

"The fight became everything? What could you boys possibly have to say to another to make you fight so much?"

The boy shifted in his seat, snapped his head to throw back a strand of hair from his forehead. Missed. Swept his hand across his forehead. A gesture, simple, that Roscoe had always connected with the farmboys, the ones who threw beer cans at the black students on Friday nights and rooted for them during the games on Saturday afternoon.

"Just words, sir. Just some silly words."

"Words like racial slurs?" Lonnie asked.

An objection was raised and quickly sustained.

"Mr. Ratliff, you may step down."

The prosecution rested its case very early. Lonnie's first witness was Juba Gregory, whose father Roscoe knew well, whose father was probably sweating in the foundry about this time of the afternoon. As he made his way to the stand, there started the scuffling of feet. Coughs. Roscoe glanced around the courtroom. Most of the blacks chose to sit together on one side of the aisle. They had supported Stone well these first two days, and Roscoe knew that it had been at a sacrifice. It was turning cold. An early winter this year. You'd wake up cold, then turn up the heat, and outside the grayness would be lifting, and by the time you warmed the car up and got on the road, the sun would be above the rim of the rolling cornfields. Yes, and stopping twenty minutes later near the court-house you'd blow into the air and be relieved that you could no longer see your breath. You'd have to do something soon about that busted muffler or leaking radiator. And you hoped Stone would win soon because the church had to keep passing the plate to help out with the legal fees. After the morning session, you'd get back to town to try to get some shopping in or maybe get in a nap before your three o'clock shift at the plant.

"Mr. Gregory, could you tell the court where you were between the hours or 4 and 6:30 P.M. on June 23rd?"

"We were just riding around, and since we didn't have anything better to do, we decided to stop by the drive-in and order some french fries or something. We didn't have too much money between us to do anything else with. So at first we just sat in the car talking. So somebody had the idea to get some beer from next door. We knew a lot of the white boys around town with phony ID's so we were going to ask one of them to get it for us. We heard about the bartenders giving the black boys a hassle about ID's when he'd let the white boys get away with it. So that's when Poon-Tang went up to this guy he said he knew . . ."

"Mr. Gregory, were you also a passenger in the car driven by Early Phillips?"

"Yes, sir."

"Would you please tell us what transpired between the hours of 4 and 6:30 P.M. on June 23rd?"

"Well, the guy didn't like too much what Poon-Tang had to say to him. That was plain. We couldn't hear them because we stayed in the car—Stone, Early, and me. We saw the boy's friend try to pull him away, but he shrugged him off and kept pointing at Poon-Tang. Then we saw both of them give the finger at one another . . ."

"The finger, Mr. Gregory?"

"Yeah, you know." And he started to raise his middle finger, and a few snickers bubbled from the crowd.

"I understand, I understand. Go ahead, Mr. Gregory." Lonnie scratched his neck and moved to the side of the stand, probably to let the jury see the boy's face without obstruction.

"So Poon-Tang ran back to the car and told us that he had some

175

business with the boy in about a half hour and that more than likely all of us would be in it, too. We took off to get some more help 'cause we didn't know how many of them would be in that bar. We went to the park and told a couple of guys to meet us at the drive-in. Then Early went home and we waited in the car. He said he was getting his daddy's .22. When he came back, Stone said that he had to go home for a minute, too. I remember we teased him about having to go home to tell his mama we were going to have a fight."

"Was he carrying anything when he came out?"

"No, uh-uh, he came back out eating a apple."

"So then where did you go?"

"We picked up Buster Mays, who was walking toward the park. Then we made two other stops. We were trying to round up as many as possible 'cause, like I say, we didn't know how many would be down there waiting for us. Plus we knew how much they didn't like blacks in there. We talked to younger guys mostly because we knew the older guys wouldn't be too excited about it. Then we took off for the highway.

"When we got there, we circled around the drive-in a couple of times, then pulled up in front of the bar. Early blew the horn to see if anybody would come to the door. We didn't want to walk into no trap. Poon-Tang hollered out the window for that guy Harold to come out, and he stepped out of the car. About that time another car pulled up alongside of us. It was a few guys who came to help out. But I was paying more attention to Poon-Tang and that door. Then I saw the guy standing in the door and start to push the door open. I could see two or three guys standing behind him. Then there was a shot from somewhere behind us, and everything got all mixed up. Harold fell back inside and Poon-Tang ran back to the car. Early had started up the car, and we was pulling at the back door, trying to get it open because it was hard to open from the outside. We finally got it open, and we were telling Poon-Tang to hurry because we didn't know whether somebody from inside might start shooting out. We could hear them hollering and shouting from in there, but nobody else came to the door."

"Mr. Gregory, did you see who shot the Lawson boy?"

"No, sir, I looked back, and from behind a tree I saw what looked like a gun barrel sticking out from behind it. It looked like a shotgun. And I could see part of a cap, too, but not much else."

"Can you describe that cap to the court?"

"A regular apple hat. That's what we used to call them. Everybody wear one now. But most of them are black, brown, or gray. This one was light blue."

"Did you know anybody with a hat like that?"

"Well, I don't remember exactly, but I think there was a couple of boys around with hats different from those the rest of us got. Barry Coleman and Spencer Turrentine."

The man paused, flexed his hands, his eyes still on the Gregory boy. There was the general riot of coughs in the courtroom, there was the restless scraping of feet.

"Were either of these boys in the car? I mean, when you later saw both cars?"

"No, sir."

"So far as you know, they were in the second car that drove up?"

"We were getting out of there fast, and I didn't recognize anybody in the other car."

"What happened next? After you left the scene?"

"We just drove around awhile. Nobody really knew what to do. Early wanted to get home, I remember that. He was on the basketball team, and he didn't want anything to happen and all. I wanted to get home just to get out of the car and think. Nobody thought all that was gon' happen. We thought it would just be another two-minute fight before somebody would yell that the cops were coming and we'd take off. We just wanted to get our licks in first, you know? We didn't want them to think we was scared or anything."

"And the Johnson boy?"

"Stone wasn't saying much. It wasn't until we were back riding

177

around the park that I saw the little gun that he had. It was unloaded and sticking out of his belt. He told me that he just had it for show. And that's when Poon-Tang pulled out his little air gun, and it wasn't loaded, and he told us that he just had his gun there for show, too. And nobody said too much 'cause we was all scared for Poon-Tang and Stone, since they had brought them guns, even unloaded guns, and whether anybody saw them or not it wouldn't look too good. Anyway, Early drove around and dropped off everybody. I was the last one he dropped off."

Roscoe did not remember all the objections, the overrulings, or the sustaineds, though there were many in the morning sessions. He just remembered the nervous witnesses, as he drove home, the boys pinching their palms, drying them along their thighs. The Gregory boy, especially, seemed frightened by it all, questioned sternly by a stranger, stared at coldly by twelve strangers, watched by an older, colder stranger above his left shoulder. A frightened truth was all the boy could tell, was all any of them could tell.

Others came to the stand after him. Those paraded through the afternoon sessions Roscoe would only hear about during the evenings when a few men would stop past the bar. Or from Everjean when she felt like talking. It would be so difficult for any of the boys to remember everything about a quick two or three minutes that shook them, but all of them would agree that neither Stone or anyone else in the first car had a shotgun. They stuck to this story in the face of the prosecutor's withering questions. Lank came down for the final sessions. Everjean, who sat with Delilah, rarely looked toward Lank, though from what Roscoe had heard, Lank had continued to be helpful. He nodded stiffly to Roscoe. With his hat off and showing his head, going bald, he looked less like a gambler and mediocre street fighter, and more like a sober pensioner.

Stone was left for last. Wearing brown, he came in with his lips tight, cheeks slightly ballooned the way he always had them just after Everjean had shouted at him. Mad at the world. He was sworn, in, and he told his story, watching Lonnie for support.

"I was picked up about four in the morning. I heard the knock-

178

ing at the door, then I later heard my mama hollering at somebody, and I got up to see who it was, and these two policemen was standing in the front room. One of them say, 'You Michael Johnson?' When I told him yeah, he told me to come downtown with them because they wanted to ask me a few questions. I asked them what for. I guess I already knew, but I wanted to say something. They wanted to know how much I knew about that boy getting shot. I didn't know whether he had died, but I guessed he must have been hurt pretty bad from the way he fell, holding his face and neck. I told Mama that I would be all right and she kissed me. Then they took me to the car and pushed me in.

"All the way to the jail, the police—there was two in the front seat and two riding in the back with me—all the way they kept saying that they know I killed that boy. But I didn't say nothing to them all the way downtown. As soon as they got me to the jailhouse, they put me in this little room and started asking me all kinds of questions. This room had a chair in the middle and a bright light over my head, and they keep asking me about where is the gun and how come I shot the Lawson boy. Then two of them would go out and two more would come in. One of them saying how famous I am around town now, how everybody know my name this morning. And it goes on and on like that.

"After awhile they took me to this table on the other side of the room and gave me a long yellow tablet and told me to write out my story. So I would start writing, and I'd get kind of nervous and stop to think about why I was in that jailhouse on that morning writing what I was writing. I didn't belong there, nowhere near there. I hadn't done nothing. Every once in a while a different one of those detectives would bust in and holler at me. He'd come in and holler when he seen I hadn't written much, and he'd say how I should make it easy on myself and just tell the truth about how I killed Lawson. Then after the hollering they'd run out of there, and I'd pick me up a pencil and draw the face of the last one to bust in. And it'd be just like the man looking in a mirror 'cause I always was pretty good drawing people's faces. That was what I started mostly doing in there.

179

"Once one of them came in there and told me that they were holding Early and that he had just wrote down something about me doing the shooting. He said that the secret was out now and that everybody in town knew I did the shooting. I knew Early wouldn't tell no lie like that even though I knew he might be a little scary. That big light had me sweating, and I got tired of them running in and out every minute hollering. But I began to wonder if Early really could have said something like that. Maybe they picked everybody up and tried to make them nervous, too, so that they would say that I did it. Then I still hadn't heard anything from Mama. In that little room, cut off from everybody and these strange white men running in and out, I felt like I was the only one in the world with any kind of sense, and these crazy people wanted to see me die or put away for the rest of my life for something I didn't do. So I started to write and I wrote and wrote, and they didn't bust in the room anymore so I knew they were hiding someplace outside where they could see me and I couldn't see them. They just wanted me to write, and I did that, telling them how we were there, yeah, but how none of us could have shot anybody. I didn't know who killed the boy—there was too much confusion and running around and bottles and rocks thrown for us to know. I had that old .22, but it didn't have anything in it. I had it to scare them with if the whole bar turned out on us."

As Stone spoke Roscoe gathered hurt. He didn't know where the hurt in his own life would end, but he knew he would be able to stand up under it. Legacy of the Old Man, that was. But still he looked for ways to understand the marriage, the fluke accidents on the football field, his inability to touch and change so much. After all, scars should be accompanied with more than the memory of the pain. There should be something learned. Once, years back while driving through the endless West and entering the plateau country just west of Salt Lake City, he saw a peeling red pickup truck slam into a large dog. He was enroute to some faceless town, which would offer a cold high school gym and seven hundred screaming fans that night. And he had regretted leaving so soon the beautiful Wasatch range and on sharp curves he would turn to look at the mountains north and east of the city. Coming out of a curve, the truck roared past him, and some fifty yards down, he saw the flash of its brake lights, then the dog. The truck slowed after the collision, then sped on. The dog spun slowly, amazingly slowly, on one leg, the other legs probably broken and the dog spinning slowly, slowly, a slow arabesque turn in that cold dawn. A broken-down dog, overgrown hound, dying with the dazed look before, Roscoe guessed, the rush of overwhelming pain, the certain death. It would lie there at the side of the road and be dead within an hour. Other drivers had done as much as he had, looking at it curiously, sympathetically, glancing up again to catch the sight of the dying animal in their rearview mirrors. Too much in a hurry through that bleak space to stop (and do what?).

And on he drove, breakfast an hour or so ahead, probably in some puddle of civilization between the inevitable hills. Mr. America in Utah. The horizon was bothered by high-power lines and occasional trailer homes. He couldn't crowd that animal out of his mind and somehow took it as a sign of his own life. He was a believer in signs, he had learned the hard way to trust his instincts. A week later, in a motel room in Reno, Nevada, he decided to give up wrestling after the tour. To come home. To think. He had run out of places. He told this to one of the wrestlers staying down the hall in the same motel, and the man laughed. Wrestling was great kicks, the man said. It was indoor work and the pay was decent. What else did he want?

Roscoe wanted more than being one of the roving champions. There were too many of them, a North American heavyweight champion every two hundred square miles. He wanted the world, more than whipping on ex-football players and lumberjacks with names such as the Strangler, the Stomper, and Okanu Hitshu. That slow death dance on the highway had revealed the sluggish moves of his life. When he reached Stockton, California, the end of the tour, he broke his contract and flew back home. He didn't want to end up by the side of the road, dying as others whizzed by, glancing up to their rearview mirrors.

Now, as he sat in the courtroom, watching the jury and the judge, he slowly realized that the boy talking on the stand was going to prison for something he didn't do. Actually, he had reached that conclusion last night while at the bar. Words and strange faces had floated across the ceiling, and he had stopped listening to two men trading lies. Then, the boy's face, the face of the boy not his, the son of the woman he could never love, the woman sought out for a short time as sanctuary against the dead end that was his marriage—that boy was doomed. The jury would not care that he carried a small caliber gun, that no one saw him with a shotgun, that no one found the murder weapon, though the boy who shot the gun had been named during the questioning. All that would be forgotten in the jury's stampede to judgment. Like the large dog in the dawn, Stone had simply been in the wrong place.

He thought of death. Stone's sentence would be a long one, a slow death. Stone would never really know much about himself and the world. He'd never chase girls again and tell lies to his buddies about his failures and successes. He'd never raise a family, were that to be his choice, or run wild again on weekends. Roscoe saw him in prison scheming to get pencils to draw with, oils to paint with. Prison, where a cigarette might be his reward for winning a fight or pointing the finger on someone, where they'd try to break him more than bad luck and coincidences had already done.

He watched the prosecutor again parade the blown-up photographs around the room. They were pictures from the autopsy, ugly holes at the side of the victim's face, darkest at the neck, this pattern of tiny holes, and thinning out down the shoulder and chest. Death was always that shameless terror. At the age of twelve he heard the older folk talking about the death of an uncle in a truck crash. His uncle was pinned inside a truck for hours, his chest crushed, and him watching the ooze of his life. It was Uncle Jack who first taught him blues songs, Uncle Jack, with the freckles, who hummed blues as he zoomed through small-town intersections against the yellow lights, his air horn gone wild as he sometimes broke to laugh at the frightened drivers. Uncle Jack also liked the Nat "King" Cole tunes, especially "Route 66" and "Nature Boy." They said he was humming songs in those death moments as men used torches to cut through the cab of the truck.

Death everlasting. No coming back, there would be, no encore. Except for his father, the never-can-say-goodbye Old Man who'd whipped, outfoxed the spirits to visit this world anytime he wanted to. Maybe he had whipped a spirit or two in a game of tonk in order to keep an eye on his number one son. But Roscoe didn't expect to beat those spirits and figured he would never return. He knew no card tricks.

Then, there finally was the long morning of waiting when he comforted Jean, when he held her for hours, and only once did he recall that only weeks before he held the woman he was still married to. If Jean guessed that, she was too involved now with thoughts of the approaching announcement to mention it. He left her only briefly, to pick up a bottle of brandy. When he returned, she was crying, scratching hard the back of one hand with the long nails of the other.

"Lonnie just called. The jury ready to come back in this afternoon."

"I think it'll be good news, Jean."

Two hours later when the verdict of guilty of conspiracy to commit murder was read to the packed courtroom, Jean's shrieks pierced the aged roof, seared the heavens, where they mingled with the ancient cries of mothers of the innocent. He remembered, too, his mother's screams as she saw the body of her husband. Would Tyrone's sound machine be able to bring all this back? He glanced at Lank, who momentarily lowered his head to his hands, then straightened to watch his son.

Stone sat stunned, shoulders slumped forward. He straightened up and jerked his head to one side. It was as if an awful weight had dropped from the heavens, a weight he may have seen falling since the early days of his life, a weight he vainly tried to outmaneuver, but falling, falling it would nick him, scarring not shattering the skull. It was now gone, past, its damage done.

Not knowing what else to do or where to go but to his furnished rooms a few blocks away, Roscoe sat alone in the bar later that night playing the jukebox. The bar had been officially closed an hour before, though Inez had sat talking with him for twenty minutes or so. He heard the rap on the door and could see Stallworth, one of the town's three black cops.

"Everything all right?" he asked after Roscoe opened the door, the damp night air rushing in around him. "I saw the light on."

"Everything's cool, Stallie. Have a drink?"

"I'd like to, but I can't now. The sergeant would love to catch me in here, know what I mean?"

"They ain't gon' fire you, man. Tell you what, let's sit in the car then."

Stallworth hesitated, and before he could protest, Roscoe had dug out two beers and was hobbling to the door. Stallworth followed him to the car and there they sat listening to the metallic bleeps and blurps from the radio. Roscoe handed him a beer.

"You know, Stallie, I'm thinking about selling the bar. But I have to sell it to somebody who will run it in the manner in which it's been accustomed. I'd hate to hear about it going down. What do you think, huh? You're pretty smart for a cop. Remember the time you warned me about taking over as manager of Toejam? I should have listened to you. My wife still rides me about that. I couldn't sleep at night knowing somebody was messing up at my bar."

"Why don't you just rent somebody to manage it for you? You still take the gravy, but you leave the day-to-day things to someone else, if you don't want to be bothered."

"Yeah, maybe that's what I should do." Roscoe turned the idea over and over in his mind, liking it more and more. "Yeah, but selling it or getting somebody else to manage it, I'd still probably hang around here everyday. Something gets into your blood and it's hard to work out. Like my Daddy never knew what a vacation was. On a holiday he'd wake up as early as ever and spend time just walking through the house humming and waking everybody else up. We hated to see those holidays coming because they'd be no fun with him waking us all up too early."

Stallworth nodded and looked to his rearview mirror. He sipped his beer, then set the can back on the floor between his feet. "I guess you just about married to that bar, eh, Roscoe?"

Roscoe looked straight ahead, and continued as if not hearing. "I might even move to Columbus. A couple of my old buddies want me to come up there and go in with them on a couple of wine store franchises."

"You leave this town, Roscoe, and it would fall apart. It would suffer, man. I'm not saying that it would collapse right away, but they need folk to stay here and make it stand for something."

"Cut the jive, Stallie."

Stallworth raised his right hand. "If I'm lying, I'm flying. This place going to hell in a hurry. That's the same thing I told Billy Africa. You know me and him came out of school together, and I was telling him that sooner or later he'd have to come back here and deal with the dudes he knew who are now pushing dope and all that other stuff. It's one thing dealing with some stranger out there in Colorado. It's another trying to put your own blood on the right track."

Static and a voice exploded on the receiver. "Say, Ros, that's for me. Probably some old lady out on the east side imagining some naked peeping Tom in her back window. Want me to give you a lift home or something?"

"Naw, I can make it OK. Plus, I got a little more to do inside. I never get so drunk I can't drive myself home."

Stallworth finished his beer and turned on the motor. "You take it easy, Big Man. Don't let that liquor talk too long to you now."

Roscoe chuckled and got out. The patrol car moved off slowly, one of its taillights out. Then the car gathered speed, and when it made the sharp turn two blocks down, its tires were squealing loudly. Two shadows, Romeo and Juliet, crossed behind the car and headed for an alley, to be swallowed in the night.

Again, the street was quiet. A wind started up, scattering paper, shaking the stop sign on the corner. Roscoe belched and crossed the street through a storm of the season's last leaves. Inside, the jukebox was still playing. Bobby Bland's "Blind Man." He poured out his beer and made himself a real drink. He never really liked

185

beer. It only filled him up and kept him running to the john. Nobody with much style sat around belching beer all night. But strong liquor took character. That was another problem with the younger kids. They couldn't take liquor the way they could when he was coming up. All they could do now was smoke dope or pop pills, then sit around mumbling about funny things dancing past their eyes. Or they sold it to others and shot anyone who didn't give them what they wanted.

The bar whizzed around his head. Grew smaller, a shrinking tomb. The bar had been nearly empty all night. The few who did come in hardly talked. Strange, its slowness. The thought finally occurred to him that he was getting drunker by the minute. He pulled the plug from the jukebox. The night air might help him. He poured a large drink in a Mason jar, added ice cubes, sealed the jar, and left the bar. He wanted to be riding out and away, driving through this night.

He had started in the direction of Stallworth's car, driving slowly through the silent streets, and eventually prowling through the town's wealthy east side. Several years before he might have been stopped by the police and questioned for driving around out here at that time of night. But now things had changed so much that they had a black cop answering the calls here. Roscoe chuckled again. Progress is a bitch.

He glanced at the columned mansions of the older families who had brought their fortunes here from New Jersey to be doubled in the booming factories like so much magic. Farther out he rode past the long squat houses owned by the town's new money: mill foremen, schoolteacher couples, managers of shopping-center stores, and here and there a "brother" who had managed to scuffle and save over the years, his children too old now to enjoy the move. But Roscoe had a sudden urge to be away from these streets, these houses that pressed in from both sides. He turned toward the expressway and even then knew that he would wind up at the river.

He sped along the highway, now, getting the car close to ninety miles an hour, watching the broken lane marker lines merge into a solid ribbon in the carlights. The Old Man had warned them about traveling on the old two-lane highways years ago. He said that if it were late and you were fighting fog or in a hurry, to straddle the medium line. ("Straddle the white line, boys, and you can never run off a strange road.") He straddled a line, hogging two lanes now for five or six miles, then nearly missing his exit, swerved in front of a rig to make the lane. He was barely aware of the fading blasts from the truck's air horn as he sipped more whiskey and laughed. He owned the night.

He remembered so many nights of depression during the college years in Columbus when he would use the night for walking. On Sunday nights, the nights after the big celebrations of football victories, the nights when the bumps and bruises would be forgotten, he would walk then, not knowing where the sudden blue mood came from. The river near campus, shimmering beneath the distant lights of the highway, washed away the confused fury buried in those low moods. The sight of the river worked as understanding fingers kneading stiffness from the back, the neck.

Two hundred yards away ran the funky stream posing as a river, and somewhere on its bed rested a shotgun. He shook his head. He had promised himself not to think about the trial for several days, but the thoughts were impossible to push aside.

A red light caught him at an intersection. Loaded with two rolls of steel, a truck rumbled through, leaves and paper whirling in its wake. Suddenly Roscoe realized that the bar where the boy was killed was only a hundred yards or so behind him. He glanced at it in his mirrors, and he thought that it looked like the kind of place that must be a bar or somebody's small church. Such a squat gray building would only know those histories. He saw two big trees in front and imagined how the Turrentine boy must have stood behind one and fired on the Lawson boy. A leaf fluttered down. Then the light changed and he rolled on.

The road followed the river's path to the next town, and Roscoe traced it, twisting and turning briefly through his own life. He was beyond anticipating now: some things are inevitable. He had anticipated at twenty. At thirty he had learned what he thought were his limits and tried to be less hard on himself. But now he wondered whether he had been a little too lax, if he had let too many chances slip through his stiff fingers, snake through the fingers as if blood, leaving a dead man fooling others into thinking he was alive. And how could he make the light to find his way? Even at forty he had only the nerve, not the method. And what about those folks who couldn't tell whether he was alive or dead? That stream had the wisdom. It knew. It knew about life and death. It knew something about direction, cutting deeply into the earth, holding secrets and making few enemies. Some of it would reach the Gulf of Mexico after the Mississippi, after the Ohio, dragging its dirt and guns and bodies with it.

In minutes he was in the next town, the county seat. The road began to bend away from the river and sprout old frame houses, then darkened stores. He passed an all-night laundromat with a solitary man staring into the face of a dryer, underwear spinning. Passed a carwash, where a couple hosed down a station wagon and then, laughing and teasing in that strange hour, ducked the spray and their own thrown rags. He turned off and sped through the streets to the courthouse, roaring to a stop in front, his front fender scraping a parking meter. He left the motor running, hobbling on one crutch toward the double doors at the basement level. An old man with his own father's face sat on a step, slowly shaking his head and held up a hand as if to stop him. But he moved past him and pounded on the doors.

"Open this muthafucka up!" He hoped to break the doors down. Two policemen stood inside, the open magazines in their hands flashing nude women. Their uniforms were Confederate-gray. They walked slowly to the door, hands drifting to holsters, to see what the big black man wanted this time of night.

"Stone," Roscoe said. "Let me see the Johnson boy, and while you're at it, let me check out that whore, Justice, too!" He laughed at the way they were looking over his head from inside. They must have expected a mob, a riot of gangbangers.

But their faces relaxed and rather than tell him about visiting hours, they winked at one another. One of the cops must have recognized Roscoe (from a football game? a clipping of wrestling matches, from the wind song?) Everybody knew Roscoe. Two other police joined them, however. They'd try to calm him down, though even now he was stabbing at the glass with the tip of the crutch. Keep him there overnight, they'd try. If he didn't give them any trouble, they'd let him go home in the morning and hope that everyone would forget the whole thing.

REFRAIN

"SON, I NEVER DID tell you about the time I spent the hour in the Cincinnati pokey, did I? Never let it be said that the old man never saw the inside of a jail. It goes back to Jack Johnson, yes sir. Well, Jack had just whipped Jim Jeffries out in Reno, and we got it over the wire back home. Of course, we had planned the victory parade the week before. We knew Jeffries had as much chance of whipping Johnson as one snowball got to drown the fires of hell. So everybody was ready when the news came about the uppercut. And we hit the streets, Shorty blowing on a beat-up trumpet he found in some garbage can, blowing that trumpet for all he worth, just playing the one or two notes he know, Ox beating on a big bass drum, and me justa highstepping. They had a old red, white, and blue ribbon around one of the statues downtown—remember it was the Fourth of July—so I just snatched the ribbon off that cold statue and wrapped it around my waist like so. And there we go just marching for old Jack. We cover about eight blocks out of the alley before the police come running up, a few at first before more showed up. Then a crowd of whites started gathering along the sidewalks, still mad 'cause their man lost to a big, grinning, bald-headed black man. So when I see them, that's when I jump ahead to really strut my stuff. 'Jeffries gone so bring us more/Johnson's got a lot in store.'

"That crazy song popped in my head, and we keep going, though we know it's getting a little dangerous. There enough colored folk downtown to keep it honest for awhile, know what I mean? So I make up more words, and the white folks getting madder and madder. That's when two cops grabbed me and run me in. Said I was disturbing the peace. Hell, Jeffries disturbed the peace when he was dumb enough to step in the ring against Johnson. Kee-kee.

"But I could tell them police wasn't too serious. They kept looking at the white crowd growing into a mob with blood in their eyes and grinning black bald-headed men on their minds. Their man Jeffries had lost in Reno, and many of them didn't *have that much else in the world to fall back on. Some of them had just got off the boat from somewhere and couldn't hardly speak English that good.*

"And that's how I remember July 4th, son. Johnson beating Jeffries. I'm a little partial that way. What else could I remember it for? The Revolution, the Founding Fathers? Shoot, who else fall for that stuff? Dummies off the boat from Europe or off the mule from Kentucky? Not me, I know better. My people been here too long to fall for that okey-doke. You expect me to stand in front of the flag all choked up? Not me! Not Roscoe Americus.

"Believe up to a point, son. Don't be the kind of fool who believe everything because it's been thrown at him day in, day out."

"Remember, Daddy, I wasn't born yesterday."

"I know, son, I know. But sometimes you seem so damned young it bothers me. Like you want to believe everything because it look, smell, sound right under you. It brings me back from the next world in a hurry."

The old man's humming was a cosmic echo.

"Another thing, son, you kind of taking that loss like he was your own son."

"I'm taking it hard because there was a time when people stood up for right and wrong. I'm taking it hard because there's something about the spirit of this town, this place, that's dying."

"Union City ain't never been much to bet on," his father said. "'Course there's a lot worse. I been through places a helluva lot worse. Went through a town once in Pennsylvania where everybody was ugly. Seemed like living there just kind of messed them up so bad inside, it showed on their faces. Ugly as sin, that place was. But it's according to how you look at it, see? When you was young, you saw things different, could only see things so high. Older folks looked out for you, like the time you wandered off from home clear to the other side of town. You were just walking with a stick humming to yourself, jabbing at bushes, hitting at puppies, having a good old time. Well, somebody passed you in a car, saw who you was, picked you up, and brought you home. Older folks always carrying on like they had responsibility for one another's kids. Always did. 'Course that depended on how

191

close the older folks was amongst theyselves. If they ain't close, they ain't gon' do too much for one another. Same way then, same way now. No difference. But here you is running around feeling sorry for yourself and trying to raise somebody else's babies before you raise your own. I got a mind to put you over my knee and wear you out with a good switch."

"Why can't we ever talk about anything without you talking about spanking somebody? We both know that wouldn't happen."

"You kind of testy today, too, I see. You should know by now that I'm only kidding. Big as you is, you'd break my knees."

"Yeah, I guess I should know that."

"You and Baby Sister getting everyone together next summer? That's good. No sense a family like this should be split up all over the world and never come together. Don't make sense."

"It's easier said than done, you know. Baby Sister, Irwin, and I might have to go after the other three and drop a net on them."

The Old Man chuckled, fished for a toothpick. "There's a lot y'all can talk about, a lot y'all can learn from one another. I never talked much, I mean really talked, with my brothers and sisters after we left out of Cincinnati and moved up here. And there were eight of us, scattered now between New York and Omaha, further than that if Rudolph haven't picked up yet and gone on out to California or Hawaii, wherever he is. But we never had a reunion."

"You never talked much about your family except for the oldest ones. I only knew about Aunt Daisy and Uncle Frank because they visited us every year."

"Oh, we were close in our way, though we never wrote much. I used to tell your Uncle Freddie in Kansas City that when his tooth ached I would feel for my jaw clear out here. Yes, we Americuses was close, but we just seem to mind our own individual businesses most of the time."

"You ever thought about Emmanuel out there chasing down that old broken-down man? Giving up his life to hound a man who has probably died by now anyway, knocked down by a bad

192

liver maybe, wheezing out his final days probably, looking over his shoulder knowing Emmanuel steady coming on and that sad old man probably dead out there somewhere in all that space, dead in some ditch along the road somewhere and Emmanuel going past him, not noticing, thinking the corpse is some poor animal just died and the buzzards not even bothering with that it has so much smell. But Manuel missing it, moving on and back in circles. The design of his life is circles within circles growing even smaller. He's got to live, Daddy. You think anybody can turn him around?"

"You can. What you expect me to do, huh? You know how that boy used to always get something in his head so bad his eyes would sort of drift away? Seem like he would be in somebody's church and—boom!—the spirit would hit him square through the head and take his mind away. The boy loved his daddy, Roscoe. He's dedicated his life to find my killer."

"It's not fair for him to trade his life for that of Jake Mays."

"It's not that simple, son. He's dedicating his life to something. There's always something to be said for that."

"Dedication is ok, if it's to something living, something real."

The Old Man ran a thumb under his suspenders and tilted his head. "Ain't I real to you now, son?"

"Yes, yes, you're too real right now. By the way, you never have told me about what you learned on that side of death."

"There's nothing to learn in death. You know, I never was religious, going to church twice a year at Easter and Christmas was about the best I could do. But I could sing those church hymns loud as any other sinner when I would go. Had me a nice voice, everybody said. If I had believed, maybe it would be different. But I didn't, so it ain't."

"So this is all it is? This life here?"

"As far as I can tell. Like I say, I might have been a little limited in my imagination."

Anger was that drumming in Roscoe's ears. "Well, if this is all there is to worry about, this life, then don't you think Manuel ought to have a chance to get in on it?"

"Jr., you keep thinking I can snap my fingers and that boy will drive home tomorrow. I ain't got that power. I visit you out of all the family, because you seem to need me the most."

Roscoe laughed. "What do you mean?"

"What I say? Death was a silent and sudden dark tunnel for me until I heard a voice, saw a pinhead of life and light that suddenly exploded, and there I was standing in your dark living room years ago. You summoned me, I didn't beckon you. There ain't nothing on this side worth writing home about. But there was you there, fumbling your life away, smacking away love that looked you dead in the face, poisoning your insides with too much liquor—I thought I could drink but you take the cake! You wanted me back for some reason that ain't all the time clear to me."

"But Emmanuel . . .?"

"My second oldest would have found a life-long ambition, anyway. He's about the most single-minded of all the kids. If it wasn't Mays, it would have been something else, something just as impossible. Bring him back and he'll stay a month, maybe two, but he'll be off again looking for the perfect place, the fountain of youth, or the forest where twenty-dollar bills grow on trees."

Roscoe shook his head. "Need, huh? Well, maybe I did need to talk with you. I mean, talk. We never talked while you were living. Oh, once in awhile you'd come in and ask how the football was going, but even still, it was hard for us to get you to a game. My daddy nowhere around to witness my meanness. On your birthdays you'd tell us about the family and your place in it and the pride and all, but your own private ideas on a lot of things I never got. You never told me—maybe you told the others—but not me, about yourself. I can understand your working all those days and nights to feed a family, keeping clothes on our backs, food in our bellies. I'm not that big of a fool not to be grateful for that. As a matter of fact, you older black daddies should have gotten medals for the stuff you did."

"Some flat-assed white man going to pin a medal on my chest for raising my family?" the Old Man interrupted.

194

"Well, maybe not. Maybe we should have the honor of doing the pinning, know what I mean?"

"A medal wouldn't have done me much good."

"Something. But what I'm saying is I also needed the talking to. I never got that."

"When you boys came along, I felt I knew each one of y'all would go further in life than I'd ever got. All of y'all were smart as whips. When you got a little older, I didn't think you'd be interested in me telling you everything that I seen or done. I didn't think it would be that interesting or that it would matter a whole helluva lot as long as you knew the story of the family. I thought the story would be enough."

"It helps. But it's not everything."

"You stop whining, now! You were going to grow up anyway. You didn't expect me to quit work, come home and sit you on my knees, and tell you the facts of life, did you? First of all, if I had done that, you wouldn't have had much food to feed your big selves, and second, you wouldn't have listened to me, anyway. You would have been too young to be ready to listen. Living is finding out all those things older folks knew you wouldn't listen to."

"Something might have rubbed off. Where was the love in your life? How did you know it? The fear? The hatred?"

"Son, it wouldn't have made no difference, I tell you. You learn those things. Hate and love? You develop tastes for them like you do beer or scotch. You just have to know what to hate and what to love, what things are worth hating and what things are worth loving."

"I'm still learning."

"I wish you luck, son. What troubled me is that I might have been wrong thinking that just being a good provider was enough, but in all that silence didn't you know I loved you? I mean, even if it looked like I turned the kids over to Earline and was scared to death about trying to raise y'all—especially that Baby Sister, I know I wouldn't be no good raising no girl—didn't you know I loved you? All of you?"

Winter of the Loving Heart

(From Terry Callier)

HE LAY ON A COT in an unlocked cell. The lumps in the cot were like fists in the small of his back, his shoulders, his ass. The hall was dimly lit, and from somewhere drifted the sounds of slurred voices. The smell of vomit was close around him. That headache was old John Henry's spike driven through the center of his forehead. He tried to close his eyes again, but failed, the eyes going up toward the dim lights. He wanted to rise and fly, to touch those colors that exploded behind the eyelids when they did close. He wanted to do something definite like bend the bars on the cell, though the door was ajar. There was a great noise rushing toward his ears like an approaching train, and as it grew louder, he stiffened. The noise roared past, and he was hovering above himself, that strange body near a puddle of vomit on the small cot. He watched the man's eyes and followed him through the dark tunnel of his pain, past the riot of voices along the way, toward the pinhead of light at the end.

Roscoe remembered the large fountain of angels downtown, a monument built in honor of the town's founding industrialist and benefactor. Even in 1964 the aging fountain showed dirty red rust streaks down its sides and through the creases in the angels' wings. He remembered, too, the warm and gray February afternoon in a week of false spring days. He had been back home for only a month. Trying to furnish his small apartment, he was shopping for a sofa. He had been to every store in town, complaining to clerks about their lack of taste. He was able to discover two table lamps, which he carried beneath his arms like two long-stemmed bouquets wrapped in dark green paper.

Rushing past the fountain in the dying afternoon light, Roscoe saw a woman, her pretty legs crossed, a woman with an unbuttoned beige coat lying off her shoulders. She licked slowly at an ice-cream cone while reading a book and occasionally smiled to herself. His love was instant, flashing brightly, hotly, and though he would fight the feeling for two years, he reeled at the force of its first blow. He slowed. Then he circled the fountain, not turning his head to look at her the first time he passed. He did not recognize her, had somehow missed her during that first round of parties upon his return. He walked around again and, not knowing what else to do, stopped in front of her. His mind raced for an opener. Roscoe hoped she would take her time tiring of his shadow, of his huge frame cutting off the dull sunlight. But she lowered the book immediately, eyed him up and down as she still licked slowly at the cone.

"Excuse my corny line," he said, "but haven't I met you before in another life?"

She brought the cone away from her mouth and tilted her head. An opening. He took it.

"You were the Princess of the Nile, the foxy Nefertiti, and I . . .? I was your ever-attentive Prince, awaiting your slightest movement, the slightest catch in your breathing, to leap to your command."

Would she run away, as if from a giant flasher? Would she signal a cop? Would she do neither of these until she caught him on the temple with her large shoulder bag, her fingers walking toward it spiderlike. But he went on, excited. He knew so little of limits then. He pinched lightly his chin, pursed his lips, and with a nod of his head brought glorious ancient history to hover over their heads, there in front of a dirty fountain.

"Yes, yes, I remember," he said. "Our slow ride together on the lazy, lazy river. See, we've been knowing one another for a thousand years."

She chuckled once, twice. "Go away, fool." She had that wide-open stare, the stare Roscoe would always read invitation into.

"Now is that any way to greet an old, old friend?"

The open book rested in her lap and she fingered the pages absently. Roscoe glanced once more to her legs. Then he looked into her face again, sizing up her crooked smile as indecisive. He sat down next to her quickly.

"In this life my name is Roscoe. And yours? Nefertiti, right?"

She shook her head. "Wrong again. And you're right about your crazy line, but I have to admit it's about the funniest one I've heard in awhile in this town."

Roscoe shrugged. "What can I say? I try to be creative."

He liked her throaty laugh, the way she held her ground. A forest flower, she was, soaking up its moment's share of sunlight, unafraid of the surrounding gloom. But where could he go from there? Could he treat her to a drink, an early dinner at one of the fast-food places around town? He didn't have much cash after the lamps. No, no, she had to get home and help her mother with dinner anyway. Besides the smallest bit of liquor made her laughing silly. He was relieved.

"You mean, you've been in town all this time and nobody's told me about you? The grapevine must be slipping."

"Maybe the grapevine doesn't know about me. I've been here two years, and I really don't know that many people."

"Yeah, well, I've been away too long if I can't find out about everything in two weeks. But can I give you a ride anywhere, at least?"

She dropped the book into her handbag, brought the coat up and around her shoulders, then stood. The top of her head barely as high as his chest.

"I'm parked around the corner. You can walk with me to the car, if that's not too tacky for an African prince who's been through some changes. And my name is Charlotte."

She chewed the stub of the cone loudly, her little finger flicking away its crumbs at the corners of her mouth. He had a sudden impulse to take her hand, but he cooled it. Instead, he fell in step beside her.

On the way to her car, he kept her laughing. The original funnyman, he was. He managed to slip in questions about her life, about her family's move from St. Louis. She had taught elementary school there and had come to Ohio with her parents. Two older brothers already away. Charlotte's mother, who was born in Union City, was sickly and had stopped working the previous year. A crane operator at the mill, her father was also head deacon at Tried Stone Baptist.

201

"I suppose you have to be in church every Sunday?" Roscoe asked.

"Well, not every Sunday. I usually spend most of the day preparing lessons for the next week. Daddy understands, I think."

His voice was suddenly that of the neighborhood gossip. "The deacon's daughter missing church? Umm-um, what's this world coming to?"

He gave little information about his own background, so interested was he in her past. He mentioned only that he lived for awhile in Toronto and had just finished a western tour.

"Tour?" she asked, stopping at her car.

"Business promotion, you might call it." He winked, feeling confident. He would reel off his heavy credentials in a more intimate setting. Occasionally he waved to passing acquaintances. Small-town streets were for setting the stage only.

Earlier he had asked whether or not she had a "steady." She hadn't answered.

"How about a movie tomorrow night?" he asked.

"It's a busy time right now. Parent conferences, meetings, and so forth. But soon, OK?"

Again, he wanted to go for her hand, any touch, her shoulder. "Some friends are having a party for me Saturday. Maybe you can tear yourself away from your work to drop by for a few minutes." He gave her the address.

"We'll see," she said, getting into her car and starting up the motor. He turned away quickly. He didn't want her to see him standing there open-mouthed. So away he moved, giving her one last wave over his shoulder as he entered the trickle of shoppers through the last warm wash of light.

On the night of the party he was king. During his brief time home he had concluded that his friends, old strangers all, were his only real fans and his only real enemies. As the fog of time cleared and he was standing in Percy Bailey's steaming and paneled basement, talking with someone he whipped in a fight at the age of twelve, or some woman whose butt he slyly pinched on a crowded junior high school stairway, Roscoe was cozy in his time, his place.

While classmates crowded around to ask about his football and wrestling ventures, Roscoe camped in a corner, leaning, gesturing grandly for them all. The men were pudgier with the inevitable potbellies. Their swollen faces showed the slow cruel work of too much scotch or gin. They looked five years behond their actual ages. The women's bodies were heavier too, the result of two or three children or simple, dull routine. Those married friends like Freddie and Ben looked at him enviously, he only five pounds over his college playing weight. No doubt they would ease up to him later and ask what life on the road was really like and how many women he really laid in those strange-sounding towns in, say, Nevada. He was the charming prodigal that evening, making their lives seem eventful and worthy of extended jokes and slapping palms.

He pulled Freddy to the side. "Freddy, the thing I can't understand is that I've been home a month and nobody's pulled my collar to Charlotte Birdsong."

"We didn't want to hit you with everything heavy at once," Freddy said, grinning. "We wanted you to have some time to get settled and get yourself together first."

"I stay together. Who's talking to her, man?"

"Everybody's tried, but nobody's getting anywhere. I would try myself but, you know, I'm married and loyal." Freddy's wink meant that he had tried and failed, too. Roscoe and Freddy went back quite a ways. Double dates and running through routines on steering girls to some secluded spot. Strange rehearsals, those were.

Freddy glanced over his shoulder in the direction of his wife. "There's nothing saditty about her as far as I can tell, though some think she's stuck on herself because she's halfway cute, been to college and a schoolteacher. She keeps to herself as anybody with any sense in this town does. Plus keeps herself neat and got her own car. And, like I say, she ain't giving up nothing." This last with a frown. He reached for the arm of a woman passing.

"Here, let me introduce you to Rita."

Rita was pretty, though a shade overweight, and lacked a sense of humor. Roscoe's best jokes dropped to the floor like wet rags, and puddled there. Like Charlotte, she had come to town while Roscoe had been away. He was getting drunk enough that night to conclude that pretty women were settling in town to wait for his return. To keep him there to get fat and soft like his friends, who took out their vengeance on high school girls.

He danced with Rita, waving his arms, rolling his shoulders, and popping his fingers, not sure of the latest steps. Not caring, really. His movements were guaranteed to fit in with any vague and current notion of hip. Rita, as flashes of dimples, as the distant woman, listened noncommitally to his suggestion of a movie on the weekend and said that she would "think about it." He danced with her once again and disappeared, surfacing again among a group of men in another corner of the basement. A loud-talking, back-slapping bunch, they topped one lie with a larger, more hilarious one. Memory worked as the elastic of their tales. In the center of the room a few wives clustered, and, along the walls, the singles looked bored. The familiar geography of such parties by their second hour.

Butch talked the loudest, crazy Butch with the short teeth. "Now that our home-boy has stopped womanizing for a minute to join us, I have to tell y'all this one about our guest of honor." A few men sipped from their paper cups and leaned closer.

"It had me cracking up for days. See, before every football season, the team had to get their physicals. This was at junior high school what I'm talking about now. A doctor would check us out, maybe give shots to those who needed them. So they had us lined up in the gym to see the doctor in this teeny little office, you understand. Roscoe here was one of the rookies that year, just in from the seventh grade, I think. So I'm standing right behind him, and he asked me what the old doctor is checking and I tell him. He check your heart plus he check you for hernia. When we get up to the little office, they leaving the door open to save time. Ole Doc whizzing them through there, checking their hearts, and jabbing a finger up their balls, and giving 'em shots like they on an assembly line or something. So then it's Roscoe's turn. He check his heart and tell him to take a couple deep breaths. Ole Doc say 'Hmmm, that's OK.' He give him a shot and Roscoe don't even flinch, y'all. The Ole Doc say 'drop your drawers, sonny.' Well, Roscoe turn around and look at me. Then he unzip his pants real slow and turn around to the Doc. 'The drawers,' Ole Doc say again because by this time Roscoe holding up the action. And he frowning too, Roscoe is. So he drop his shorts and step closer to Doc. Then Doc reach for Roscoe's balls. What he do that for? Roscoe here shoot both hands down there and covered up like a virgin who just been pinched. By this time, Lou—y'all remember short Lou, don't you? Dude used to make us do all them pushups on our fingertips? Well, Lou he about ready to fall out laughing. Roscoe heard me snicker, so he try to loosen up a taste. Lou say, 'Come on, Americus, we ain't got all day. The doctor ain't gon' hurt you. He just checking to make sure you don't have no rupture.' But when the doctor pushed his finger up there on the side and told him to cough, ole Roscoe just turned his head, shut his eyes, gritted his teeth, and grunted. Did the same thing when Doc stuck his finger on the other side, too. Boy, I laughed so hard I thought I'd never catch another breath. We called him Tough Nuts for the next couple weeks."

Roscoe shared in their laughter, shared in the old memory hauled out like a musty, bad-fitting suit cut in some ancient style. They'd all get around to airing such pieces before the party ended.

He interrupted the laughter, grinning. "Course now, Butch ain't gon' tell y'all about the time he was caught stomping around the field with his badfoot self." Butch chuckled and threw back his head.

"I don't think I remember that one," put in Horace, perpetual agitator, still wearing his hair the way they all did as seniors in high school. He still had the flair for red ban-lons with gray sport coats. "Tell us something new tonight, Ros."

"Hoss, I think you will remember the little incident in high school that made us give Butch here the name of Cave Man. You were on the team, too, man. Anyway, for the rest of y'all, Gator had us out on the field in the rain for two hours one day, had us getting ready for the Dunbar game. Se we had our shoes outside of our lockers so they could dry. Nobody liked practicing in the rain because it left the shoes bent-up and the jerseys funky and feeling like cardboard. The next day we came in, suited up, and went out to practice. It was still a little muddy from the day before, so everybody grumbling about that, catching mud in the eye and so forth, especially us linemen because we the ones who have to get down in the mud and roll around like pigs. I noticed Butch was not running like his usual self. The scrub team was catching him from behind on end runs. It looked like his legs or feet was hurting him because everytime he run he would frown and go 'oomph-oomph.' And Butch could make some faces, y'all, ooe-wee! That dude could make some faces. Look like Dracula chewing on a nail. Anyway, we're in the huddle and Gator comes and says, 'Williams, you're running around like a little old lady today. What's wrong?"

"What he say then, Roscoe?" Horace asked, a smile playing at one corner of his mouth.

"Butch unsnapped his helmet strap and frowned up like he going to cry. 'Coach Gator, my feets hurt.' Well, when we heard that we got scared then, because the game was only two days away, and Butch was our bread and butter. The quarterback would run him over me, and that'd be a guaranteed ten yards everytime, if you see what I'm saying. So Gator took off his cap and scratched his bald head. 'Williams, did somebody step on your feet? It's not that ankle again, is it?' Then he dropped down on one knee like he inspecting a thoroughbred's legs. But all of a sudden he fall back laughing, leaning on the other coaches and still laughing.

"'Butch Williams, no wonder your feet hurt. Your shoes are on the wrong feet.' Man, I'm telling you that huddle was no more good, everybody laughing and looking over at Butch's shoes and him standing there like he done peed on himself, and we just laughed all over again. The next day everybody started calling him Oomph-Oomph. Even in the games, we might be in a bind, and some joker would trot back to the huddle and say, 'Give the ball to Oomph-Oomph,' and everybody would crack up, and Lamb, our quarterback, would have to call time-out. Next thing you know these inventive bloods calling him Cave Man and making up a dance called the Cave Man Stomp." They all laughed at that one, all remembering and stroking that bad-fitting suit hanging in their memories as if they might have have worn it once. Roscoe was warmed up and not to be stopped.

"Splivs used to be something else with nicknames. Remember Skinny Roger before his family moved up to Cleveland? When I got to be a senior on the team, we started making the sophomores shave their heads during the first week of summer practices. Somebody noticed that Roger's head under all that hair was real little like a peanut and when he turned to the side it looked like he got a little hook there on the back of his head. That's when Skeeter spoke up and started calling him Captain Hook. Then Horace here come along and say 'Naw, that head shaped like a question mark so they called him Question Mark for two weeks. And if that wasn't bad enough, somebody else came along—who was it, Geronimo or Chester?—and took the cake. Started calling poor Roger *What*."

The men howled and slapped their bellies, refilled their paper cups with scotch or gin and laughed some more. Then, mysteriously, as if on some signal of subterranean vibrations, the group broke apart, and the men danced one or two dances with their wives and girl friends, who had started fidgeting in the center of the room. In another half hour or so the men would drift to the bar and start another rhythm of shucking and jiving.

Roscoe had been too busy to notice Charlotte's entrance. After he had refilled his glass and promised himself that he had poured his last drink, that he would walk a straight line out of that basement and not stumble or crawl as some silly, younger dude might do, he saw her smiling at him over her shoulder as she talked with another woman. He interrupted their conversation with no style whatsoever.

"I see you made it after all. How about this next dance?" He reached for her hand.

She said nothing, but allowed him to lead. It was a fast number,

207

and Roscoe again dealt with the few steps he knew. After the music ended, she teased him as he dabbed his wet forehead. "I see you take your dancing seriously."

"How do you mean?"

"I just checked the way you were concentrating. You ever consider auditioning for American Bandstand?"

He laughed uneasily. He didn't like being laughed at. "I don't take my dancing half as seriously as I take my women."

"That must be very, very seriously."

Roscoe nodded and reached for her hand again as a slow tune started. Out of the corner of his eye, he could see the men beginning to cluster again in the corner. They'd just have to do without him for awhile.

"No sense starting anything unless you do it all the way. That's the way I live."

"I see," she said, a smile struggling.

He tried to pull her close while they danced, but she resisted. He decided not to force things, knowing his history of fumbling approaches and scaring away perfect angels. Nevertheless, his fingers played lightly on her back as they talked. But, he thought, would she be the type to play hard to get? She wasn't playing the Virgin Mary role now. How far would it go anyway? And he hadn't planned to come home and get saddled with a long term arrangement so soon. Scout around a little, have a run at the field first, and then take time settling on one or two. He didn't mean to love her.

Years later he could still see himself dancing that night, glancing at Charlotte's smiling face. He would notice a sudden bored look and take that as a challenge, her style. He wondered what would be different if he had left her then to share more aimless jokes with his friends. Instead, he made a date with her for the movies.

"Why is that woman looking so hard this way?" she asked him as they danced. Rita, it was, unsmiling Rita, and Roscoe remembered that she might be thinking over his earlier invitation. He'd have to break the bad news to her gently. But it was also his sudden cue to circulate, to not kill off his chances with the others.

208

And, yes, those first months were the core of dreams. Women were generous with their attention. Old girl friends from high school, divorced with a child or two, whispered over the phone that despite their marriage and/or another man, he had always haunted them. He smiled and, wanting to hear more, told them to stop kidding. He saw Charlotte a few times during those months, but their times together were inconsistent—at one moment, laughing and relaxed, at another, tense and silent. He attempted to convince himself that his interest in her would shift with the next wind.

In addition to working as an assistant high school coach, he started teaching gym at the high school during that first autumn. He figured that the head job would be his in five years. He enjoyed working with the younger players, though he didn't like the methodical play calling by the head coach and his top assistant, a shouter by the name of Gonzaga ("Call me Gonzie"). Despite the predictability of the offensive plays, they had a winning season during Roscoe's first year. During those Friday night games he would look up into the crowd of five thousand, watch them suddenly explode to eighty thousand roaring fans in the great horseshoe stadium in Columbus, waves on waves of roars rushing from the top rim into swirling around and frightening enemy players into dozens of mistakes. It was enough to drive the thumbs to the ears. Still ringing his ears would be during the week when he taught indifferent students the subtleties of volleyball. It would take awhile to get used to the smaller crowd and to the work that was only one step, sometimes one giant step, away from playing. He couldn't cold-turkey that dream.

Another problem was the alumni. They were the most loyal team supporters, these red-nosed businessmen who played for the team some ten years or so before. They'd glad-hand the coaches, give them discounts on hamburgers, hardware, or socks. One bought the staff a set of navy blue blazers, so they wouldn't look too much like plain-clothes cops as they fidgeted on the sidelines. These men were pests. They weren't like the brothers who drank wine and hung around the fence during the practice sessions. They knew something of limits. The businessmen would elbow their way into the confusion of the steamy locker room at half-time, cornering an assistant coach or quarterback and whiskey-breathe revelations of magic plays that would get the team out of some jam. Then they would be diplomatically hustled out by one of the firmer coaches.

After his second season as a coach, after too many times of having his player selections overruled and anonymous fans stopping him on the street to tell him whose son deserved more playing time, Roscoe got out. His friends told him to be patient, that the head coaching job was his if he played his cards right. But he resigned in an evil mood and to everyone's surprise took a job at the steel mill and helped coach the little league football team on the weekends.

The mill job was something to tide him over while he got his thoughts together. When he decided to move back home, he had given little thought to what he might do, to what work he would throw himself into. The only clear decision was to rent out the old house and share the small profits equally with his sister and brothers. He could coast maybe another year on his wrestling savings, but sitting around all day had never been his idea of paradise. At the same time, he never liked taking too many orders. At the mill the foreman, one of his former fans, gave Roscoe steady work, and Roscoe did it without the man coming around five times a day to check on him. When the foreman did come around, they talked football and how hard it was becoming to get good tickets for the Ohio State games. Although such conversations became monotonous to Roscoe, he preferred it to the chatter of unimaginative men who liked to pound on the helmets of teenagers. His father had said two things about such situations: "Why work for someone dumber than you? You can't learn anything that way." And, equally forceful, though not yet an urgent problem, "You just can't work for ugly folks."

The steel mill wouldn't be new to him. He'd worked there most summers while he was in college. It was the only work around that paid well when he was growing up. After that, there was only shining shoes, unloading boxes for department stores, or mopping and polishing office floors at nights. Maybe he'd try his hand with a bar and maybe even pick up where the Old Man left off, except his place wouldn't be one for random hell-raising. It would be a place where all could come and have a nice time without the nervous looks and the expectation of a fight breaking out on a Saturday night. Maybe in a year or two he could tie that idea down.

With his decision to leave coaching and the high school, Roscoe felt that a drastic overhaul in his life and ways was necessary. A single decision can act on life's plans as a wrongly placed piece of wood can help bring down a flimsy yet intricately designed house. For example, he decided to see less and less of Everjean. He had convinced himself that they would never grow in any direction, and five years from now they'd be complaining about the same things to one another and having roof-raising sex twice a week while he was still chasing other women.

"I suppose you don't have any more time for me?" she said one day over the phone. "I suppose you going back to your little schoolteacher. Well, I'll tell you one thing when you get tired of her, too, don't you come darkening my front door. You hear that, Mr. Roscoe Americus, Jr.?" He hung up the phone gently. That from the woman whose bed and cooking he sought regularly during the first three years after he got back, from the same woman who accepted his gifts with soft shrieks, who leaned on his shoulder crying when she was down. No gratitude at all.

He had set his sights on Charlotte. Although she could be so frustratingly proper at one moment and so impulsive the next, he wanted to be with her longer than with any other woman he had ever known. All the women he had met over the years and the one or two he still wrote or called occasionally would be forgotten. Why go on fooling oneself about time and distance? He was home and, no longer the wrestling champion, Saturday afternoon idol of small towns and National Guard armories. He was lonely and restless without her.

One evening Charlotte called, the summer's breeze in her voice. "I hope you don't think it's too forward of me to call on you this way, Roscoe." She giggled. "I usually wait for my men to call me . . ."

211

"I know, I know," he said. "Except this time you just can't help it, right?"

"I swear, Mr. Roscoe, you read me like a book." He could imagine her eyes wide in mock surprise. He was skeptical of that remark, however. "But, look, I'm calling about tomorrow. How about going horseback riding instead of the Sidney Poitier movie? It's going to be nice tomorrow, and wouldn't it be fun to try something like that? I haven't done it in years."

"I don't know a damn thing about horses. I haven't been on one in years, and that one was just a pony when one of those jive-time carnivals with one clown used to pass through town."

"There's no mystery to it, Roscoe. You'll enjoy it."

Anything could happen. He saw himself on a runaway horse, the horse rearing suddenly, its hooves slicing the air high above their heads. He saw himself falling without flair to the forest floor. A futile Lone Ranger.

"Aren't you the man who's been telling me for two years that you'd try just about anything once?"

"That's definitely what I'm about, but I also said that I wouldn't try anything that would kill me."

"I bet you'll have that horse eating out of your hand in no time. You're a real charmer, you know." Could he refuse that?

The brightness of the next day stunned the eyes. The fields of young corn were shimmering as they drove ten miles or so outside of town to the riding stables. Then he turned the car onto a winding gravel road that brought them to a paved parking lot. Near a barn not far away, moving slowly through the slight shade, were peacocks.

Roscoe had only seen pictures of the birds, and he remembered the greenish-blue "eyes" in the feathers. Once a year, a grade-school teacher would pass them out in her art classes, in the same automatic ways that the school principal would pass out twigs of exotic trees on Arbor Day. No one knew what to do with the feathers at home (put them in a vase? tickle a sister's neck?) in the same way no one knew where to plant a tree the species of

212

which no one was sure about. So many of the young trees wound up as switches against a child's leg. Each year the students would look up the word *peacock* and remind themselves of something they had never seen before.

When two of the peacocks screamed, Roscoe shivered. There were several in the barn's loft, and he thought that even stranger. The birds looked too proud to bother flying.

"Beautiful, aren't they?" his Charlotte said as they headed toward a stable.

"I haven't decided yet."

On the bar in large gold letters was the insignia CIRCLE GOLD. The barn was clean, almost antiseptic. A motel for horses, it seemed. Rock music came off loudspeakers, and cowgirls in tight jeans moved their shoulders to the music as they groomed the horses.

Charlotte calmed him all the while. "See? They're just big pretty animals."

"So are lions."

Then she led him to a high-ceilinged barn where a few people walked their horses slowly in a circle. A smiling woman greeted them, and they made arrangements for their guided ride on the trail. Roscoe asked for the tamest, tiredest horse available.

"That's Candy," the woman said.

Roscoe shrugged. "OK, Candy it will be then." Candy was a brown-and-white pinto with bloodshot eyes and a back going to sway.

"Make friends with the horse," Charlotte said, stroking the long jaw of her own horse. "Let her get used to you."

He was a little surprised that the horse's mane which looked so stiff and wiry could be so soft. He stroked its jaw, too, though pausing when the horse bared its huge yellow teeth as if grinning at him. "Good horse," he whispered. "Good horse."

There were a half-dozen other riders, and, one by one, they mounted. Roscoe watched them closely and concluded that it was just a matter of bouncing high off one foot and swinging the other

213

leg over. Just like they do in the westerns. Then he watched Charlotte, who sprang up easily and turned to smile encouragingly at him.

When he could stall no longer and the other riders began to glance his way impatiently, he slid his left foot into one stirrup. He swung the right leg high, though it wasn't quite high enough and he managed to kick the back of the saddle. He caught himself without falling.

"You almost had it," Charlotte said. "Bounce higher this time."

There might have been far less aggravation if he had stayed inside and rode this broken-down horse around the ring slowly. He tried again and missed.

"Need any help?" asked their guide, craning her neck from up in front.

"No, I got it." Damn high-butt horse. He bounced mightily the third time, he remembered, swung up, and landed squarely in the saddle like a giant Chisholm Kid from the pages of an old Pittsburgh *Courier*. Candy tossed her head in approval, he guessed, and Roscoe noticed that the guide gave the signal to move ahead. With no help from Roscoe, the horse moved slowly foward, methodically, as if for the thousandth time.

Roscoe rode in the middle of the pack, slowly getting accustomed to the movement of the horse under him. Like his first time in a boat, when he sweated and prayed to have his feet on the solid ground once more, it would take long, agonizing minutes before he would be comfortable. But how did he get talked into this one in the first place? Aside from Charl's flattery, was it his guilt over forcing her to sit through so many pro football games and boxing matches? Is this her payback and his acknowledgment of it: don't force anyone into anything? She had poured that sweet rap into the phone, that soul-sweet tidal wave of nostalgia about summers on an uncle's farm in Tennessee.

"I'm no expert with the horses, Roscoe," she had said during the drive out. "I got this scar on my chin when I fell off a pony and my chin caught a rock. I nearly broke an arm another time. So understand that. But I can tell the head from the butt. When I

214

was little and visiting Uncle Jessie and Aunt Kate, I used to ride out with one of my cousins early in the morning, and the horses would just be walking easy as you please through the wet grass. We'd hit the woods and there'd be places in the valley where the fog hadn't lifted yet, and it would be as if you were riding through clouds at the top of the world."

Roscoe had snorted at this. It sounded beautiful, a world where he would want to enter, but how connected to his fear? He might have his spinal cord snapped helping her chase after some god-damned dream. There was no mist now, no wet greenness of a Tennessee morning, but just that shimmer of a spring afternoon. He tried to imagine such a morning as Charlotte had described. He could. Mostly the silence interested him and the power of directing the huge beast under him. He tried to imagine himself young, too. Early morning in a field, hunting with his father and Emmanuel, and the Old Man telling them to cut out all the loud talking if they wanted to go home with a rabbit, quail, or pheasant. There was the silence to fall into, no echo coming, while the land slowly burst with day.

They were barely out of sight of the barn when Candy stopped to nibble at the leaves of young trees growing along the trail.

"Give her a kick," the rider behind him said.

Roscoe kicked hard.

"Harder!" yelled the rider.

The horse nibbled up the arm of a tree and Roscoe, leaning forward, gasped at the sudden space below them. They were on a cliff and the horse, enjoying the leaves, stepped close, step by step, toward the brink. Roscoe swallowed hard, pressure building against the inside of his forehead. His gut knotted. How dumb were horses? Had they fallen off of cliffs in search of leaves?

"Kick her," Charlotte said, calmly.

But Roscoe looked instead from the lip of the land into the tree-tops far below. He grabbed one of the skinny branches and slid his feet far back in the stirrups. If the horse were stupid enough to fall, he wasn't going with her.

"Kick!" someone shouted.

215

And he did, harder this time, hoping he hadn't broken the sad horse's ribs, probably brittle as hell at her obvious age. Again he kicked for his own survival, to walk away from this ride and see another morning, and the horse nibbled at another leaf, then turned quickly as if suddenly remembering her chore, and, tossing her head, found her place in line again.

Roscoe breathed easier. The tightness in his stomach eased.

"Good horse," he assured. "Good horse."

Charlotte turned around to watch him from time to time, a worried look on her face. "I'm cool, Charl. Why you keep checking me out?"

He settled in the saddle again, rocking to the rhythm of the horse's walk. Then he watched Charl's hips moving to the same rhythm, an oceanic sway. Hypnotic, it was. Her horse's tail slapped casually at a fly buzzing at its haunches. His stomach unknotted even more then, and suddenly Candy was just a simple beast, hardly a threat at all, following the behind of another horse ahead of her. And the woods were hardly ominous, tall trees that touched the sky somewhere beyond all that greenness above. He wanted to touch Charlotte. Now he would touch her and, guessing that she would unfold behind that touch, allow the mystery of the heat and the dizziness to send them down some uncharted path through the brush, hidden from view and let ferns cushion them and let peacocks roost in the trees overhead and scream their glory through the silence.

"Lovely, isn't it?" someone said lamely from behind. He grunted, not sure who the words were meant for.

Broad shafts of sunlight cut through the trees to throw puddles of light on the forest flowers and shrubs. Calls from invisible birds punctuated the snorting of the horses as they moved up an incline. Strong around them was that smell of pine that he called *turpentine*. And he noticed a stream running its crooked course just below and off the trail.

"This is a pretty place to get lost in, Charlotte," he said, not caring whether the others heard or not.

"Lost is right. But if you think this is something, wait until you see the ravine." Her smile collected sun. Then she pointed to the deep gloom off to the right.

"Oh, hell, not again." Roscoe groaned, stiffening in the saddle. But it would be minutes before they would reach the gorge. He let his mind drift, not wanting to think about his horse pausing to admire the view, a choice leaf blocking its view, then long horse head reaching for it. No, not that. It was better to go back to the first day he met this woman. In their beginnings were those words and the fountains and the false spring day. And since that time she had opened up parts of him that he did not realize even existed. For him, possibility was the sum of the needles on that tall pine. He could be a cowboy, for example. He could go into politics and work himself up to mayor. He could run a profitable business and retire at forty. He could become the town's power broker, or at least, one of the brokers. Whole careers would depend on a *yes* or *no* from him. He could do all of that. And more, much more.

"There, Roscoe!"

He looked to where she was pointing and caught his breath. Some twenty yards off was the dropoff, and below there was nothing, not even the tops of trees. Across the chasm was the green wall of a foothill. He imagined a fast river below, though he heard no sound, a river gurgling and cutting more deeply than the fast creek they had seen only minutes before. And he imagined that on the other side of some great falls, fishermen would be out in small outboards fanning flies and hauling in bluegill the size of a large man's palm.

Roscoe tightened the reins on Candy, hoping that a frenzy for leaves wouldn't seize her. The horse simply snorted once or twice, tossed her head, and moved closer to Charlotte's horse, which promptly slapped her nose with its tail.

For minutes they rode along in silence until the guide took them up a path that broke sharply from the canyon. As if entering suddenly onto a new stage, they broke from shadows into the brightness of a large meadow. There were several hitching posts arranged along the rim of the meadow, and they were instructed to dismount and give the horses a breather.

"We'll take about fifteen minutes here," their guide announced. "You can get off and walk around if you want to."

Roscoe and Charlotte tied up their horses and found a shaded spot away from the other riders. Roscoe lay on his back, knees drawn up. Charlotte lay propped on her elbows.

"I should have brought along a guitar to serenade you," she said, turning to him. "After all, this one is on me. You enjoying yourself, Roscoe?"

"Except for a dumb horse, I'm having a ball. But as far as that serenade, you don't need a guitar. I'll just whip up a rhythm and you can deal on that." He patted his thighs. "OK, now go ahead and lay something on me."

She improvised a tune, scatted for a bar or two, then threw back her head and laughed richly. "Sarah Vaughn, I ain't."

He wanted to be a juju man, like old Luther Barnes claimed to be, and chant out a spell that would have all the others in this meadow disappear, and they would make love on the lush carpet of grass. Crush-clover smell would be their incense. He told her that and she stroked his arm.

He pressed on. "Why don't we ease on back up in the woods?"

"Just like two kids all steamed up with the love fever?" she teased.

"Uh-huh. They won't miss us. We'll tell the guide to go ahead and we'll catch up."

"I don't think she'd go for that, especially after that episode with your horse about to go over a cliff. She doesn't want you out of her sight."

"Can't you tell her that you'll be responsible for me?"

This time she patted his arm. "Our ride will be over in twenty minutes. We can always walk and find a spot somewhere." She winked. "That is, if you haven't cooled off by then."

Chuckling, he lay on his back. "We've got to make a decision."

"What do you mean?" Her face was serious now.

"I mean, we're at the point where it's time for us to either take off with this feeling between us or cool the whole thing down."

218

There was silence except for the snorts of horses, the song of birds, the whir of butterfly wings past the ear.

"I'm saying that I've made a decision. At least for me I have, Charl. Let's get married. You know, the good old-fashioned tie-up."

Her smile was a confused one. Her face clouded as a summer day can cloud so quickly in the afternoon, confusing picnickers. Her hand stopped its movement along his arm. He wondered whether he could call back the words, but, no, that was just the quick glance back at some old self. Possibility lay ahead.

"You really know how to catch a woman off guard, don't you?"

"Look, we could be somewhere having dinner by candlelight and some turkey ease up to us playing the violin just before I pop the question, but, hey, you know that's not my style. This is as good a place as any to tell you how I feel about you and that I want us to be near one another always so I can keep telling you. It's time we get on to the beginning."

"I just don't know, Roscoe . . ."

"I know, I know. But you had some idea, didn't you? At least how I felt? Maybe even I didn't have any idea that I'd spring the question today."

"I need time, Roscoe. Wow, I'm going to really need some time on this one."

He raised up on his elbows then. "Time? What's there to think about?" Then, after a long pause, he nodded. "Time? All I got is time. Sure, baby, take your time, take all the time you need. Just remember that I'd steal a couple of stars for you, and when you get bored with them, I could toss in the moon."

What was time to a man who could walk away from careers as one walks out on a dull game at half-time? What was time except another opponent to be pinned in the best two out of three falls, a chump and willing partner who catered to his rhythm? What was time, really, for one such as he? For Charlotte, it would be a warm place where memory would shadow expectation, a place from which she would emerge willing. Yes, yes, take it.

"Let me ask you something, lady. How many times have you been loved?"

"Twice," she said.

"That's a lot. That's twice as many times as I've loved and one time more than I felt loved." Then he reminded her of the good times over the past year and a half. He gave her the music of it so softly. Then he breathed loudly. "I bet you ain't never been loved this much before."

Then he tried to close his eyes on the blur of butterflies playing across the meadow. But she nudged him.

He looked to the other riders, surprised that they were looking in his direction. He started to ask what they were staring at when he realized that he and Charlotte were delaying the rest of the ride.

"Come on, Charl. Let's not hold up the show. Besides, I'm ready to do some serious riding now."

The rest of the trail was no less lovely than the first part. The hills grew steeper, the woods even lusher. Roscoe was a stranger on his own homeground. He didn't realize that any nearby country could be less monotonous than the rollaway flat plains that surrounded the town. His words to Charlotte slipped back into his thoughts as easily as broad shafts of sunlight snaked through the tops of tall trees at that time of the afternoon. A stupid wild trick with no style, he confessed. He had assumed that she would fly into his arms, that she would have finished the sentence for him. Instead, there was that slow intake of air, held for so long that he looked up at her, his own lungs burning with the air held in, then she not meeting his look, staring just above his head, it seemed, slowly began to breath again. It was her sitting still like that for an instant that chilled him, that made him want to fill the silence so much. It was that picture of her that he wanted to wash away with laughter. So he joked through the last minutes of the ride, relieved that she was howling so loudly by the end, laughing a little too loudly even at his one-liners. Like the one about Candy being eligible for Social Security.

And for the next week and the week after that, he'd remember that meadow so clearly, its smell of clover and promise. He'd see it as the stage for the dance of ghosts, and there would be small game playing through its mornings. Where the sun leaned in. They would talk everyday, and, at first, he preferred not to bring up marriage. It went unsaid, untouched, as if some deep secret only they could share, grown sacred in their sharing, and to reveal it would be the severest form of treachery. But there would be more to tell—there was always something forgotten!—and he would call her back. Other times he preferred to move through the long days rehearsing the nights' conversations. Despite it all, he stammered, stuttered, fumbled his words. Then he would tell her that he loved her, and in hearing those words he convinced himself that, despite what he had told her about having loved before, it was the only time in his life that he ever meant them. That was all he was trying to say.

One month later she answered him. "Yes," she said as if answering a child's question as to whether the sun really rises in the east. "Yes, Roscoe."

Roscoe wanted little fuss over the ceremony. A drive to Indiana would be enough. They'd find a motel, and the next morning they'd be married by a sleepy-eyed, bourbon-drinking justice of the peace, and the man's wife, curlers blossoming through her hair, would stand in as a witness. But, though Charlotte thought the idea exciting, her mother insisted on a large church wedding. Charlotte gave in.

"She calls this one her last request. She's one of the greatest mamas in the world. So I'd like to go along with it, Roscoe. I'm not excited about all that preparation either. But we can bear up under it, can't we?"

Roscoe had gotten along with her parents very well, especially with her mother, and there had never been any problems, not even during their futile attempts to get him to church. Grumbling, he went along. As the day drew near, however, he thought more and more to a drive to Indiana along two-lane roads. There was a certain magic to that that the glitter of a large wedding would frighten away.

His friends showed up in formal wear, looking as stiff and as uncomfortable as he did. There was a reception and pictures to cap a ceremony that the town would remember for years. Their pictures would be in the Sunday paper on the "Wedding Bells" page and older women would say how beautiful Charlotte looked, and younger girls would read the details, about the color and cloth of the dress, and grow restless for their own day of days. Those few hours were a blur, and Roscoe only remembered the spotted hands of the minister, a fly buzzing among the flowers (and hoping it wouldn't land on his nose) and Charlotte smiling through her tears.

He plotted the honeymoon for Ontario. When they stopped briefly at Niagara Falls, they took pictures of one another. They conned a stray tourist into taking a picture of both of them leaning against a railing, the mighty falls behind them spraying them, a rainbow through its mist wrapping low around their shoulders. But he told her that, all in all, the charm of those falls was a bit small-time for their needs.

Ontario was hot that August. They drove through Toronto, heading north to Georgian Bay on Lake Huron where they would find a motel and swim and sleep and make love and swim. Roscoe knew the area from his year in the Canadian league. Anna, a Jamaican waitress in Toronto, had been his guide then. He remembered the surprisingly blue and warm water, though he had forgotten about Anna.

Charlotte liked the area, too, and that pleased him. One day he would like to guide her back to all his favorite places and hoped that she would like them as much as he did, maybe they would also tell her more about him. Places like the hilly stretch of land in northern Georgia and southern Tennessee; the six hours' worth of Rocky Mountains west of Denver on Highway 40; Red Devil's Bar-B-Q Shack on Scovill Avenue, Cleveland; the sand cliffs of San Gregorio Beach south of San Francisco; the Old Colony Bar and Restaurant at 128th and Lenox, Harlem; Key Largo, Florida.

That Canadian August they lingered on the beach long past the time all other swimmers had left. He remembered how wind whispered off the great lake and the soft snap of the blanket Charlotte shook out, then spread. For long minutes they tried to hear their own breathing above the lake's own rhythmic beat. They had toweled each other dry and wore old sweatshirts, but they could feel chill bumps sprouting. The sand was packed hard beneath them. They lay close to the water, close enough for the water to wash over their feet, cover their ankles as it came in.

On their last evening there, Roscoe found no words proper for the peaceful moment. Needed none. He pulled Charlotte on top of him and he stroked the back of her neck with two fingers. "Just trying to keep you warm," he said. He made light circling movements with his fingers, traced half-moons on her behind with the other hand. He smoothed away her chill bumps, licked them away from her throat.

She chuckled. "I thought you said that you hadn't recovered yet from this morning, Mr. Man."

"Losing my head, again, I guess."

They laughed again as the water, a willing blanket, washed warmly up their legs this time. Charlotte began to move slowly. Slowly. He pushed up her sweatshirt, undid the top of her swimsuit, and kissed one of her nipples. She stopped and looked up the beach. "Roscoe, what if someone comes along?"

"We'll treat them to something that beats the movies by a mile." He had glanced up the beach, also. The beach was theirs, the world was theirs. The water rushed over their knees and Roscoe wondered whether they were on a downward tilt, headed feet first into the lake. Maybe they would be sucked away like this, pulled into the great blue and warm lake, locked in the foam and fury of their hunger.

The water caught his hands kneading the backs of her thighs. Roscoe entered her as the water receded, and Charlotte ground down upon him, and they rode through their world, the new world, they discovered here, of sky and sand and water, three days old, this world, and they would chart its mysteries, leaving no maps to find their way back, keeping its best secrets between them. The water started its rush again, and they broke into laughter at the delicious thrill of it.

"Don't get me laughing," she said. But she laughed anyway, and watching each other, they rode further this way through their release, a long and life-exploding release. And they lay together, conspirators, somehow expecting car motors and shouts to start up on the road far behind them.

"If anybody saw anything, they'll spread our legend far and wide." Roscoe pulled on his shirt. "We'll be known as the two spirits who steamed up a whole lake. These Canadians already figure we're from another planet as it is."

They didn't leave immediately. They sat and watched the sun slip behind a distant hill. Listened, as evening stole over the continent. And Roscoe, never passing up an opportunity to swim at dusk or dark, snatched off his sweatshirt and ran into the water.

"Roscoe, what are you doing? The air's too cold for that."

He laughed and swam a few strokes, then floated on his back. He remembered, remembering, the hot nights at home, when a few of them would tip through the park to the pool, scale the fence, careful of its barbed tips, then slip into the pool as quietly as beavers. A sharp-eyed neighbor would mistake them for sea monsters and call the cops. They'd get to the corners of the pool and keep still as the police car patrolled the pool, its spotlight raking the middle of the pool. They were never caught, except for Bobby that time he panicked and ran, wet and naked, luckily getting over the fence before the cops caught him in their spotlight not even thinking about running him down, just kept the light on his bare ass. Roscoe was the one who later found him shivering in high weeds and brought his clothes.

When Roscoe came out of the water, Charlotte sat with the blanket tight around her and was breathing across her fingertips. The wind was whipping up the sand, and it drove them away, howling after them as a cranky spinster drives mischievous kids from her peach tree. Drove them to another corner of their world.

Back home, the world of their daily movements soon settled

into an easy pattern: for Roscoe the steel mill, the bar that he bought and started to furnish, and home. Each day Charlotte taught her students, returned to grade papers in the afternoon, curling up in a chair wearing Roscoe's faded jerseys that fit her like smocks. Roscoe cooked his famous stew once a month, helped out with frying fish, using a batter passed down in whispers among the family and swiftly committed to memory. If then the rhythm became monotonous, it seemed they would be the last ones to know. There were no limits on their love. To count the ways they had their fun was to count the grains of sand even a child's hand might hold.

Barflies kidded Roscoe when he tended the bar. ("We don't see you at all the games anymore, Ros." Forgetting that with two jobs and not knowing anyone well enough to run the bar so he could take off a day or two now and then, forgetting that they didn't see that much of him, anyway, since he was never one to make himself too common in the streets.) They noticed that he shied away from the flirtations of women customers, though with enough tact so they wouldn't shout to the world that he was hopelessly housebound. His friends understood even if the women didn't. Why waste time running the streets when you have the finest woman in town waiting for you at home?

Once, in bed, Charlotte talked about infidelity with more than her usual curiosity. Roscoe was lying on his back, listening to the late-night sports scores off the TV. She waited until they were off before she spoke.

"What would ever make you play around, Roscoe?"

"Nothing could make me creep on you," he said, after a moment's pause. He raised his right hand. "I'm a born-again man."

"No, I mean, it is possible. Everything is possible. We've been happy these six months and I want to do my share to keep us that way."

He frowned and closed his eyes to consider the possibilities. Of course, he still took the time to evaluate a nice pair of legs and a firm, rounded behind like any other man. Marriage didn't put your eyes out, after all. And Everjean with her magnificent hips had

225

come on strong ever since her break-up with Lank, letting Roscoe know that, despite her angry words and his marriage, anytime he ever got restless she'd welcome his shoes beneath her bed. But what would make Charlotte dwell on this? Were the lies and rumors starting already? Was she hurt by some fragment of a lie she overheard in the beauty parlor?

"Well, let's see. If you ever became a nag, yeah, and grew fangs and started to hollered and scream and go to my throat everytime I came in late. I never liked to be hollered at, and none of us were hollered at when we were growing up. If someone screamed at me, I'd go into one of those trances and start shivering. A football coach tried it once, and once I came out of the freeze I caught him upside his head. So hollering and screaming on the part of my wife? Uh-uh. Start that stuff and your butt goes out in the cold."

She didn't laugh when he did. Only nodded. "What else?"

He was surprised and a little irritated that she wanted to discuss this matter so calmly, just like she was discussing the kind of house they might buy once they struck it rich or something. Ranch, Tudor, Colonial, Normandie?

"If you can't take care of business anymore, if I have to rope you and tie you up to get you to bed, then that's serious grounds for creeping."

"You got all you can handle now. Just don't you get old on me."

"Uh-huh, well, you stay like that, and we'll be walking around at seventy-five with big smiles on our faces. Although I keep it under my hat, I believe that a steady diet of good downhome loving can cancel out hardening of the arteries, rheumatism, and clashing zodiac signs. Without good loving, folks walk around like this." He made a face guaranteed for laughs. Keep it light as possible, this song she's started. Otherwise her humming of it will force the birth of a jagged blues.

He shifted in bed and cradled her head. "Of course now, if love flew out of this marriage, for no good reason just took off like some big eagle one morning, and we had done all we could, well, that would just drive me crazy."

Again, she nodded, but when she spoke, she seemed to be

226

speaking to herself. "But even still, suppose it happened later? Suppose there were children and suppose we were really on top of our careers, would it be worth going on? Would you tell me, then? I mean, if it would ever happen? Would you tell me that you had no more love for me?"

"Would I have to tell you?" He raised up on his elbows. "Damn, Charl, what is this? We barely getting started and you talking about ending it."

She shrugged. "I guess my brother's separation from his wife last month might have something to do with it. But I'm a sentimental fool anyway. I'd try to close my eyes and try to think that we carried this moment, now, or even the past three months with us. I'd tell myself that bad moments could be waited out, that everything else was bullshit."

He smiled, missing her point. He remembered when she seemed embarrassed to say "damn" and he'd tease her about her strict Baptist upbringing. Both knew, however, that if there was any strictness in her parents it was reserved for her two older brothers, not her.

"Look, don't worry about what you might hear out there floating around. Gossip is all it is. People tired of their own lives and the jails they've created for themselves and lost the keys. I've told you a thousand times what I was into before we married. And if I hadn't told you, small as this town is, you would have heard it before I told you. But all that is past now. You're the now and the hereafter. Understand?"

Her head nodded beneath his hand, and he fell asleep knowing that she must understand.

By winter there were rumors, though few and as random as the snowflakes that warm December. Who of the bored fleshy women in Gloria's Beauty Salon, of the yawning laborers in the poolrooms, of the righteous strolling home from church—who of these had seen Roscoe talking with so-and-so for over twenty minutes in his very own bar? Others had seen him on a street corner downtown talking with Miss so-and-so who grinned and stayed in his face. And wasn't that him and Everjean parked over at the swimming pool yesterday evening along about duskdark? If it wasn't Everjean, it was somebody who could pass for her twin. The women were those who did not like Charlotte. They thought her aloofness aimed at them, not the shyness that it was. They took that to be her arrogance over her schoolteacher job and perhaps knowing a mystery or two that books revealed. The men were angered and bored with the treadmill of working at the mill for low pay and trying to raise large families. Imaginations running red-hot, some of them cast out a web of gossip, hoping that it would snag on something they thought missing from their own lives.

"Some good storytellers in this town," he would tell Charlotte, over and over again. "And they don't mind peeping into the lives of others when the material from their own lives runs thin."

He saw Everjean that winter, carrying her four-month-old son. They smiled at one another in an intersection downtown. Roscoe assumed that by the way she eyed him she was gauging the effect of marriage on him. Was it killing his spirit softly or giving it wings? Most anyone could see that it was good for him, but some folks didn't want to believe what they saw.

He and Charlotte usually spent their evenings alone, though they could tolerate one another's friends. Occasionally some friends would drop over to see him, and they'd play whist or watch a game on television. With Charlotte around, genuinely trying to make them welcome, these men would accept the bowl of chips or sandwiches she'd offer. Yet there'd be that strain, that awkward need to fill up silence. But the ease would come in time. They saw her and thought that too raucous a laugh, too bawdy a joke would somehow soil the air around her. Then too, there was Roscoe's jealousy. Which was legend. He was known to stare down men's thoughts.

In his turn, Roscoe endured the parties of schoolteachers and young professionals that they were continually invited to. They'd talk to him about football but, when talk turned to sports cars or group charter flights to the Bahamas, he would head for the punch bowl for a refill.

"Think your schoolteacher friends will give my bar some of their business?" he would tease Charlotte.

"I don't see why not."

"You know, I think they're still trying to figure how I give up that job of teaching and coaching to work at a mill and open a bar."

"You bring it up like you're bragging."

"Maybe I am."

"I'm happy that you're doing what you want to be doing, but holding it over their heads doesn't prove anything. I'm not in your corner because of the job you have, but for the man you are."

"Sounds sweet, but you know that if I got busted down to street sweeper or the bar collapsed and all the niggas decided to boycott my ass, you'd be on a bus back to your mama's house."

"Oh, Roscoe. Not that again!" As she did dozens of times, she'd look at the ceiling and throw up her hands. "That line is getting old. What are you trying to prove to everybody? That you bigger inside than they are? That you take more risks than they do?"

He did not have an answer. Clumsy, he felt, as if he'd tracked mud on the carpet she had spent all day cleaning.

In the spring a semipro team was put together, and that was when the thought of a comeback first fluttered across his mind. Whoever said you couldn't stop, look back, and retrieve something you might have lost in your life? He wasn't thirty yet and a number of players had gone directly into the pros from sandlot teams. Younger players, spoon-fed on his legend, begged him to try out for the team. Yet, fifty dollars a game was the best that the owners could pay for a man of his ability and experience. Not exactly NFL scale, and there would be no fancy ads on television that he dreamed of doing. At least, not yet.

The cheers never die in your ears. Younger, while he practiced with the high school team, he noticed former high school players who did time in dreary jobs, who hung around the practice field every day. Clutching the wire link fence, they would watch the practices through August's great heat, criticizing loudly from where they stood. They would idle near the exits afterwards, then walk home the freshly scrubbed players and tell them about great games from the fog of the past, about surefire plays and patterns. They shared all their secrets, but the younger players did not hear. Could not hear. Saw them as hopeless middle-aged men who had missed their plane to fame, had been missing planes all their lives. In college, too, Roscoe would get phone calls or short notes from former players, and they'd mention a trick or two, all legal they would add, or suggest a mix of honey and raw eggs that would give him the strength of a crazed bull elephant. He remembered all that along with the cheers. He vowed to never become like them, promised himself years ago that when he got out of football he would forget the roar of the crowd on bright October afternoons, a band playing a tune that raced the blood, the taut thighs of the cheerleaders cartwheeling past the bench, the backslaps from strangers after the game. He promised himself these things but realized in that first year of his marriage that he had lied, that he was too weak to forget them and that one day he might even have them again.

"Roscoe, do you really think it's worth it?" Charlotte asked when he lingered over the idea of a comeback. "You might go out there and break a leg or mess that knee up all over again. For a lousy fifty dollars? Isn't that what you call chump change? I used to play flute when I was in high school. I won so many awards we ran out of space for all those medals and citations. I could try it again, but you don't see me crying for the good old days, do you? Sometimes you have to stick to the decisions you make in life."

"Me? Forget about the past?" He chuckled. "Look, I'm from a family where the sons seem to live the same lives as their fathers. I've got a brother now whom I haven't seen in over five years because he won't let the past die. Don't tell me nothing about time. It's like a hungry lion. You learn to make friends with it early or it will maul the hell out of you."

Charlotte thought that he would try out, and was surprised when he didn't, telling the younger players that he simply didn't have the time. Instead he quit the job at the mill. The bar was doing very well, and if he could devote full time to it, it could do much better. His plan was simple: do more tomorrow than you do today.

230

He had no choice; the first child was due in May. He bought a fledgling dry cleaners next door and knocked out the adjoining wall. The dry cleaners became a busy poolroom. He decorated and redecorated the bar, making it a place comfortable enough for anyone to happen in. It would be a place for a beer after work and for a fellow to bring a woman friend on any night and not have to worry about sprinting for the door amid flashing knives and flying fists. Roscoe's Place, he first called it. He later changed the name to the North Star Café, surrendering to the inevitable.

By the time Mayisha was born, the bar was the biggest thing to hit the town in years. On weekends, they were there in droves. Roscoe had hired a woman to cook fish sandwiches on Friday nights, and hot spicy ribs would follow in the summer, he promised.

In addition to the usual teddy bears and rattles, he had bought a small football for his firstborn who would logically be a son, according to family history. When he learned that the baby was a girl, he kissed his wife and showed the ball to the screaming infant. "Women will be coaching teams by the time she grows up," he told Charlotte. "She'd better learn the sport." He tossed around the football with his daughter even before she could walk well and took her to see high school games when she reached the age of five.

Mayisha went with him everywhere, her presence cleaning up the language of the snaggletoothed tale-spinners who sat on crates in front of the corner grocery stores. Mayisha in the bar in the early afternoon eating a fried fish sandwich and drinking a creme soda that smeared her lips red. Mayisha at home sitting in front of the full-length mirror on a bedroom closet door, sunlight striping her as she reached for the dust motes dancing through the light. When he wondered how things might have been different with a son, he would shrug it off as some outdated arrogance.

"You see Mayisha more than you see me," his wife kidded one day. "You aren't trying to turn our daughter into a fullback on the sly, are you?"

"No, just showing her what the world is like while she's young.

231

When she gets twelve, it might be too late. Kids grow up so damn fast these days. Plus, since she is a girl and will one day be a foxy young woman who'll have dudes lined up on our doorstep, she'd better get used to men now."

"I never thought I'd hear that from you."

"Yeah, the problem with too many women is that they never learn to be comfortable around men, to be friends with them. Most of them want their daddies all over again or some dude they saw on the movie screen once handing them the world on a silver platter. I don't want my daughter chasing after some goofy mess like that."

"Where do I fit in all that?" Charlotte asked.

"You were one of the exceptions. That's how come I married you."

"No, I mean in teaching our daughter about men."

"I'm just giving her the inside view. 'Course I know you've got a lot to teach her, too."

"I was just making sure I fit in there somewhere."

"You right in the middle, sugar. Right in the middle."

And Charlotte had joined a social club or two. She traveled frequently, taking those charter flights with other schoolteachers to Honolulu, Montreal. Roscoe had turned down the trips, trusting no one to mind the bar. He'd stay at home with Mayisha, though Baby Sister was always willing to invite her niece up for a weekend or so. He was content to watch his daughter grow. Sons would come later, he knew.

Roscoe would encourage Charlotte to take night courses, to upgrade her status in the school system. He wanted her to be the first black woman principal in the system.

"How does that sound? Think about it for a quick minute. You, Charlotte Americus, the first lady principal in this funky town. I bet all your friends would be up in your face then, trying to eat cheese. Have to shoo them away with a broom."

"It's a headache running a school. Just teaching is fine with me."

"You gon' tell that to Mayisha when she run for governor of the state or something like that the year 2000? That's the trouble with you black folks now. You fight like crazy for your freedom and get satisfied being just average. You want somebody to give you orders while you roll around heaven all day. Shake up some chumps! Baby, you the best. If you weren't, you wouldn't be with me here in this house. You should run things. You have the best school in this part of the country and I will run the best bar. We'll get them going and coming."

She had laughed and gone along with his suggestions. Dutifully. They were growing toward something larger each day, they felt. Discovery. These were the best times. Roscoe would bring home dozens of flowers when he stumbled upon a type he liked. One season it was giant yellow mums. The house would be flooded with the burst of small yellow suns. Then there would be a dozen blues albums as his mood dictated. Six pairs of shoes on one shopping trip. ("Couldn't decide among the first three pairs and they had a boss sale on the others.") He would never wear them all. His taste would settle on one pair and the other five would get lost and dusty somewhere on the closet floor.

Just as quickly he could fall into the foggy valley of depression. Caused by the slate-gray color of an afternoon sky or a stray comment overheard. He would take walks then or drives along the river. None of this did Charlotte understand, though she tried. She was the level-headed one, the woman shunning the swift rises, the sudden falls. Such surprises were, well, childish, she argued, and he should learn to control his moods better or otherwise he'd go out with a heart attack or something.

"Sometimes when you get in your moods, there's no place for me at all. You close yourself up and walk away and I don't know where you are. It's as if you've moved to some other world and I'm left here, helpless to watch and wait for you to get back."

And get back to her he would always eventually do. Charlotte would be there in the middle ground, more puzzled than before and always wondering whether it was something she said or failed to do that made him that way. And why was she just noticing this then? Had it always been this way, and only after the dust had settled after each episode, was she finally seeing those moods? In her confusion she'd tell him that he was acting like a kid, a big kid, to go stalking off like that.

"Cut the 'kid' stuff, Charl. I'm not a kid. Find another word."

"You are a kid. Only a kid could to the things you do. Buying those two smelly racoons that time and wanting me to help you clean them and cook them. And . . . and staying away like you did most of last week. We didn't know where you were. The house could have burned down for all you care."

"I got home both nights, if you remember. Or care to. Saturday I was at Baby Sister's. You knew that."

When she mentioned that she was pregnant again, he hoped that their preoccupation with the new child's coming would blunt any edge on their petty problems. But instead, their arguments seemed to mushroom and he was at a loss to explain why. Charlotte was infected by his bug, her temper tantrums were volcanic, her composure a terrible shambles. Roscoe withdrew. Went on fishing trips, though he hated fishing. At the bar, where the crowds soon leveled off, the newness fading, he listened to other men complain about their marriages, and though he never really listened to such complaints before, considering them ways to get conversations started about other matters, he listened closer. But there was little that he could learn.

He remembered, too, a conversation he overheard years earlier, in the Old Man's juke joint. Stuff, a man recently married, was complaining to two other men. "What can I do now? I married one woman to spite the woman I really loved for five-six years. And now Phyllis done broke up with the dude she was going with and she want me back. Spite tells me to forget about her, but what I feel deep inside tells me something else."

There had been silence after this revelation. The men shook their heads and in turn sipped their beers or jabbed at pigs' feet cooling in sticky pools on paper plates.

One of them finally spoke up. "Just be a man, Stuff. Be a man."

Stuff nodded and lit a cigarette. Not yet fourteen, Roscoe was confused. He didn't know whether to be a man meant that Stuff

234

should divorce the wife he didn't love and marry his true love or live up to the commitment he had made, no matter how empty of love. He felt sorry for the man, who started whistling a blues song in that breathy way which is both humming and whistling. Later he would learn that Stuff would stay married, yet still see his Phyllis as much as he wanted to.

Just be a man. He would go to his wife and tell her that he loved her, that they had been through rough times before and come through them, their relationship better than before. They were long-distance runners, a singing team of the long breath. Nothing could turn him around. But the stiffness was there. Strangely, Charlotte quit her clubs.

"You ought to get out more, Charl. Talk with the girls and whatnot or whatever you want to do. Isha is no problem, I'll sit with her. Staying cooped up in this house making you look down on the face. The child in your belly needs joy and good feelings."

"Don't tell me what to do. *I'm* not the child, you know."

And she became the stranger. He could not blame anything on the pregnancy; it wasn't simply moodiness. They both wanted more children, and she had looked so happy that afternoon she told him, even before seeing a doctor, that she was pregnant. No, it couldn't be that. His answer was worse than hers. She was acting stuck-up. She was looking down on him as a simple bartender. Once during an argument he had hit her, a clip on the shoulder, a swing that he wanted to check and afterwards wished he had. The blow was in no way dangerous, she was two months pregnant then, but through her tears she reminded him about the rich every chance she got.

The child was a summer's girl, born into a gray muggy August day when the air was still and oppressive. Charlotte's labor was six hours long, during which, at her suggestion, Roscoe broke for lunch. He went to a rival's café instead of to the bar where he would normally fix himself a sandwich. And while he ate his roast chicken, mashed potatoes, and collards, he compared the day briefly to the one on which Mayisha was born, to the cold gray January day with the cloud cover breaking late in the afternoon, a crisp clear night coming. On that muggy day, clouding up after a bright morning, he hoped again for a boy. He glanced around that café at all those crowding in to get a quick hot lunch. As there was life in his bar, there was life in this place, an impatient, funky, finger-licking, belching life that crowded him, helloed him. Life and all there was to come beyond any silly arguments and misunderstandings he and Charlotte would stutter through. He had cried there, jukebox blaring, laughs exploding, large-hipped waitresses weaving in and out of the kitchen. He had cried, thinking of Charlotte in the hospital, the young nurse attending and measuring the cervix opening and saying calmly that there were a few centimeters left to go yet. He cursed his stupidity for forgetting so easily, so easily always, that through confusion, pain, struggle, and blood, there would be crying, spluttering life, unpredictable, mysterious. That would be all he would know.

The new daughter was named Grace, and she got a baseball bat as her coming-home toy. She soon joined her sister as a sidekick to her father. In the silence that seemed to gain like a glacier between Roscoe and Charlotte, the girls were the sparks of life. Roscoe rediscovered circuses and carnivals. Zoos. He grew a beard. His temper calmed a bit and he found himself cursing the barflies less often. It was calm there in the eye of the hurricane.

At night he and Charlotte would lie back to back after an argument, not touching, or, when they did touch, exaggerating their jerks away as if stung by scorpions. He would get up, light a cigarette, and walk through the dark to the front of the house. He would pause at the bedroom of his daughters and listen to their breathing, then continue to the front room where he'd turn on the stereo. He'd finished the cigarette there in the dark, listening to a scratched Drifters' or Miracles' album. The back bedroom was a deep and terrible cave then where evil dreams snaked about.

On one such night his dead father just appeared. A smoke figure, though as definite as fire, he stood over Roscoe, who lay on a couch. The familiar yellow suspenders, the hat cocked to one side of the head, the cigar, the short and straight figure—it was all too familiar to be startling. As he did the first time, the father talked as if he were resuming a conversation that had been broken off to attend to some twenty-odd-year emergency in, say, Georgia.

"I never told you, did I, how I met your mother? Well, it was during depression times. I was standing on the sidewalk in front of your Uncle Wilbur's place. He used to run a garage where he fixed cars. He could fix anything that drank gas and had wheels. 'Course business wasn't turning much in those hard times. I was between jobs and was helping on what little bit did come through, but mostly I stood outside on the sidewalk to see what there was to see. Anyway, I'm out there, and it's late October, around my birthday, and I can smell leaves burning somewhere. I'm stand-ing there, son, and this woman coming my way, just as straight and tall. So I kind of hitch up my pants, you know—oh, you should have seen me! I was a real sport in those days or least I thought I was. I puffed my cigar, too, and I'm thinking of what to say. She looking as fresh as new corn with that open look in her face. Across the street, some fellows nudging one another and saying, 'Ros, man, Ros! Here come one I bet can't hear you.' And I winked at them and, as she come close to me, I tipped my hat.

"'Howdy do.'

"She shook her head and just smiled. 'Can I escort you to where you're going?'

"'It's a terrible long way out to the white folks' side of town.'

"'I got the time,' is what I said.

"'Maybe tomorrow,' is what she said and she kept on walking. 'Course I didn't feel too bad because I didn't want to take no long streetcar ride clear to the other side of town.

"But everyday I made it my business to be out front when she passed. She was a fine-looking woman, your mother. And a lady, too. My brother Wilbur told me after that first day, 'Ros, that Earline ain't no run-of-the-mill woman. She's special and you treat her right, you hear?'

"I jumped salty when I heard my own kid brother talking to me like that. How else would I treat her?

237

"Then one day I rode out there with her, I been stalling all that time. I rode to the end of the line and walked with her up to the door of one of them big houses. I could see her face going from happy to servant-woman. I understood how come she had to do it, but that didn't mean that I liked it all, Junior. The first time I took her out to one of the colored cowboy movies, a real funny one like they used to show Friday nights at the Strand Theater. And she had the sweetest laugh, you wouldn't believe.

"Well, pretty soon, we just naturally started to courtin'. I wanted it so that she wouldn't have to wear that servant-woman mask no more, not even for me. 'Course Wilbur kept giving me those funny looks, like he thought I was up to no good, and I had to tell him to mind his own business, heh-heh. One thing led to another and we got married."

The son snorted. "You never told me that one before."

"You seemed down tonight . . ."

"You just saying that to make me feel better? How do I know you're not just making that up!"

The Old Man rubbed his hands together. "We all start out with hope, that's all. I'm pulling for both of you in this one. If it don't go beyond tonight, well. . . . Son, remember you're a man of many lives. You take after me. They say a cat got nine lives? Hell, you got at least twenty and might find enough love somewhere to fill up all twenty."

"Well, this is the only life I know and this ain't hardly living."

Then nothing. He was left suddenly alone with the night and the music. He took another belt of scotch and finished another cigarette. Then that night he went back into that cave to find Charlotte crying, whimpering.

"There's no need for that, Charlotte. Let's just say we weren't in the mood tonight. Either of us. There's no sense in blaming." He would curl up and try dreaming.

"That's the easy way out. Something terrible has happened between us these last two years. And I don't know what to do about it."

238

"It's just a bad-luck spell. We'll ride this one out and grow and look back and say what kind of useless jive did we dare let hang us up? But whatever it is has been there for the past five years. Not just two. If you haven't noticed that, then you've been walking around with your eyes closed."

Roscoe turned on his back, his hands clasped beneath his head. She sat up, shaking her head. "It's not necessary to call me stupid. Maybe I missed so much because I was so busy taking care of you and the kids and doing the work around the house that I didn't have time to notice."

"I suppose you're hinting at some kind of sacrifice the way you usually do about now. You didn't do me any favors, woman. Any work you did around here was to keep that dream alive in your head—a cozy home, a nice little marriage, and your life laid all out with no problems. If there are any problems, just close your eyes and they'll go away. If they don't disappear, then blame them on me. Isn't that how it's always worked? Blame me for holding you back, for making you like the other tired women in this town? Afraid of taking their life by the wings and running with it?" The tightness in his head was a sudden thing. He had come back to bed seeking peace. He had noticed his voice growing louder.

Miles away, a train moved through the night, that slow empty freight that rolled along the backside of town around one o'clock every night. Roscoe could even hear the clicking as wheels hit the seams in the railroad ties, and marveled at the way sound carried at that time in the morning.

"You're going to wake up the girls hollering like that, Roscoe." He heard her take a deep breath, then hold it.

"Let them wake up! It'll do them some good to hear this. Maybe they'll grow up with some sense and their feet on the ground and not tipping around dreaming tired fairy tales."

"I hate you."

"You don't really hate me. You hate the fact that the little cozy world you dreamed up for yourself at the age of fourteen is crumbling. Time or bad luck or something is making it crumble and it's falling. You hear me, Charlotte? It's falling."

239

Her fists to her ears, she sat up in bed and rocked and rocked. Her soft shrieks growing longer, tearing, as if a jagged knife through velvet. He thought to the next morning, to its dawn breaking, and he asked himself how he would make it through that day and what had really helped him make it through all the days. Why had he stayed during all those bad times? The girls? He was a coward, too, he told himself. Never would he use the girls as an excuse to stay in an impossible marriage. Especially cowardly was his staying after their love had died the long death of an animal, wounded in its own nest to watch the slow steady ooze of its lifeblood. At least the death of love could have been something larger, worthy of legend, worthy of them—at least that much before they had run out of memories.

"Why don't you just leave?" she asked after awhile. "Just leave me to my fairy tale, as you call it. I just wanted us to be happy. Is that so bad? Is that what you call my fairy tale? You're still trying to remind everybody that you're Roscoe Americus. Everybody knows that. Who you were, who you are. Those who don't probably couldn't give a damn either way."

"Don't push me, Charl."

Then there would be a few more days of moving silently around each other, each waiting for an ambush at the slightest excuse. It was during this month, the last month, that Roscoe began to see Everjean as a stranger no longer. Running into her in the town's shopping center, he rediscovered the jokes that made her laugh in that year before he met Charlotte. She would return his teases and his looks, knowingly. She and Lank had divorced. She asked Roscoe over for a beer after work, and he said he'd think about it, remembering the shambles in which he'd left his own home.

Twice a year he would clean his small pistol. He never fully understood why he kept it around, since no one with any good sense would try to break into his home while he was in it. Of course, the town was going to hell. Young dopeheads, possible superstars or geniuses, were getting their color television sets and cameras the easy way—jimmying back doors or windows. But they knew his house was off limits. At least, so far.

Unlike other owners of businesses he had kept no gun on the premises. A shoot-out was useless if someone got the drop on you anyway. There had never been any attempts except that one time, fourteen years back, with Lemon, Coot Jones's boy. Lemon had done a little time at the Boys Industrial School and had been in and out of jobs for two years. One night he had come in the bar, nursed a beer, and chainsmoked, watching the door, playing the jukebox steadily. Roscoe had begun to notice him and had planned to say something to him. That was before he turned to face the gun, a small .22.

"Give me the money, Roscoe."

"Boy, get that gun out of my face."

Shaken, the boy looked wildly around. Raised his voice. "I ain't playing, Mr. Roscoe. Give me the money."

Roscoe did not move, did not flinch. "Lemon, if you don't put that gun away I'm gon' tell Coot and he'll whip you ten times worse than I will."

The boy cried. "Goddamit, you gon' get hurt if you don't give me what I ask for."

"Well, you gon' have to shoot me to take it." Roscoe turned to clean glasses. He dried off one, set it down, and looked into the boy's eyes. Then slowly, without a word, he reached out and pulled the gun from Lemon. He handed Lemon a beer and told him to sit down, then noticed the open-mouthed stares of those who had slipped in from the poolroom.

He raised his arms and shouted, "OK, everybody, either place your order or get back to the poolroom. Ain't no pool tables on this side."

Roscoe had not seen Lemon since that night. And he had kept the gun for weeks. Finally, he gave the gun to Everjean, who was complaining about break-ins in her neighborhood.

One night, after cleaning his pistol, he pushed a clip into it and walked to the back room. Charlotte's breathing was barely audible. So still she was. Grace coughed in the other bedroom. There was a swish of tires as a car passed out front. His stomach knotted. Rarely did one ever know the pain of another. And how did you rescue those in pain? Yourself? Let the two-nineteen train ease your worried mind? He chuckled at the old blues line.

Roscoe could still barely make out Charlotte's position, though he knew she would be on her side, knees drawn up and locking one hand. And he suddenly relaxed. At one with the night, he was, standing there. As calm as they say one feels freezing to death, sight and hearing blurring as death steals up the bones. He noticed that the gun was near Charlotte's temple. Once or twice a moan slipped from her.

Now was the time he needed Tyrone's time machine. He could reach into time and collect those good moments—the energy in that meadow, that beach in Canada. He could gather the words, as one gathers clay from the bed of a stream, and ball them up to marvel at his effort. But then what? And why had his own efforts in the past months brought him nothing? After all, the machine could only capture the past, not recreate it.

Moments went by, ticked off by the sudden pounding in his ears. The peace gone again. There are instants of understanding and love and strength as there are instants of betrayal and blindness. Feel them in flesh and bone and blood quicker than thought. The gun barrel was at his mouth, cold and brackish to the tongue. He decided to leave in the morning, to destroy nothing more of the dreams of this woman.

He walked outside to the back porch. The chilly air of the spring night was good to his lungs. A breeze brought the smell from the blossoming dogwood trees in the front. It was a good night. The new moon had long lost its redness and was pale as it broke through a cloud cover. He brought the gun up slowly and with relief at a motion beginning, with peace more than rage, he fired one, two, three shots at the moon.

During a December morning two weeks before Christmas, Roscoe locked the door to his room. Then he carried two suitcases with him down to the car. The sudden cold slapped him suddenly awake, stole his breath in a blast of vapor. Fumbling for his keys he blew across the tips of his fingers. Hawk sure out here

*this morning. He revved the engine once, then pulled down the
street to the corner stop. There, crossing the street were Romeo
and Juliet in long heavy coats, stiff thread dripping from the edges
of the coats. They limped along arm in arm, the vapor shooting
from their mouths and noses. When they got to the corner, they
kissed. He laughed and shook his head. They'll probably outlive
us all. Roscoe honked and waved to them as he pulled off. Away
then past the bar which he slowed to inspect. He would need a
new sign after he got back. The old one peeling with letters missing: NORTH S AR CA E. He hoped he was doing the right thing
leaving Inez in charge. Couldn't too much go wrong in a few
weeks. And he didn't plan to be gone much longer than a month.
He would find Emmanuel and have him gather his things to come
home with him. Maybe even convince him to buy into the bar,
and they'd expand it into something really nice. They'd set the
town on fire, just the two of them, and, if all the brothers returned, all the cowards and lying judges would have to slink to
the hills. After all this time, though, it would take a little effort
to persuade Emmanuel. They might not even recognize one another at first. Emmanuel might have a beard or something by
now. Broad and pigeon-toed he'd still be, yeah. On the way back
they'd turn a few places out just for practice. Then they would
pick up Billy Africa and bring him in on it. Clean up the home
base at last.*

*But Roscoe first would drive the old Chevy west, toward the
setting sun, and when the car would break down, if it must, he
would hop a bus, and if that moved too slowly, he would hitch-
hike, and when the cars of anonymous travelers gave out, their
motors smoking, he would run, footing his own road through the
mountain snows, run to free his brother, bearing the rainbow of
his life as a loose collar. Run, he would, without pain, without
guilt, with only joy, yeah, laughing, wet-eyed joy, clean on into
the sun.*